Allure of Home

Book 1 of The Gifted Series

By Ana Ban

Allure Of Home by Ana Ban

© 2016   Ana Ban. All rights reserved.

The author can be reached through Facebook @anabannovels

All Persons Fictitious Disclaimer:

This book is a work of fiction. Any similarity between the characters and situations within its pages and places or persons, living or dead, is unintentional and coincidental.

ISBN: 9781520207568

1.Romance 2.Fantasy 3.Paranormal

First Edition

Printed in the USA

This book is dedicated to the memory of
Glen and Betty Smith
(a.k.a. Grandma and Grandpa)
You are loved and missed every day.

Table of Contents

CHAPTER 1

Never in my life will I forget the smell that drove me to near madness. It was a combination unlike any other, a mixture of stale bed sheets, overcooked lasagna and unwashed bodies no longer able to function at their full capacity. Not that I blamed Saint Mary's. Every nursing home smelled the same.

I was there, sitting beside a hospital style bed with a water bottle in one hand and a hand of cards in the other. Luckily, my grandmother was still lucid. So many others could not say the same.

With a shaky hand, she set down a group of threes.

"Good one, Grandma," I commented loudly enough for her to hear. "Take a sip for me while I pick up the next card."

Handing her the bottle, resting it against the bed so she only had to sip through the straw, I picked up a nine and discarded it. Up until two months earlier, I had thought gin rummy was a type of alcohol.

"Done?" I asked her. She nodded her head feebly and went for the next card. The Parkinson's medication caused her to lose what voice she had left at 86 years. Scooping up the bottle, I watched as she laid out the last of her cards, beating me once again. Shaking my head, I smiled at her. "Got me again. All right, it's nap time. Let me clean this up, and I'll get you settled."

She didn't resist. There was no point anymore. I gathered the cards and set them aside. By now, I was an old hand at the workings of the mechanical bed and had her quickly situated. Leaning down, I dropped a kiss on her head. "I'll be back for supper," I promised. Grabbing my purse, I stopped at the nurse's station on my way out.

"Hey, Janet," I said to the upbeat nurse that had taken a special liking to my grandma. "She's sleeping, and I'll be back for dinner."

"Oh, great! I'm off before dinner, but I'll check in on her before I go. See ya later, Jade."

With a smile and wave, I continued out the door. When the wind hit, I shivered and pulled my sweatshirt closer against me. It was early May and the temperature in Wisconsin was still winter. Of course, I'd been living in the south for many years and it was a shock to the system to return to the north.

There were days I missed Florida. The oppressive humidity, the year-round surfing opportunities and, mostly, the food. If you wanted a good hometown meal like steak or hamburger casserole, Wisconsin was your place. Otherwise, the variety was severely lacking. The thought made me long for my own kitchen with the ocean view. But only briefly. There were more important things in life, and one of those was lying nearly helplessly inside the building at my back.

Sliding into the second-hand car I'd bought for the duration of my stay, I blasted the heat and pointed in the direction of home.

Home. It was a funny word. Until 18, Wisconsin was my home. My whole family lived there, and still did. My two older sisters, Amber and Emma (short for Emerald) were married with children. My younger sister, Pearl, was married with children. All my high school friends that I'd lost touch with over the years were now married. With children.

That made me, glaringly, the black sheep. Not that I had anything against marriage, or kids. I just knew it would take more than a man to ask for me to settle down. Most thought me a cynic, a lone wolf. It was true. But deep down, I was a hopeless romantic. And I refused to take anything other than happily ever after.

The drive was short. It was always a little surreal pulling up to my childhood home. When I left at 18, I hadn't been back except for extremely brief visits where I stayed in the one motel in town. Now, at 25, I was back to living with my parents.

And to tell the truth, it was nice. Sure, I didn't have as much freedom as I was accustomed, but there was something I'd been missing all these years. Closeness. All three of my sisters lived within minutes of my parents and visited at least every other day. We had big Sunday night dinners after church- another guilt trip by my mom, like when she talked me into staying with her instead of a hotel- and I was getting to know my nieces and nephews. All ten of them.

Up until now, to those children I was a face in an old picture that sent cool Birthday and Christmas gifts. Now, when they saw me, they didn't just say 'Who's that, mommy?' They actually knew my name.

As a group, we could be a little intimidating. The four of us all had blonde hair and green eyes, a combination of German and Irish that left us with fair features and strong stomachs. My three sisters were tall with long legs while I was the midget of the family at 5'5. Of the ten kids my sisters produced, six were girls and carried the same features. Two of the boys had dark hair, but their eyes were the Callaghan green. My older sisters tried to convince me once when we were younger that I was adopted, but I merely laughed and pointed at a reflection of us. It was undeniable.

Pulling into the dirt circular drive, I parked in the grass and headed up the walk. The door was rarely locked, which only bothered me after living in a larger city. In a town of less than a thousand, it hardly mattered. I passed by a tidy garden that my mom planted religiously each spring. I thought she was pressing her luck a bit with the weather, but she claimed it was gut instinct. Since she's had fresh vegetables every year since before I can remember, I couldn't argue with her.

This time of day, I had the house to myself. My dad was the only realtor in town, and most days my mom followed him into town to help with paperwork and other office business he didn't like to deal with. More than anything, she went into town for the gossip.

Stepping into the kitchen, I saw a note left for me.

2

J,

At the office. Look over the seating chart for the picnic for me?

-M

I sighed and shook my head. The infamous picnic, chock full of family members from far and wide. I still didn't quite understand how it could be called a picnic when it had a seating chart, but instead of arguing I indulged my mom. Grabbing a snack out of the fridge, I sat down at a stool and studied the poster board dutifully. Beneath her earlier note, I scrawled,

M,

Cybil and Rebecca still not over the green bean squabble. Everything else fine.

-J

Duty done, I headed upstairs to my room and checked my e-mail.

My days were consistent, also another big change for me. I spent almost the entire day with my grandma, from breakfast to dinner. Usually, I took a small break between breakfast and lunch, and another between lunch and dinner. I also stayed home Sundays. That was another long dispute with my mother. Something about getting burnt out and taking some time to myself. I came extremely close to laughing in her face. Time for myself? I wanted to say. What do you call the last seven years?

But I didn't bring that up. I just stayed home Sundays.

Sifting through the garbage in my inbox, I deleted it all and sat back. It was already starting. I rarely heard from my friends down in Florida, offers for work were dwindling and I couldn't even work up enough energy to care. Very few understood the decision I made to go on a prolonged sabbatical and I realized no matter how many times I attempted to explain it, it didn't matter. I'd truly become that eccentric photographer everyone believed me to be anyway.

The doorbell rang and I welcomed the intrusion. More than likely it was a sibling with a gaggle of children. As an afterthought, I grabbed one of my cameras off the desk and headed downstairs.

3

It was Emma. She had the least number of children of my three sisters with two, one boy and one girl. They were both too young for school yet, so they got to accompany Emma on all her outings.

"Hi Suzy," I said to the 2-year-old. She ran inside and jumped into my arms in a practiced move.

"I got a puppy!" She said enthusiastically, holding up a worn stuffed animal.

"You sure do," I said, stroking the animal on the head. "What's his name?"

"Puppy!" She exclaimed before squirming out of my arms and racing off for the living room where Grandma kept toys.

"Hey Emma," I said, giving her and the newest nephew a squeeze. Michael was 3 months old and didn't do much other than sleep and eat.

"Jade, I'm glad I caught you. Mom's going crazy with decorations, and I told her I'd help but now I'm overloaded. Do you have some time to help me?"

Doing a mental eye roll, I smiled reassuringly at her. "Sure. Let's set up in the kitchen, so you can put Mikey in the seat."

As we walked past the living room, I glanced over and had to stop. Suzy was reaching for a high shelf with the puppy in one arm and a look of pure innocence on her face. Silently I crept to her side and snapped a picture. Immediately she zeroed in on me and gave me her best smile. I snapped another. Not for selling, but Emma would probably like it.

Before going to the kitchen, I reached up and grabbed the object of her affection- a Barbie doll reserved for the older girls- and handed it to her. I doubted she could destroy it too easily.

Emma was sitting at the table with magazine after magazine spread out before her. Mikey was happily sleeping in the baby rocker.

"We only have two weeks left, and nothing has been ordered. What do you think of rose and graphite?"

"Looks like a mental institution," I told her without thinking. Her stare warned me of my misstep. Quickly I pointed to another color scheme. "How about this one? Brown and turquoise. Rose might offend some of the males there."

That seemed to mollify her. I knew none of the men would even notice the color scheme, and if they did it would be too much work to be offended. So, we went through balloons, plates, table cloths and banners in the colors and wrote out the entire order sheet. Halfway through, Suzy ran in with a Barbie head in one hand and a leg in the other. When Emma asked how Suzy got the doll in the first place, I ducked my head and searched one of the magazines intently.

"So," Emma said as we were packing up. By the tone, I knew I was in for it. "Gerry has this friend Jason that works at the factory with him..."

"No," I interrupted her. "No, no, no."

"He's really nice, and great with kids, and he really wants to meet you," she continued as if I hadn't uttered a word. "He'd be a really great father."

4

"Emma," I sighed. "For the last time, I don't want to meet anyone right now." Hardly a day went by without one of my family members attempting to set me up.

"Oh, nonsense. Everyone wants to be with someone." I shot her a look which was ignored. "Well, just come over for dinner on Friday. Gerry and I will be there, and the kids. Oh, and he has puppies, so I'll tell him to bring them too."

Puppies. *Plural*. Wonderful.

"We'll see, Emma. I've got to go, dinner is in half an hour."

"Okay, okay. I'm bringing the kids by in the morning, so I guess I'll see you then."

"Sure thing," I called after her as they trooped out the door. Glancing down at my hands, I shook my head at the decapitated Barbie that had been placed there for me to deal with. "I know how you feel," I muttered.

CHAPTER 2

Friday afternoon was the face-off with my mom.

"Jade Callaghan, when someone invites you to dinner, you accept. You will not stand up your sister and all the hard work she has put into this."

This time I gave in to the eye roll that was forever poised for execution. "It's spaghetti. From a jar."

"You will go and that's final." She crossed her arms and stared at me. The stance worked every time. I grabbed my coat and slammed out of the house.

This was the fourth time I'd been bombarded in two months. And that was only the amount of times I'd been tricked or persuaded into actually meeting the men. The rest I'd been able to squirm out of. I thought briefly about creating an alternate identity. Or were guys into mental illnesses nowadays? Maybe my alter ego could be a serial killer. Or a man. Or a mute. It was something to think about.

I pulled into the small two-bedroom house that Gerry and Emma bought the year before. It was cute, white siding with blue trim and, of course, a tidy vegetable and flower garden in front. How Emma managed two children under age 3 and a garden was beyond me.

Shoving open the door, I was met by the smell of garlic bread and spaghetti sauce. I knew, without looking, there would be a pound of hamburger browned and mixed in with the can of Ragu and a box of noodles. Once again, I felt that sharp pain for the little Italian place down the street from my house, or at least my own kitchen that was stocked with fresh garlic instead of garlic salt in a tub from the bulk aisle at the grocery store.

I was three steps in the door when Suzy did her flying hug and my arms were full of 2-year-old. Gerry was on the couch holding Mikey, and from the noises in the direction of the kitchen, I guessed Emma was putting the finishing touches on dinner.

"Hey, Jade," Gerry greeted. I sat beside him and stole a sip of beer from his can.

"Hey, Ger. Don't know how you can drink that stuff."

He merely grinned at me. Suzy bounded off my lap in search of toys that could make the biggest mess possible before dinner. She managed to unload a box of gigantic Legos- all 500 of them.

"Nice," Gerry muttered.

"And you want me to jump on this bandwagon?" I asked him with a sideways glance.

"Hey," he protested with one palm up, the other securely wrapped around his son. "This was all Emma's idea."

"Sure, it was," I grumbled before standing to go in search of the accused.

I found her pouring the noodles into the sauce and meat mixture, as I thought I would. With a one-armed hug, I asked, "Need any help?"

"No, thanks, I'm fine. Would you like a glass of wine?"

"Sounds perfect," I told her and grabbed the bottle. The front had a kangaroo on it and it was red. Worked for me.

"Jason's on his way. He stopped at home to pick up the puppies," Emma informed me. I downed half the glass.

"How many puppies does he have?" I asked her.

"Three," she responded happily.

I nearly groaned. Puppies, to me, were like babies. Nice when they were sleeping or playing. When they needed a diaper change or started to cry, they were best handed off to their parent.

"Lovely," I murmured, and finished the other half. Not sure why I bothered with sarcasm, it always seemed to be lost on my siblings. Guess it was just a coping mechanism.

Pouring a second glass, I heard the sound I was dreading. A car door and three little yipping bundles of fur.

"Oh, he's here," Emma purred as she took the bread out of the oven. "Just in time. Take this in the dining room, would you?"

I hefted the platter and strode into the other room. Gerry and who I assumed to be Jason were standing in the living room, watching the three pups climb all over Suzy. *She* was having the time of her life, at least.

The man beside Gerry was... vertically challenged. Maybe it was just because I was standing in the next room and things got smaller with distance, but he looked like Frodo standing beside Gandalf with Gerry beside him, and Gerry was not all that tall to begin with.

Short's okay, I admonished myself. Give the guy a chance. I'm sure he's perfectly nice.

And he's blonde. Great.

I didn't date blonde men. Sure, it seemed an unnecessary prejudice, but that's just how I was. Fair featured men just did not attract me.

Okay, so he's blonde, he's short, and he has three puppies- one of which is doing his business on my sister's rug as I contemplate the situation- but I'm sure he's interesting and intellectual.

As I was staring at the puppy in the corner, its head suddenly whipped around and fixed me in a puppy gaze. With a bounce to his step, he headed for the door and stood patiently waiting to be let out.

That was weird, I thought to myself, but Emma interrupted any further musings.

"Jason! So good to see you," I heard Emma say from behind me. "This is my sister, Jade."

He turned, and I got my first frontal view of the now infamous Jason. As he approached, I realized that he really was as short as he looked from far away. When I, the midget, feel self-consciously tall, you just know it's bad. And, just as I suspected. Blue eyes.

"Hi." He extended his hand and I shook it tentatively. His palm was sweaty, but he did have a nice smile for the brief moment that he flashed it before he looked away.

8

"Nice to meet you," I said. He nodded, staring at the wall. Thus ended our conversation. Looks like no go on the interesting and intellectual.

I sat at the table, resigned to an evening of screaming children, crazy puppies and dull conversation. The nursing home would win this competition, hands down.

When Jason left that night, he uttered two more words to me- which made it a total of three throughout the entire evening- 'good night.' Although, it was sort of mumbled so may even be classified as one word.

"Isn't he cute?" Emma whispered to me as Gerry walked him out.

"Mmhmm," I murmured, hoping that if by some miracle Emma grasped my sense of humor, it wouldn't be now. I helped her with dishes and made my escape.

That night, I sat in the room at my parent's house and looked through the pictures I'd taken the past few days. There were so many nice things about digital- immediate review, computer altering and I wasn't out the cost of developing. It did cheapen the process somewhat, though. That's why I still had an entire dark room set up in my house, plus I used the guest bathroom here when I needed. From the first time I ran photo paper through the chemicals when I was back in high school and saw the picture come through, I was hooked. It was still a place of joy when I had the time to develop the old-fashioned way.

There were quite a few good shots, I thought happily. At least there was that. The kids were a great source of inspiration, and since I'd talked all my sisters into signing releases I could use those photos. Plus, the wildlife was incredible- any given morning, I could spot deer, red tailed squirrels and twice there were black bear, right outside the kitchen window. From far away, at least, they were much cuddlier than the crocs I've photographed on occasion.

My thoughts straying away from my desktop, I stared out the window. The stars were an amazing, glowing sheet across the sky. In my travels, I've found the best places to see stars were in the middle of the desert and right here, in my parent's back yard. The moon was on its way to full. Inspired, I checked the calendar. Interesting. Full moon the day of the picnic. I'd have to get some shots in that night.

As the day of the picnic approached, my mom grew more and more anxious. In the last few days, I began sneaking in and out of the house just so she wouldn't spot me and order me to help her with one thing or another. Once, my timing was off and I was roped into tying little bows around bags of rocks. When I asked what they were for, she ranted on about how I was ungrateful and no one appreciated her creativity. I'm still not sure what the bags of rocks were for.

Close to two hundred people were expected at the picnic. With four daughters, my parents had the least number of children in the family. My mom came from seven and my dad came from twelve. Four was chump change in this genetic lottery.

Both sides of my family had been living in the same area for a few generations, so our picnic included the Callaghan's and the Stryder's. My great-grandfathers fought in the war

9

together, my grandmothers were best friends and, I managed to find out, had always planned for my mother to marry my father's younger brother. But Uncle James joined the army at 18, and my mom's sights were set on my dad instead. It worked out for the best, I always figured.

There were so many stories of the Callaghan's and the Stryder's intermingling, but until Isaac Callaghan proposed to Madeleine Stryder, there was no mixed blood. Friends, neighbors and now family.

The bulk of the family still resided in the area, though a few managed, like me, to escape. Most would be back for the annual event. Aunts, uncles, cousins and more cousins. That was the thought going through my head as I prepared Grandma Stryder to leave the nursing home for the day. I wheeled her out in the simplest wheelchair I could find and loaded her into the front seat of my car. She smiled happily and seemed to understand the general concept of leaving for the day, though I couldn't be sure. Her short-term memory was getting worse and worse.

It was still a shock to me to watch her visit with friends that she'd known since grade school. Back when she still had her voice but her memory was going, she could recall in vivid detail any event before she was 30. After that, it was the luck of the draw.

She sat now, quietly as always, staring out the window. Occasionally her head bobbed to the Frank Sinatra I played softly for her. Nothing was wrong with her taste.

We reached the park that had been completely transformed by my mother's and sisters' hands. By volunteering to pick up Grandma Stryder, I managed to weasel out of the majority of setting up. The place was already packed, the children running amuck and the adults starting in on the drinks. My mother ran around playing hostess while a band played oldies unobtrusively in the background.

When I pulled up, my car was immediately surrounded by helpful relatives. Uncle James pulled Grandma out of the car while two of my teenage cousins set up the chair. Aunt Judith hovered nearby, taking control of the chair once Grandma was situated.

It was quite overwhelming, taking in the sheer amount of people that claimed relation to me. I stared out in wonder, recognizing less than half of them on sight. Amazing, I thought. Each year, the total expanded incredibly, and the children grew so quickly I had trouble placing faces with names. Taking a deep breath, I joined the festivities.

Immediately I was cornered by a great-aunt. She stared at me through bifocal lenses and pointed a crooked, shaky finger at me.

"You," she said, her voice as shaky as her hand.

"Hi Aunt Maude," I said politely.

"Any children yet?"

I grimaced. "No, not yet."

"Pregnant?" She pressed.

Hm. Was I packing on pounds I didn't know about? "No, not pregnant."

"Husband, then."

"No husband."

"Boyfriend?" This last sounded desperate.

"No, Aunt Maude. No one special in my life right now."

She stared at me through squinted eyes for a full minute before turning away. Amber, my eldest sister, approached with little Sandy in her arms and was caught in the cross-fires. Without risking a glance back at me, Aunt Maude jerked a finger instead.

"*That* one's never going to get married, is she?"

Amber, bewildered by the comment, stood silent. Aunt Maude wandered off without another word. Amber shot me a curious, wide-eyed look.

With a shrug, I answered her unspoken question. "It's Aunt Maude."

"All right then," she said, with one last odd gaze in our aunt's direction. "I figured you could use some support. Guess I was right. What do you say we make the rounds?"

"Sure," I said with fake enthusiasm. Once again, the sarcasm was lost on the sibling. Something, deep down in my gut, told me I just received a preview of what the day would be like.

Finally, an hour and 14 aunts later, I snuck into the shallow woods and found a tree stump. Kids were running freely throughout the thick vegetation, and I kept an eye on the lookout for injuries or fights. The most trouble they could get into otherwise was being attacked by a wood tick. That job was for the parents.

I sat on the stump with my head propped on one hand. Every year we had this picnic, and each year I endured the questions. Why did they bother me so much this time around?

Perhaps it was being forced to deal with my own mortality from spending all my free time at the nursing home. Looking back on my grandma's life, from what I can tell it was a happy one. Sure, they never had much money. Most of my mom's childhood was spent on military rations and homegrown vegetables. The house my grandfather still occupied had been paid off a good 50 years earlier, for a ripe sum of $9,000. That included a three-story house and 20-acre lot. Their profit margin on that particular deal had to be incredible.

But what did possessions mean, in the long run? Like they always say, you can't take it with you. Even now, I knew if I could see the picnic table my grandma was perched at, that she would be surrounded by her children, grandchildren and great-grandchildren. Love. What more could you ask for?

Grandpa Stryder still looked at her like a teenager. He would hold her hand when they sat, tease her until she blushed and kiss her on the cheek when he thought no one was looking. Watching the two of them made my heart feel just a little bit heavier. One day, I wanted that. The kind of love that really did last forever.

The problem was, so often it didn't. Men just weren't made like they used to be. I had three very strong examples of good men- both my grandfathers and my own father- and with them, happy marriages. In a way, that made it just that much more difficult. I couldn't even blame my deficiencies on my family.

11

For a while I sat on the stump, my camera swinging freely from my wrist. Without a doubt, I'd gotten some amazing shots, which would later be sorted through, printed and sent off to the appropriate parties. We did the group shots immediately, so outfits and faces were relatively clean. Now the kids could play without furtively trying to stay clean.

The sun filtered through the trees and hit my face. It was a nice day, as far as the beginning of June went for Wisconsin. But, I knew, my mother wouldn't have had it any other way. Turning my face up, I soaked in the precious rays and prepared myself to head back into the battle field. To make myself feel better, I toyed with the idea of creating secret marriages and scandalous rendezvous to torture any more aunts that might be wandering around, waiting to pounce. I knew I wouldn't dare attempt to pull it off, but the thought made me feel immensely better anyway.

Heaving a sigh, I stood and took one last look around me before heading back into the clearing. The small park was just on the outskirts of town. The trees were gorgeous here, I thought, taking a sharper look. And the slight hill would be a great place to catch the full moon rising. If I stuck around for an hour or two, I could get some nice shots through the trees. There shouldn't be any interference from people. Smiling, I turned and headed back. At least I had something to look forward to.

Immediately I was cornered by Pearl, my younger sister. Pearl started having babies almost immediately after graduating, and although she was the youngest of us, she currently had the largest following. Three girls and two boys, each spaced a year apart just like my sisters and I were. The youngest was now 2 years old, and Pearl was making noises about another. Merely thinking about it made me exhausted.

"Jade! Where have you been? He's here!"

Groaning, I glanced over to where she was pointing excitedly. Not another one. "Pearl, what have you done?"

"His name is Rick, remember I told you about him? His daughter goes to school with Ashton, and we got to talking and it's just a shame what happened to his wife, but he's been single for three years now and..."

Cutting her off, knowing if I didn't she could go on for hours, I smiled and said, "Pearl, I really am not looking to meet anyone right now, you know that. Please, can you just leave it alone?"

Her bottom lip stuck out in a practiced pout. "He came here just to meet you. Just say hello, it won't kill you."

"It might," I muttered, but allowed myself to be dragged along. Though she drove me crazy, I, like everyone else, always found it impossible to say no to Pearl.

"Rick! Rick, this is Jade," Pearl made the introduction and ran right into an excuse. "Oh, dear, Ewan's up to no good. Chat, will you?"

I stared after her for a full 20 seconds before offering a bland smile to Rick. He had brown hair, at least, so Pearl was paying attention. He was good looking, in the boy next door way, with hazel eyes and an easy smile. I held out a hand. "Nice to meet you," I said.

12

"You too. Pearl's told me a lot about you," he responded. Wow, nine words. He was beating what's his name with puppies already.

"Great," I mused. This earned me a flash of a smile.

"Of course, she's told me a lot about pretty much everyone. Gotta love her though."

"Too true," I agreed and managed a small grin. "Want some punch?"

We wandered to the food table and I could feel at least a dozen eyes on me. Some would call it paranoia, but I just knew my family too well. By now, Pearl started the gossip train and it wouldn't be slowed until sometime tomorrow.

"Quite a shindig," Rick commented. "Everyone here's family?"

I nodded. "Everyone but you. At least, not that I know of." I raised an eyebrow in question.

He laughed. "Don't worry, I was transplanted to the area. No blood ties that I know of. So, three sisters?"

"Yup. Three married with children sisters, nonetheless."

"Must be rough," he said and took a sip of punch.

"You have no idea," I responded, staring out at the sea of relatives.

"You'd be surprised. Small town, single guy with kid. I'm constantly being set up."

I eyed him again, feeling more at ease. His tone was a mixture of amusement and annoyance. "You have a point. So, why'd you agree to come here?"

He shrugged. "Pearl said you were the good-looking sister."

I burst out laughing. "Honest, at least. Which rug rat is yours?"

Pointing out a dark-haired girl about five, he said, "That's my Cassie."

"She's gorgeous," I told him.

"Thanks. I like to think so, but I always figure I'm a little biased."

"You have good reason to be. She's in school with Ash?"

"Yeah. I think she has a crush on him."

I laid a hand over my heart. "Already? Man, they start young."

It was his turn to raise an eyebrow. "How old were you when you had your first crush?"

"Three," I responded immediately. It earned me a laugh. "What can I say," I continued, "some of us are early bloomers."

"Look," Rick said, and I glanced up at him again. "I'm not really looking for a romantic thing, but I really don't have too many friends. Would you be opposed to hanging out sometime?"

I studied him for a moment. Maybe I was delusional, but I believed him. "Sure," I said. "You know where to find me."

He smiled again. A friendly, non-threatening smile. "Great. I've got to take off, but I'll be in touch."

Calling out for his daughter, he shot me a parting grin and walked off. No more was he out of range than Pearl popped up beside me.

13

"So? What'd you think? Cute, right? And totally nice. Are you guys going out? You should come over for dinner, or we could..."

"He's nice, Pearl. We're going to try the friend thing."

She paused, looking disappointed. After a moment's thought, a smile brightened her face. "Relationships last longer when they're based off friendships. I'm so happy for you!" Throwing her arms around me, she gave me a quick squeeze. I started to protest but she was already off, talking off someone else's ear.

The picnic ended, mercifully, just after 4:00. I managed to evade a good fourth of the people that were out to question me, which made me feel good. Of course, that left the other 75% to test my patience. My mouth hurt from forcing a smile for so long.

Playing the good daughter, I helped clean up and pack the cars. Grandma Stryder didn't quite make the full day, and I'd already brought her back to the nursing home earlier in the afternoon. It had been a long and eventful day, and I was happy to be done with it. All I could think about was my planned photo shoot for that night, and the absolute solitude that it would guarantee.

With my car stuffed to the max, I drove it back to my parents to unload. My mother had a shed specifically for party supplies, so with the help of my brother-in-law's, we got it unpacked and shoved into the compact space.

Once they left, I hauled myself onto a kitchen stool beside my mom. She was exhausted, sitting with her head in her hands, but with a huge smile on her face. I was just plain exhausted.

"It was a great day, Mom," I told her.

She turned her head towards me. "Thanks, honey. I think so too. How did the pictures turn out?"

"I think pretty well. I'll get them all uploaded tomorrow, and you can pick out which ones you'd like to send where."

Nodding, she turned back to stare at the counter. "There's some brownies leftover," she told me.

"Sold," I said, and slid off the stool to find them.

As dusk hit, I was packing up my cameras and equipment I would need. The evening had taken a cold turn, so I threw on an ankle length white coat as I headed out the door. It was past deer season, so I hoped that I wouldn't be mistaken for a fawn's tail and get shot.

I had gloves and a hat with me, just in case, but left them off for the time being. Over the last couple months, my body had gotten acclimated to the temperature again, and the light breeze actually felt nice. Definitely needed the coat, though. I wasn't that thick skinned anymore.

I drove the five minutes back to the park where I'd spent all day. Now, it was quiet and empty. Perfect. I parked as close to the woods as possible and began my trudge up the hill. Checking my watch, I noted I still had 15 minutes before it would rise. Plenty of time to set up the tripod.

I positioned myself in the prime position to catch the moon as it made its appearance. The night was clear, thankfully, so the stars were also readily apparent. With my new lens, I was hoping to get some wonderful night shots.

For half an hour, I stayed on the hill, shooting from every angle. Again, the benefit of digital. As the moon rose higher, I switched out my memory card and began to pack up, to take some shots from the ground.

For an hour, I did so, using the silvery light to take shots not only of the moon but of the foliage of the woods. A mom and baby deer approached from the East, and I got some excellent shots of them eating berries. An owl hooted and a wolf howled from somewhere in the distance. After a while, I just stopped and stared around me. It was absolutely gorgeous. In my wanderings, I came to another clearing and I realized that I was no longer near the park, but in an unfamiliar part of the woods. A stream of panic rising, I shot looks around at the trees to try to distinguish which direction I'd come from.

I still had one camera dangling from my wrist, its usual position when not in use. The wash of moonlight on the white of my coat gave off an eerie glow as I came to realize I was completely, and utterly, lost.

Being able to tell direction at night wasn't much help when I didn't know which way I'd come from.

Turning in another slow circle, I suddenly felt eyes on me. Images of ravenous wolves, huge bears and predatory birds flitted through my mind as my eyes searched the shadows. Something was out there. My heart began beating too strongly in my chest, thudding out one beat after another. It wasn't just my imagination, I knew, but something really was out there, watching me.

In another slow turn, I spotted the slightest movement to the West. Squinting, I attempted to peer through the thick trees but it was hopeless. I darted my eyes back and forth, remembering it was easier to see out of your peripheral in the dark than it was to see straight on, but there was nothing. Perhaps I *was* going crazy, after all.

Another scan and there, just to the left of where I'd spotted it the first time, another movement. Standing perfectly still, I watched the same spot for more. No, I wasn't crazy. There really was something out there.

Something big. My heart sped again. Big, but not... animal. Human? It was coming closer, and I could just make out an outline. It *was* human.

My first instinct was to speak, to say something reassuring. But something stopped me, so I merely stood there and stared. The person was edging closer, moving in a slow circle as they did so. Not an animal, no, but stalking me just the same.

15

Finally, after what seemed an endless space of time, the form came into view. If I could breathe, I would have sucked in air. It was a person, yes. A man. A man without a shirt on. His skin was a deep, rustic color and looked copper in the moonlight. His hair was black as pitch and flowing freely towards his shoulders. He was wearing black pants and, if I was not mistaken, no shoes.

Slowly, still without a word between us, he approached me. I could feel his eyes on me and the strangest sensation throughout my body. It was as if everything inside me turned to liquid, and I only remained standing by sheer will. The soft light caught his eyes, black obsidian sparkling at me through long lashes. The liquid feeling spread and my will was lost.

I fell into blackness.

CHAPTER 3

I was crawling through sludge.

There was no other name for this thick, murky material hindering me from movement. Wanting to give up, to just slide back into the hole that was calling my name, I struggled for memory. I had been somewhere. Somewhere light, and pretty. Where this darkness crept up from I did not know.

The woods. That's where I was when this dread took over my limbs. It wasn't right, didn't feel right. I wanted to be back in the woods. With my cameras. With the moonlight. With *him*.

The thought shook me into consciousness. Who was the figure that suddenly popped into my mind?

It was thinning now, the darkness. Now noises were seeping through. That owl, the one from earlier in the night. The soft rustling of the wind in the trees. And a voice. A soft, soothing, deep voice that I wanted to curl into and fall asleep with.

Sleep. Back into that darkness? No, I couldn't do that. I didn't even have my cameras. Somehow, I had to get up and find them.

Slowly, I slid my eyes open a crack. Darkness. Just as slowly, I closed them again.

"No, you don't," I heard the velvet voice whisper across my skin. "Come back to me now."

Every morsel of my being wanted to obey. Anything for that voice.

Of course, if I disobeyed perhaps it would speak again...

"That's it, you're almost there. Just open your eyes again, let me see you."

My eyes. Sure, I could do that. I'd been doing that for 25 years, hadn't I?

Something equally as rough and yet just as gentle as the voice rubbed my cheek. It felt nice, perfect. It stopped. No, I didn't want that. I turned my head into the warm object.

"Yes, you're awake. Now just open your eyes, and I can help you out of here."

Why would I want to leave? If I left, that voice and that warmth would disappear.

Whose voice was that?

With a start, my eyes shot open. An object was in silhouette against the softly lit night. As my eyes focused, they widened with shock.

The object was a face. An undoubtedly masculine face.

The mouth curved and my focus was immediately diverted. It was wide with bright teeth shining out at me. Everything inside me was encouraging my hand to lift, to stroke along the smooth lips. Instead, I narrowed my eyes.

"Who are you?" I asked, and was pleased when my voice sounded steady and slightly haughty.

"Talon Wolfchild," he responded in that deep, soothing voice. "And who are you?"

17

His question sounded a little too mocking for my taste. Sticking my chin out just a little, I told him, "Jade Callaghan."

"Oh."

"Oh?"

He smiled again, and I realized then that I was actually laying in his lap. Without waiting for a response to my question, I struggled out of his hold and to my feet. He copied my movement, except that his was smooth and noiseless.

"Yes. Oh. I've heard of you." He answered as if I hadn't had a moment of complete dysfunction.

Feeling safer now with a few feet between us, I slapped a palm to my head and groaned. "Great. Which relative was it?"

His smile still in place, he held out one hand, where my camera was held securely by its strap.

"Oh," I said again, my brows knitting. "Thank you."

"You're welcome." He waited patiently for me to take it- I did so without the least bit of contact with his hot skin- before he answered my previous question. "Amber."

I nodded. Of my three sisters, Amber was the least likely to set me up. She went on a string of it during high school, brothers of best friends and that sort of thing, and mostly gave up the practice since. I remembered her mentioning someone named Tal briefly about a month ago, but I couldn't recall any details.

I wasn't going to give him the pleasure of knowing he'd been spoken of, even if it was forgettable. "My sisters like to talk."

"I've only had the pleasure of meeting Amber, but I can imagine. Of all the things she told me, she never mentioned an inner ear problem."

I awarded him with another narrow look. "What?"

His smile widened briefly. "An inner ear problem. A common cause for fainting."

My breath came out in a huff. "I do not faint."

He kept a serious look on his face, but I could see the smile hovering around his eyes. "I'm afraid to tell you, you do."

"That is absolutely ridiculous." I had my hands on my hips now.

"Ridiculous, yes, but true. How else do you explain how you came to be on the ground, lying in my lap? Not that I was complaining."

My face turned beat red. "Well, I..." I trailed off, struggling to come up with a logical explanation. They escaped me. Instead, I let out something akin to a growl before spinning on my heel and heading into the woods. I still didn't know where I was, but I didn't care. I'd rather walk all night than put up with his blatant-

"Where are you going?"

His voice was close, way too close for comfort. He was so silent in the woods I didn't realize he'd begun to follow me.

"Home," I said through clenched teeth.

18

"You may want to turn around. This leads to the next town. Thirty miles away. The park, where I'm assuming you left your vehicle, is the other direction."

Without a word, I spun again and kept my pace. I didn't have to look to know he was beside me.

"I'm sorry, you're angry. Let me walk you to your car and you'll never have to see me again."

"No thank you," I spoke with as much polite disdain as I could muster.

"All right. Though, I did spot some bear earlier. And some wolves. Big, hungry wolves."

My step faltered. Tough it out, I admonished myself. You were born and raised in this country. Large, frightening animals looking for a snack didn't put a damper on your plans.

"I'll be fine, thanks just the same. And where are your shoes? And your shirt?"

Though I couldn't see him, I sensed the infuriating grin return. "Does my bare skin bother you?"

"Of course not. It's just... aren't you cold?" I couldn't help it. My curiosity got the better of me.

"No, actually. I'm like a hot cup of chocolate on a snowy day."

This made me glance over. His eyes were on me, laughing again. I shot my glare forward again. "What?"

"That's what you told me, on your way back to consciousness."

"What are you talking about? I did not."

"You did. You also said I smelled like campfires and evergreen."

My face had gone crimson again. Thank goodness for the dark interior of the forest. I still had a feeling he knew.

"I don't believe you. Besides, if what you say is true, I was unconscious when I said those things, so that means it doesn't count."

He caught my arm and spun me towards him. The heat from his body seared into me. He *did* smell like campfires and evergreens.

It was silent for a full minute as he stared into my eyes. My heart was pounding wildly, though I couldn't be sure if it was from fear, excitement or exertion.

"Oh," he finally murmured. "I think it does." Slowly, he lifted the hand that held my arm and slid one finger down the length of my cheek. Abruptly, he pulled away and pointed. "There's your car."

I glanced over and was surprised to see my car not 20 feet away. Not trusting my voice, I stomped to the driver side and yanked open the door. When I turned to look back, he was gone.

"And then! And then he had the nerve to grab me, to stand that close to me with all his bare skin and campfire smell permeating the air while he insulted me! I just- I can't believe it!" Slamming a group of Jacks down, I glanced up at my grandma. If I wasn't mistaken, she was smiling at me.

"Oh, don't look at me like that. I know what you're thinking. But he was such a jerk. I never want to see him again."

A smile still on her lips, Grandma Stryder laid down a group of seven's and the fourth Jack off of mine. She was out, and she won again.

"Good game, Grandma," I told her. The venting had helped. There was no one else I could have talked to about it, not yet. My mom was always a good sounding board, but she was too desperate for me to be married for me to rant about a man. Amber would get an earful later, but I wanted to be more composed than I was currently.

The truth was, I'd been up most of the night. All lousy night, I'd tossed and turned. When I did manage to drift off, his face was in my head. And for all my trouble, I had circles under my eyes and a pounding head. Stupid men. This was why I just avoided them when at all possible.

With a sigh, I rose and cleared the cards. It was nap time, which meant I had to go home and check out the pictures I took of the moon. At least if they turned out, part of last night would be salvaged.

Dropping a kiss on her forehead, I left Grandma Stryder's room and checked in with Janet. She promised to look in on Grandma Stryder before dinner, so I headed to the car and drove home.

When I arrived, there was a beat-up truck in the dirt drive. Glancing across the yard, I saw that both of my parent's cars were gone, which meant that our visitor was either going to be waiting a while or had something to drop off, because they weren't there to see me.

Getting out of my car, I started across the grass just as the driver stepped out of the truck and I stopped dead in my tracks.

At least he was fully dressed today. Though, to tell the truth, it didn't help much. He was sporting a tight, black tee and worn in jeans and was carrying a bag in his hand. A very familiar looking bag.

My palm went to my forehead again. Figures. My camera bag, which had my tripod and other paraphernalia in it. Of course I would leave it so he could find it and bring it back to me.

He approached me cautiously, similar to the night before. His smile was easy as he held the bag out by two fingers. "Yours?"

"Yes. Um, thank you."

"I promised you wouldn't have to see me again, but I thought this stuff might be worth the hardship."

I shrugged. "It's just the tripod. Now, if it was my Nikon, we'd have a different story on our hands." Taking the bag from him, we stood awkwardly staring at one another. Common courtesy battled hard with personal feelings, but ingrained manners won out.

"Would you like something to drink?" If he heard the animosity in the words, he chose to ignore it.

"I'd love something to drink," he said with that grin. In the daylight, I noticed a small dimple in the corner of the right side of his mouth. It transformed his features from masculine to boyish in the blink of an eye.

With a sigh, I turned and started for the door. I didn't bother to look and see if he was following. I knew he would.

Without much ceremony, I dropped the bag on the floor in the entryway and slipped off my shoes. When I got into the kitchen, I took out a fresh pitcher of lemonade and poured two tall glasses.

"Here," I said and slammed it on the counter before him. He'd chosen a stool at the counter, the same stool I always sat at. Wondering why that bothered me so much, I leaned against the counter and took a deep sip. The sweet, tangy taste helped calm my nerves.

"You don't live here," Talon said. I wasn't sure if it was a question or a statement. I answered anyway.

"Not usually."

"Somewhere in the South. You still have a bit of a tan."

I glanced down at my arms. Anyone in Florida would have laughed at my pathetic, minute coloring. Here, I was darker than 99% of the people. "If you say so," I muttered. "What do you want?"

His grin returned, and he drank half the glass in one smooth gulp. "I was only trying to be polite by returning your bag."

Moving my shoulders restlessly, I knew I had to be somewhat nice. "Thanks for that. What else do you want?"

"To see you," he told me. He didn't seem to have any problem being blunt. "Amber told me what time I might be able to catch you here."

Rolling my eyes, I groaned, "Great."

His eyes sharpened on mine. "What?"

Shaking my head, suddenly amused, I explained, "You obviously don't know my family too well. Within an hour, the entire town will know that you came looking for me. By tomorrow, we'll be engaged and by the end of the week, no doubt, we'll be expecting a bundle of joy." Shrugging, I finished, "It's a small town."

"Hm," he murmured, stroking a hand across his chin and considering me. "I thought maybe a scandalous affair, at most. But marriage and children?" Shaking his head, he finished off his glass. "I'm not quite ready for that. I should go."

This took me by surprise. "Really?" Too late, I realized there was disappointment in the word.

He rose and brought the glass to the sink. "Really. I have some work to do. Maybe I'll stop by in the middle of the night and toss a rock at your window. That should get the neighbors talking."

Before I could stop him, he took my hand and kissed my fingers. "Until next time."

A strangled noise escaped my lips. It was supposed to be something witty and aloof, or at the very least cohesive. I didn't even manage to move until he was already out the door.

"There won't *be* a next time," I grumbled. There. That should show him.

Snatching up my bag, I stomped up the stairs to peruse the pictures. It's too bad I didn't get any of him last night, I thought before I could censor myself. He looked almost ethereal, with the pale moon and his dark features. I sighed. The way he looked, anytime, was not supposed to be on my mind.

Just who was he, anyway? How did he know Amber, and why had I never seen him before? The town only had a thousand people, for goodness sakes. Twenty percent of those were related to me. He definitely wasn't.

It didn't take long for Amber to call. I was actually surprised she waited as long as she did. Perhaps she thought it would give Talon and me more time alone. I snorted at the thought. Right. Just what I wanted.

I picked up the phone and pulled off a perfectly composed voice. "Hello?"

"Jade, it's Amber."

Amber always sounded so sedated. I couldn't stop the small grin, knowing she was bursting at the seams with curiosity. "Hi Amber. What's up?"

"Oh, I just wanted to make sure Tal made it over there. I wasn't totally sure on the time."

"Yes, he did." There was dead silence, and I had to suppress a giggle. This was killing her.

"Well, I didn't realize you two knew each other."

"We don't, really."

More silence. She was trying very hard to remain diplomatic.

"All right. I'm happy to hear he caught you. I guess I'll let you go, then."

"How do you know him?"

"Me? He's doing the remodel on my kitchen." Oh. That's right. I knew she'd mentioned him, but I must have zoned out on the details. "And... how do you know him?" She finally blurted out, obviously relieved to have the opening.

"Oh," I began, and decided to have a bit of fun. "Like I said, I don't really know him. I was lucky to catch his name after we got up off the ground last night. I can't believe he didn't freeze, he was hardly wearing any clothes."

I was pretty sure the phone dropped out of Amber's hand. There was a thump and some scuffling before her voice came over the line again. "Wha- what?"

This time I did laugh. "I was out taking pictures last night, and I must have crossed onto his property or something, because we ran into each other. I... fell down... and he helped me back up. That was all." There was no way I was admitting to fainting.

"Oh. Okay. That's nice." Amber was still a little flabbergasted over my initial telling. "Are you all right?"

"Sure. I must have hit my head though, because I left my camera bag there. That's what he was bringing back to me today."

"That's nice of him. Are you seeing him again?"

My smile disappeared and I responded more sharply than intended. "No."

"Sorry, I thought- well, that was nice of him, anyway. Um, would you like to join us for dinner tonight?"

"Can't tonight. Emma's roped me into another dinner with some guy."

"Tomorrow, then."

"Just you, Jack and the kids?" I had to check.

"That's the plan."

"All right. I'd like that."

"Okay, I'll see you at 5:30. Bye, Jade."

"Bye, Amber." Hanging up, I checked the time. If I went down to the nursing home, I could help Grandma eat and be back at Emma's on time. Shutting down my computer, I grabbed my purse and headed back to Saint Mary's.

Somehow Emma had coerced me into dinner with another prospect. She was definitely the sneakiest of the four of us. One of these days, I would get even with her.

Tonight, the man's name was Reginald. No joke. I asked if he had a nickname, but I was told he preferred to go by Reginald. To each his own, I told myself.

Reginald was older, and balding. Though, for points in Emma's direction, what little hair he had left was dark. A nice beer belly was sagging over the band of his pants and he had an odd habit of smoothing his eyebrows. The only conclusion I could come to was that since his eyebrows probably had more hair than his head, he wanted to enjoy it while he could.

Over dinner, we got the lovely pleasure of listening to 20 years of complaints about the factory. Though he could pull off much older, I did manage to find out he was 40. Obviously, the years at the factory had not treated him well.

"Me and the boys hit up Duffy's last night," he was saying currently while engorging on stuffed peppers. "Closed the place down. Shoulda been there, Gerry."

"Next time," Gerry told him good spiritedly.

"Yeah, we were wasted," he gave Suzy a toothy grin, which she stared at blandly. "Can still pack 'em away," he emphasized this with a pat on his belly.

"Never could have guessed," I muttered. Emma held her hand to her mouth, stifling a giggle.

As dinner wound down, Reginald shoved back from the table and winked at me. "Heading over to Duffy's now. Want to join me, sugar?"

I think I puked a little in my mouth. "You know what, I have to be up early. Maybe another time."

"Anytime you want, just gimme a call."

I'd rather chop up and eat every phone within a mile of me.

Helping Emma with the dishes, I found myself staring out the kitchen window into the darkened trees. It seemed every house had its own forest around here. The sun was still setting, but the trees were thick enough to secure the darkness.

My thoughts drifted, and against my better judgement, went straight to Talon. My inexplicable emotions around him were better than another evening with the likes of Reginald. Even puppy guy was less obnoxious. But thoughts of puppy guy didn't last long. Talon was front and center in the daydream.

"I'm so sorry," Emma said from beside me. When I glanced over, we both burst into giggles.

"Reginald," I said sarcastically. "I mean, really, what dumpster did you two pull him out of?"

"Hey," Emma said. "It wasn't me. Gerry just told me he had a friend at work who was lonely. I should have known to ask more details."

"Please, please," I begged, "*Please* be done with setting me up."

"I wouldn't have to if you would meet men on your own."

Emma's comment was met with silence. I should have known better.

"Jade Rose Callaghan, did you meet a man?"

"Not... exactly."

"Tell me everything."

Scrubbing at a small spot on a pot to stall, I moved my shoulders restlessly. "There's nothing really to tell. It was odd."

"Odd."

"Yeah. We met in the woods. I was out shooting pictures, got completely lost, fell down, and he was there. He helped me up, and then brought me some camera equipment that I left there earlier today." I left out the part about me fainting, deciding 'fell down' sounded more plausible.

She sighed. "Sounds romantic."

"Romantic isn't the word I'd use," I murmured.

Enchanting. Mysterious. Familiar.

I gave my head a quick shake. Where had that come from?

"Anyway, I probably won't see him again," I told her, and ignored the hard twist in my gut the words produced. I didn't want to see him again, I admonished my stomach. I didn't.

As I drove home that night, the sky was still brightly lit with the setting sun. It wasn't a long drive, but the furthest of my sisters. I was going along an abandoned road, trees rising up on either side of me, when I glanced over and caught sight of a figure in the woods.

My heart skipped a beat and I slowed, trying to catch a better look. It was some kind of large animal, dark and majestic as it raced through the trees steady with my car.

24

Slowing more, I was hoping to make out what kind of animal it was. Wolves were common up here, as were bears and deer. A wolf seemed most likely, for the speed and color.

Unbelievably, it was keeping pace with my car. Slowing more, I squinted out into the woods. But as the car came to a stop, the figure was gone.

Disappointed, I drove home. Maybe I'd see it again, another day.

CHAPTER 4

The next day was hectic, but no more than usual. I was looking forward to a nice evening with Amber and her kids, sans another Reginald. As I was driving up Amber's driveway, I spotted... an old, beat up truck. Aggravated, I sat in my still running car and contemplated turning around and leaving. Amber would be upset, but she would get over it. Eventually.

Just as I shifted into reverse, the door sprung open and three blonde mops of hair flew towards me. Too slow. Shoving the car back into park, I opened the door and pasted a smile on my face.

"Hey, guys!" I said to the three bundles of energy as they climbed into the car before I could get out. This group included Jack Jr. who was four and went by Junior, Penny, who was two and a half and Sandy, who was just over a year. Once I managed to grab the two girls, I was able to stand up and walk towards the house with Junior attached to a leg.

When I walked in, Amber was setting the table and through the window, I saw Jack grilling something that smelled delicious. From the direction he was talking, I figured Talon was out there with him.

"Amber," I said curtly.

Her face brightened when she looked up. "Jade! I was hoping that was you the kids were attacking, and not the delivery man again."

Depositing the kids on the couch, I followed her into the kitchen and stole a piece of fruit to munch on. The construction was near completion and didn't get in the way of preparing meals. "What's he doing here?"

Glancing up, looking almost surprised, Amber replied, "Tal? He was working here this afternoon, so I invited him to dinner." She turned towards me, eyes too wide to be innocent. "You don't mind, do you?"

"Would it matter if I did?"

"Nope. Bring this out, would you?"

Every battle with my sisters was a losing one.

Carrying in the platter of fruit, I set it none too gently on the table and made whatever other noise I could. Chairs were shoved in, plates rearranged and silverware moved. I was just getting into a good rhythm when my concentration was broken.

"This is becoming a habit."

Spinning at the sound of the voice, I glared at the intruder. His shirt was smudged with what I recognized as drywall and dirt. "Bad habits are meant to be broken," I answered him.

"Here," he said, holding his hands out. When I simply stared at him, he lifted the candlesticks out of my hands and slid a box of matches out of his pocket. Setting them in the center, he struck a match and lit the three. "There. Now everything is properly arranged."

"It's fine," I huffed, crossing my arms over my chest. Eyes narrowed, I watched him. "What are you doing here?"

He glanced around, that same annoyingly innocent look Amber attempted on me. "I was invited. I learned long ago to never pass up a home cooked meal."

My glare was obviously losing its touch. "Whatever," I said smartly and walked off. The kids were in the living room, playing with an assortment of matchbox cars and stuffed animals. Immediately, Sandy ran to me and lifted her arms in the widely-accepted motion of 'up.' Obligingly, I lifted her into my lap. Three seconds later she squirmed down again, so I contented myself to watch the kids crash their cars into monster teddy bears.

Though I refused to look up, I felt his stare from the doorway. He stood there, all smug and good looking. My arms tightened automatically around Sandy, who had already climbed back into my lap. Good looking? Where did that thought come from? The last 24 hours, my brain has been running amuck. It was time to reel it in.

Besides, if I was going to be honest, good looking wasn't the correct adjective. Gorgeous. Drop dead. Exquisite.

No, no, no. I wouldn't even think it. My eyes snuck up, slowly, beneath my lashes. Good, he was watching the kids. And I was wrong. Not even exquisite quite cut it.

"Dinner!" Amber called out, and I nearly jumped. The kids ran out before I could gather them, so I was left with a guardian at the gate. Throwing my shoulders back, I walked right past him without a sideways glance.

"Tense?" His voice was too close again. It made the hair on my neck stand up.

I sat in the chair he held out, because making a scene now would be a bad idea with the audience we had. "I'm fine," I told him curtly. He smiled, I know he did.

We were seated next to each other, which was a small blessing. At least I didn't have to look directly at him. Though, it presented its own dilemmas. Like his smell, and his heat. Was he running a fever? People weren't supposed to radiate body heat like that.

"Jade was telling me that you helped her when she fell the other night," Amber began the conversation over the squeals of the children. I felt my whole body tense, even more so than it was already.

There was a slight pause and I thought for sure he was going to give me away. So smooth that I must have only noticed the pause because I was the one caught in the lie, he answered, "Yes. The woods can be treacherous at night, even with the light of the full moon. It's not wise to wander off on your own. Right, Jade?"

I stared down at my plate. The steak was less appetizing than it had been when I first smelled it. "Right," I mumbled.

"Luckily, I happened upon her just as the incident occurred. She had no injuries that I could tell, except perhaps her temperament. It seems she's much sweeter when she's near unconsciousness."

Amber choked on a laugh and Jack paused with his fork halfway to his mouth. If I could spit daggers through my eyes, I would have done so.

It was time to switch tactics. He wanted sweet, I would give him sweet.

I smiled and even managed to bat a lash. "You're absolutely right," I said, my voice pitched higher than normal. "I have been so utterly rude. In fact, let me refresh your iced tea." Before he could reply, I upended my drink on his lap. "Too sweet?"

Everyone, children included, was completely silent. Amber and Jack's mouths were hanging open in shock. My glare was set on Talon, and his eyes were alight with amusement.

"You're right. Much too sweet. I like my girls with a bit of grit." In one swift movement, he pushed his chair back, stood and pulled me up by my arm. "Do be so kind as to help me clean this up."

His grip was hot and hard. My momentary struggles were useless. Pulling me down the hall, he swung me into the bathroom and locked the door behind us.

"Just what do you think you..."

"Quiet," he ordered. Grasping my upper arms, he shoved me against the sink and stared straight into my eyes. "I see only one solution to this problem."

I opened my mouth to protest but it was too late. His lips met mine and I was sunk.

It wasn't angry, as I'd expected. It wasn't sweet and gentle, like in the movies. It was... perfect. And too short.

"There," he said, pulling back. "Are we better now?"

I stared at him.

"I'm leaving now. Sitting through dinner with wet pants does not sound enjoyable. Have a good evening. I *will* be seeing you again."

The last sounded like a threat.

He left, and I stayed standing there, propped up by the cabinet. What in the world just happened? After a few minutes, I made my way back to the table. I was met with wondering stares, which I ignored. Instead, I cut into my steak and stuck a piece in my mouth.

When I left, barely any words were spoken. I can only imagine what Jack and Amber were thinking. Feeling bad about the mess I'd made, I did scrub down the chair before I headed out. Luckily, with a house used to kids, the chairs were easily wiped up.

It took until I drove home, got into my pajamas and lay down on the bed for my thoughts to catch up with me. While I'd never been the sweet one like Pearl, this was entirely new for my personality. Pouring a drink on Talon's lap was a little extreme, I knew that now. Why did it feel so right at the time?

And his reaction to it. Amusement, clearly, was the emotion on his face. Then, in the bathroom...

Nope. Not going there.

What was wrong with me? I liked men. No, I didn't want to get married immediately, but I genuinely liked men. There were many that I dated, and squabbled with, but nothing like this. No one brought out such intense reactions in me before. It had me worried.

There was just something about him. Something I couldn't quite put my finger on. Not bad, but not good either. Sighing, I shoved a pillow over my face. I'd worry about it in the morning.

But I wasn't so lucky. That night, I had my first dream about Talon Wolfchild.

Crouched in the tall, wild grass, my form was utterly still as I waited for the prey. A person could walk a foot away and not spot me, this I knew. This skill had been practiced and perfected since I was a youth, and was one that came naturally, easily, even then.

The javelina was a skittish animal with tough meat, but we needed it. The harvest had not yet come in and supplies from earlier in the season were dwindling. As it neared, I could hear its heart beating, its life-giving blood rushing through its veins. It snorted, just a low grunt, but I remained still. Timing was everything.

In a lightning fast move, I leapt and lunged the arrow into its throat. Quietly, I prayed over the body and sent the spirits my thanks for the life sustaining food. Then, I carried it back.

She was washing clothes at the small stream. The light reflected brilliantly off her midnight black hair and bronze skin. She was absolutely beautiful.

"Mother."

She turned then and her smile filled my soul with happiness. The meat would make her happy.

"Dear Talon," she said in a voice that was light as feathers. "Well done."

Though in many respects I was considered a man, I still had the form of a boy. Soon I would be 15 summers. Mother approached and laid a hand on my head. "Father will help you clean it," she told me. "Go to him now."

I nodded and walked between the two tents we occupied, where the cook fire was being prepared. Father was ready for me, and we worked quickly. When we had a portion roasting and the rest packed in salt to keep, I watched my father's eyes light with love and knew my mother had returned. It was like that with her. People were willing to do anything for one of her brilliant smiles.

As I woke, the dream cleared until only a faint remembrance remained. Tossing and turning, I knew it was still much too early to wake, but my mind would have nothing of it. Finally, exhausted, I dragged myself out of bed.

Shuffling my feet, I trudged down the stairs and pushed the button for coffee. It was only rarely that I drank the stuff, but I had a feeling I would need it today.

The coffee began brewing instantly, having been prepared the night before by my father. Isaac and Madeleine Callaghan were two that could not function before their second or third cup. As the aroma filled the air, I got down two mugs from the cupboard and the creamer from the fridge. My dad would be down soon and would appreciate the gesture.

Taking my seat at the counter, I sipped and watched out the window. The sun was already up, though just barely, and some deer were enjoying the early morning quiet. Today, I just watched them. So often I had my face behind a camera, and without stopping once in a while to just enjoy, what point was there to life?

A few dark clouds were springing to life on the horizon, which meant a morning downpour. That was perfectly fine by me. Not only did it mean good lighting later in the day, but it also suited my mood. Perfectly.

Only minutes after the scent of coffee wafted upstairs, my dad was down and in search of his caffeine fix. He mumbled an incoherent good morning to me, poured his mug with just a dash of cream, and sat beside me.

We sat in companionable silence until he finished his first cup and was pouring his second. When he sat again, he cleared his throat tenderly.

"So. I hear you were a bit clumsy last night."

I shot a quick look at him, but saw the small smile playing at his lips. "Wonder who could have told you that."

"You know me and little birdies. Talon Wolfchild, isn't it?"

I nodded and resigned myself for a lecture.

"Nice young man. Bought the old Wilson place. Hear he's fixing it up right nice. Good thing, it's a shame how long that place had been sitting empty. Also, doing Amber's kitchen, isn't that right?"

Grumbling an affirmation, I kept staring out the window.

"Fine work, from what I saw the other day. Can't find good work ethic much anymore. Amber told me he was ahead of schedule."

He waited for a response, but didn't get one. "Done some volunteer work, too. Rebuilt the playground at the school and made the ramp for Mrs. Winchester when she had her accident and got confined to a wheelchair."

I sighed. "Are you trying to make me feel guilty?"

"Of course not. I'm your father, after all. If this young man did something against your wishes, why, I'd like to know so I can pay him a visit myself."

Rolling my eyes, I rose from the stool. "He didn't do anything against my will." Thinking briefly of the kiss, the coffee cup slid out of my hands and into the sink. I realized what I said was true. Risking a glance back at my dad, he had an eyebrow raised in question. "We just don't get along, that's all."

He shrugged and rose casually from the stool. "All right." Taking another mug out of the cupboard, he poured a cup for my mother, black. As if a thought just occurred to him, he turned back at the doorway. "By the way, your mother and I are visiting Naomi this morning. So, you know, you're off the hook, if there's somewhere you need to go."

Looking quite pleased with himself, he turned and left. I stared after him.

It was a struggle. First with myself, and then with an apology. Finally, I decided on a buffer.

At the store, I picked up a fresh baked loaf of French bread, some cream cheese, honey and eggs. There were a few specialties I had in the kitchen, and as yet I hadn't found anyone that could resist my stuffed French toast.

The drive through the wooded driveway was tough. Since I wasn't in view of the house, I could come up with a million reasons to leave. Go back to Grandma, like I did every other morning. Use the amazing light to shoot pictures. Claw my own eyes out.

But before I knew it, the rickety old farm house was in sight and I was stuck. I parked in front, and counted to ten with deep breaths before I opened the door.

The house looked empty, but I could hear pounding from around back. Curious, I detoured there instead of trying the door. My dad mentioned Talon was fixing up the place, so if there were construction noises, that would be the place to look.

The old house had some definite charm, though it was falling apart from lack of use. Already I could see repairs to the wrap around porch, which had yet to be painted. I found myself curious about the inside, but that thought was sidetracked quickly when I rounded the back.

He was there, much as I'd seen him the first night. Shirtless, though I again had a jacket on, with a pair of black work pants and, at least, some old work boots. He was incredible. Since he hadn't spotted me, I took my time admiring the build of his back and arms as he swung a hammer. To this point, I'd never understood the appeal of construction men. Now I got it.

His hair was pulled back at the nape of his neck and hung just below his shoulders. I drug a hand through my own, suddenly self-conscious. The bangs my latest hair dresser talked me into were going awry, and the rest of it hung limp and loose towards my lower back. My sisters and I all had the straight hair curse- even after hours of primping and curling, our hair would hang straight as an arrow.

Lost in my thoughts, I jumped when he turned and caught sight of me. A smile spread easily and he replaced the hammer before coming closer to me.

"Um, hi," I managed. Very smooth.

"Good morning," he answered, stopping just short of a few feet away.

For a moment, I forgot the reason for my visit. "I, uh, well- I thought I'd make you breakfast."

"Breakfast."

"Yes, you know, the thing you eat in the morning?" Closing my eyes, I took another breath and tried again. "I felt bad for last night, so I was hoping this would make up for it." There. That could be considered an apology.

"You don't have any iced tea in there, do you?" He asked, gesturing towards the bags.

"No. Just some hot coffee."

"At least it's something new and different. Would you like to go inside? I just have a little to finish up here, and then I'll join you."

"Uh, sure," I responded. I wasn't expecting such easy acquiescence.

"The kitchen is complete, I assure you. Just head in through that door, it'll be on your right."

Deciding not to speak, I just nodded and started towards the back door. Behind me, the sounds of hammering continued.

Coming in through the back door, I slipped my shoes off and went through a short hallway. When I reached the first set of doorways, I stood in shock.

The kitchen was gorgeous. It was big and open with top of the line appliances. Off an arched doorway was a curved dining area, surrounded by windows looking into the yard. I was in love.

Setting down the bags, I snuck into the room opposite the kitchen only to be disappointed. The walls and floors were stripped bare. There was no furniture, no lights and no window coverings. Looking up towards the ceiling, I saw delicate, and very detailed, wood trim. It looked as if Talon was restoring it to its former glory. The thought made me inexplicably happy.

Returning to the kitchen, I unpacked and rummaged around until I found mixing bowls, a cutting board and a skillet. Brand new knives were waiting in their wood block. I almost salivated over the thought.

After a brief search, I found the spices I needed and set to work. Just as I was placing the first batch in the warmed skillet, Talon walked in, pulling a shirt on over his head.

We studied each other for a brief moment before I broke. "I love the kitchen," I told him.

He grinned. "I'm glad. It was the first thing I finished. Two months," he said, taking a look around himself. "It was worth it."

"How much of the rest of the house do you have done?" I asked. This was easy ground, where I didn't have to fake interest.

"The master bedroom is nearly complete, and I'm working on the bath now. That," he said, pointing outside where I'd found him, "is the new cabinet."

"Better bring that in before the rain," I told him, stretching to look out the window. "You wouldn't want it to get ruined."

"I'll be sure to do that."

I turned again, feeling slightly awkward. "I'm making French toast," I told him. "One of my specialties."

"Sounds delicious."

Flipping the first batch over, I said, "These should be done in a few. Would you mind setting the table?"

He obliged me, setting us up in the little sun room off the kitchen. Thinking about it, I realized that was the only place we could have eaten. From what I saw of the room next door, he didn't have much furniture otherwise.

Sliding the toast on a plate, I set the next on the skillet and brought the done ones to the table. Talon was ahead of me, setting out butter and syrup.

"Perfect," I complimented him. "Try some while it's hot."

He pulled out a chair for me to sit, so I did and served us both. Taking one bite, he smiled up at me.

"This is wonderful. What's in it?"

I smiled back. Worked like a charm. "Cream cheese, honey, vanilla and nutmeg. Then I put cinnamon in the eggs before coating them."

"There's more in there, right?"

My smile widened. "Of course. You can have the whole loaf, if you want."

"I just might. Thank you for doing this."

Dropping my eyes, I felt my color rise. "I wouldn't have if I hadn't doused you with my drink last night."

"Once again, well worth it."

Sliding my chair back, embarrassed and nervous, I mumbled something about flipping the toast. I rushed back into the kitchen to compose myself.

Talon seemed to understand my need for space, because he didn't follow. Silently chastising myself on yet another unnecessary swing of emotion, I waited until the last batch was cooked and brought them all back to the table.

I offered him a big, fake smile. He studied me for a while, but seemed to think better of whatever he was going to say. Instead, he took another helping and started a new subject.

"How's your grandmother doing?"

My eyes shot up, momentarily surprised before I remembered Amber. "She's okay. With the drugs she's on, she's lost her speech, but I know she still has an idea of what's going on. Beats me at cards every time."

He laughed at that, and the dejected look on my face. "She sounds like a wonderful woman. Both you and Amber speak about her with such love."

I nodded. "Our family is extremely close. Both sides, which I know is highly unusual for most."

"Your mother and father's families have been in the area a long time?" He asked.

"Yes. Generations."

"And you left."

Feeling a little uncomfortable again, I shrugged. "Got antsy, I guess. Couldn't wait to get out of here at 18."

"Where did you go?"

I thought back to the early days, when I took off in my car without a clue. A wry smile twisted my mouth.

"South. I made stops along the way, got a few jobs here and there and finally ended up in Florida."

"You're a photographer," he said, and I figured Amber had filled him in on that too.

"That's right. I took some classes in high school, and loved it. When I was down in Florida, I was interviewing for newspaper photographer positions." I laughed abruptly, making Talon's eyebrows raise. "I got my big break a little unconventionally," I explained.

"Tell me about it," he offered, sitting back in his chair. There were only a few pieces of toast left on the platter.

"Well, I was on my way to an interview, and somewhere between the fourth and fifth floor, the elevator got stuck. There was a storm outside, which before I lived there I would have called a hurricane, and the power went out. I was in that elevator for three hours." I paused, taking a sip of juice. "Three hours is a long time in a small space, so I got to know the man with me pretty well. Eventually it came out that I was looking for work, and that I was a photographer. Since I was on my way to an interview, I had my portfolio with me. He asked to see it, loved my stuff, and wanted to know if I'd ever done private sittings."

I paused then, remembering the know it all 18-year-old I'd been, and how that moment felt. "I said that I could, and the next day I did photos of his family. His name was James Royce."

Talon asked, "*The* James Royce?"

James was a multi-billionaire and a huge public figure. It wasn't surprising that Talon knew of him. "Yup. From there, I went straight up. Before long, I had more contract offers than I could manage. Now I mostly freelance, though once a year he has me take new photos of his family. I have an agent that I send my pictures to, and she handles everything from there."

"Gives you freedom."

"Yes, it does. I've traveled all over, and get paid to do it. Now, I can stay here as long as I need and not have to worry about my bills piling up."

Fiddling with my cup, I asked him, "So how did you end up here?"

"What do you mean?"

"You're not from here, right? So, where'd you move from?"

"I've lived many places. Most recently I was in New Mexico."

"That's a long way from here," I commented, meaning more than the distance.

"It is. Sometimes I miss the desert life, but I'm acclimating rather well."

"Why did you choose Sun Valley?"

He smiled. "The land called to me."

It was my turn for my brow to raise. "Does it use the phone for that?"

His smile only widened. "Sometimes. Perhaps one day I'll show you."

"Maybe," I answered noncommittally. "Anyway, I better go. I missed breakfast with my grandma, and she'll miss our morning card game if I don't leave soon."

"Of course," he answered, and stopped me from clearing the table. "No, no. I'll get it. Thank you again for breakfast."

"Sure," I said, picking up my purse and heading for the door.

I made it down the steps before he stopped me. "Jade?"

Spinning around, I looked up at him. He was leaning casually against the railing, the wind rustling his clothing. "Come to dinner tonight."

"Oh, I don't think..."

"Don't think. Just come. I can make it as late as you need."

There was that war within myself again. One of these days I might implode.

"If you say no, I'll just call your sister."

Letting out a frustrated sigh, I succumbed. "Fine. But I might bring iced tea."

He smiled. "Let's try for 8:00. Is that late enough?"

"Yeah. Fine," I repeated, and walked off to my car. I knew I was going slowly insane, but perhaps I'd already lost my mind.

CHAPTER 5

The day was at once too long and too short. It's not that I was looking forward to my evening plans. Not at all. I was merely curious. Partly, I wanted a tour of the rest of the house. Partly, I wanted to see his culinary skills. Most of all, though, I wanted to see if the strange phenomenon from the morning was still evident.

I liked him, I realized.

It scared me.

And excited me.

And aggravated me.

There was no real reasoning behind it. In our very limited conversations, we hadn't hit on any real common ground. More often than not, I found myself thinking harmful thoughts. Yet there was some indescribable pull that I felt, and no matter what reasoning I gave to avoid him, I realized this: in some fashion, for some bizarre reason, Talon and I were irrevocably tied together.

It was these thoughts that kept the day much too long, and much too short. Grandma had a bad day. When she slept, we couldn't wake her. She barely ate, at breakfast with my parents or at lunch with me. During our morning card game, she threw the cards on the floor and started crying.

I didn't know what to do anymore. It broke my heart watching her deteriorate in front of my eyes, and I was helpless to do anything about it. Research on her diseases just wasn't far enough along to be of any help.

Over and over again, Janet told me to go home, but I refused to listen. This was my grandma, and I would be there for her.

When she fell asleep for the night, I finally dragged myself to the car and noticed the time. It was five to eight. I desperately wanted to cancel dinner, but I didn't know Talon's number. Or if he even had a phone. With a groan, I made the drive out to his house, preparing to say thanks, but no thanks.

I parked in front of the house and hauled myself out. As I reached the steps, Talon came out the door and extended a hand. Without a word, I took it. He led me inside, down the hall from the kitchen into a front living room. To my surprise, there was a couch. Nothing else in the room was completed, but there was a single couch where he sat me down.

"Bad day?" He asked, sitting on the end and propping my feet in his lap.

"Yeah," I said. Then, with narrowed eyes, "What are you doing?"

Slowly, he was removing my shoes and setting them carefully on the floor. Sliding off my socks, he took my foot in his hands and began rubbing.

"Never mind," I told him, leaning back. "Don't stop."

It was heaven. His hands were warm and soothing on my soles, and as I lay back I felt totally at ease. Between my lack of sleep the previous night and the emotional day, it took only minutes for me to be out.

When I awoke, it was to the smell of garlic and some kind of sausage. Sliding my eyes open, I noted the pale light and figured it had to be close to 9:00.

"Feeling better?" Talon asked. He was standing in the doorway, watching me.

"Actually, I do. Thanks. And sorry."

He smiled and walked towards me. "Come, have something to eat."

"It smells wonderful. What is it?"

"One of *my* specialties," he said. Still holding my hand, he led me back to the room off the kitchen. "Pasta with fresh vegetables and Italian Sausage."

When I walked in, candles were burning brightly on the table and a vase of fresh flowers sat in the middle. As he'd done twice before, Talon pulled out a chair for me to sit.

"Is that," I paused, feeling a tear come to my eye, "Fresh garlic?"

"Of course," he answered, sitting beside me.

"It's wonderful," I breathed.

He chuckled. "You haven't even tried it yet."

"Doesn't matter," I told him. "It's not from a can, it's fresh and there's not three pounds of beef mixed in. You have my vote."

He scooped up a helping and waited for me to try it. "Mm," I said with my mouth full. "Even better than it smells. Thank you."

"You're very welcome. I take it you're not very happy with the meals you've been having lately."

I rolled my eyes. "If you could call them meals. One of those things that never bothered me until I moved away, of course. There's just so many wonderful dishes and flavors out there. I can't believe people are afraid to try them."

"My thoughts exactly. Perhaps you'll let me cook for you more often."

Raising my eyes to meet his, I thought about my answer. Normally, it would have been an automatic no. Maybe I was maturing. "We'll see."

"I can work with that," he told me. I had a feeling he could.

Once the meal was finished, I rose and cleared my place. We set the dishes on the counter, but before I could start to rinse or wash, he asked, "Would you like a glass of wine?"

It only took me a second to consider. After my day, a glass of wine sounded perfect. "That'd be nice," I said.

We took our wine back into the room with the couch and sat at opposite ends. I curled my feet beneath me, feeling more at ease than I had in months.

"Do you want to talk about it?"

"Not really," I answered honestly. "At least not tonight. I was actually just thinking about how relaxed I feel, and talking about it would ruin that."

"It's okay to take time for yourself," he said.

I nodded but didn't comment. Definitely didn't want to get into that.

38

"There *is* something I'd like to talk about," I ventured. He looked at me inquisitively, so I rolled my shoulders and sank deeper into the cushion. The wine was helping my confidence a little.

"About last night," I went on. "About what happened after the iced tea incident."

"Oh?"

"Right. It's just that- well, not that it wasn't nice, but..." I let out a breath. "I just can't do a relationship right now. My family is all trying very hard, but my focus is elsewhere. Not that I didn't enjoy tonight, I did, but..."

"But you'd like to keep this platonic." His voice was very flat when he said it, his eyes on his drink.

"Yes."

"Fine."

"Really?" I let out a breath I hadn't realized I was holding.

"But I need a promise on something," he continued.

Uh oh. "What?"

"When you are looking for more, promise me to look here first." His eyes met mine, and I wanted to agree to anything he asked of me.

"We'll see," I said again.

"I can work with that."

We both smiled, and I finished off my wine. "I should go."

He nodded. "Let me drive you back."

"Bad idea. I *am* living with my parents, so my car disappearing would not be a good thing."

He shook his head, smiling. "I'll drive you in your car, and I'll walk back."

"Are you crazy? What if..."

"Remember the night we met? I was out walking then. I go out almost every night. I'll be fine."

"Will you take no as an answer?"

He shook his head.

"Fine. Let's go."

He pulled into my parent's driveway and rushed around to open my door.

"Thanks," I said awkwardly.

He slowly, and deliberately, took my hand in his. My heart beat quicker until he gave it an easy shake and released it.

"Good night," he said, and waited for me to walk inside. When I did, I turned around with a wave, but, once again, he was gone.

39

CHAPTER 6

The next week brought with it more bad days than good with my grandma. It was disheartening and frustrating. It also took up most of my time, so there were no run-ins with Talon.

On Saturday, I went grocery shopping for Sunday dinner at my mom's request. I had a feeling that she was forcing me to get fresh air, and I didn't put up much of a fight.

In the meat section, I was perusing the roasts when a vaguely familiar voice made me glance up.

"Jade?"

It took me a second to register, but when I did I smiled a friendly smile. "Hey, Rick."

His little girl, Cassie, if I remembered correctly, was sitting in the basket and staring at me.

"Hi there. I'm Jade, Ashton's aunt."

She kept staring at me.

"I was going to get in touch with you the next couple days. How does dinner and some drinks at The Spade sound?" Rick asked.

"Actually, it sounds great. What day did you have in mind?"

"How's Monday?"

"Perfect. Can we meet around 7:00?"

"Sure. I'll see you then."

I picked up my roast and gave them a wave. Cassie was still staring at me.

An evening without pressure or family. It sounded too good to be true. I finished the shopping list and headed home.

Sunday afternoons were a nut house. The entire family gathered: Jack and Amber, with Junior, Penny and Sandy; Gerry and Emma, with Suzy and Mikey; Micah and Pearl, with Ashton, Aspen, Ewan, Ella and Kalia; and, more often than not nowadays, Grandpa Stryder.

Today's menu included roast, mashed potatoes, green bean casserole and apple pie for dessert. Luckily, it was a nice enough day that the children were sent outside to wear off some energy before dinner. The men stood around watching them and discussing manly things while the women took over the kitchen.

I was on apple duty when the doorbell rang. Since my station was the cleanest, my mom asked me to get the door.

Wiping my hands off on a towel, I pushed my hair out of my face and pulled open the door. I shouldn't have been surprised, yet there I was, stock still.

"Are you going to invite me in?"

Talon stood at the door, an amused smile on his face and a small bag in his hand.

I didn't step back. Instead, I crossed my arms and glared at him. "What are you doing here?"

"I was invited."

"My family sure seems to enjoy feeding you."

"I brought a peace offering," he told me, holding out the bag. I peered into it. "Wine and a garlic sauce for the potatoes. Fresh garlic."

He dangled it in front of me like a carrot. "Fine," I finally muttered. Taking a step back, I waved him through.

As he passed, he bent and kissed me on the cheek. My glare darkened.

"Many cultures kiss friends on the cheek to say hello," he answered my scowl.

"Not mine," I muttered to his back as he found his way to the kitchen.

"Oh, Talon, you made it!" I heard my mother coo from the doorway. When I entered, I could have sworn she was batting her lashes.

"I don't make it a habit to turn down beautiful women," Talon answered smoothly and kissed her hand. Color stole into my mom's cheeks and made me roll my eyes.

"Amber, so good to see you," he went on, seeming not to notice his effect on the room. Turning towards my other two sisters, he studied them a moment before saying, "You must be Emma, and you must be Pearl. It's a pleasure." He repeated the gesture with each of them as he had with my mom, making them giggle.

"This is for you," he said, turning back to my mom and holding out the bag. "Some wine and a sauce to mix into the potatoes, if you'd like to use it."

"Why, thank you. That's so kind," my mom seemed abnormally flustered.

"Talon, the men are gathered outside, if you'd like to join them," Amber piped in.

"Though I'm sure I would enjoy the company in here much more, I should do the man thing," he said, with a wink towards me.

The second he was out of the room, it exploded with exclamations.

"He can come to dinner anytime!"

"Am I melting? I feel like I'm melting."

"If I were 20 years younger... hell, if he comes near me again..."

The only one not speaking was Amber, but she was enjoying the pandemonium. I was silent also, but not nearly as amused.

"All right, which one of you do I get to hurt?" I asked when it had calmed enough to be heard.

Amber held her hands up immediately. "It wasn't me this time."

"This time?" Pearl was sharp. "You mean you've had him for dinner, and didn't invite me?"

"First time I've met him," Emma said. All eyes turned towards our mom.

"All right, you got me. It's just that when I heard about your little *incident*," she shot me a look, "I thought it only right I invite him over. When I happened to run into him at Amber's..."

"Ugh. Never mind. I'm not sitting by him."

"I will," Emma and Pearl said simultaneously, then craned their necks to look out the window.

"Okay, married women in the room, stop gawking at Jade's man." My mom, luckily for her, turned away to smile.

"HE'S NOT MY MAN!" I yelled, but to no avail.

"Way to go, Jade. I mean, I wanted you to get together with Rick, but now I see why you declined." This was from Pearl.

"I didn't decline! I'm seeing him tomorrow!"

All eyes turned to me. "What?" They asked in unison.

My cheeks flushed this time. "As friends, that's all. We're going to dinner."

"Well, well," Emma mused, "Looks like Jade's got herself two men."

"No, I don't. I don't have any."

"You didn't see the way Talon was looking at you. I'd say you do."

I didn't bother with a reply. Anything I said would just dig me deeper. Instead, I sliced the last of the apples. The knife hit the board with a satisfying *thwack*. I smiled, imagining a different target than the bright green fruit.

The dining room table sat 30, and was in the largest room in the house. Around the table, chairs were interspersed with high chairs and boosters so the kids could sit with the adults. My mom had a firm disbelief in 'kid tables'. They were her grandchildren, and they would sit at the table with her.

Despite my protests, I was seated next to Talon. It was either that, or baby duty. If I had been asked, I would have picked the latter.

Since I wasn't, I was sitting squeezed between Talon and Pearl. My grandfather was at the head of the table one direction, with my father opposite. My mom sat at my dad's right side, with Amber beside her. The rest were clumped together by family, with baby Mikey between Talon and Emma. He was too young yet to have anything but milk, but he joined us anyway.

Pearl was currently leaning over me to speak to Talon. Always a natural flirt, Pearl couldn't pass up the opportunity to bat her lashes at an attractive man. Not that I was worried- she was head over heels in love with Micah, and had been since she was 10 and he saved her cat from a tree. He had been 16 at the time, and thought of her as a little sister. Six years after that, he'd come home from college to find Pearl all grown up. They'd been inseparable since.

"I hear you're rebuilding the old Wilson place," Pearl was saying.

"That's correct. I just finished up the master bath yesterday."

"I always loved that place. Maybe I could stop by and see it when it gets done," she said hopefully.

"You're always welcome. Micah and your children, also. Could you tell me their names again?"

"Of course. This is Ashton, Aspen, Ewan, Ella and Kalia," she recited down the line, gesturing towards each mop of blonde hair as she went.

"Those are all trees, if I'm not mistaken?"

43

Pearl smiled happily. "That's right! I've never had anyone know that until I told them. We have a thing for themes in our family. I was going to do a flower theme, like all of our middle names, but out popped Ashton and I couldn't very well name my boy after a flower. So, I went to the next best."

"They are beautiful names, and beautiful children."

"Oh, thank you," Pearl smiled shyly, then extended a hand to meet Micah's. "I had some help with that part."

The men exchanged a grin behind her back. I shook my head and dug into the mashed potatoes. Stifling a sigh of pleasure, I savored the spices before swallowing. If nothing else, the man knew how to cook.

One good thing about so many people at the dinner table, I could completely ignore someone without seeming to. Conversation was a constant buzz that served as a buffer between me and the person whose heat I could feel across the scant few inches that separated us.

Grandpa Stryder was at the end of the table, telling jokes to the children that we all hoped they wouldn't understand for a few years. Last week, he told us all that we could give up drugs, alcohol and sex, but it wouldn't make you live longer. It would only make it *seem* longer. Amber and Emma had covered their children's ears, while Pearl and I had giggled hysterically.

"Talon, this sauce is delicious," Emma was saying over the baby's head. I knew for a fact that all my sisters were happily married, and yet they couldn't seem to keep their eyes off our guest. Not that I blamed them.

"Thank you. I'm glad you enjoyed it."

"I might have to steal the recipe from you," she said with a flirty smile. I tried not to roll my eyes again.

"Nonsense. You don't have to steal it, I'd happily share." Talon sent her a huge smile, dimple included, that had Emma's eyes going hazy.

I shoved my chair back. Mumbling something about using the bathroom, I started off down the hall. There was only so much I could take.

Closing the bathroom door, I ran cold water over my face. What was my problem? Handling men had always come so naturally, easily. Too easily. Why was this one so much different?

Staring at myself in the mirror, I was forced to admit the truth. Because I'd never been so attracted before.

It wasn't just physical- though, as all the females in my family could attest, physically he was extremely attractive- but I felt this other pull that had never been present in my other relationships. A pull that made me want to place everything in his hands.

I shook my head forcefully. No. I didn't get emotionally attached. That wasn't my thing. I was a free spirit, a lone wolf. Not some lovesick teenager. With a quick swipe of a towel, I pulled open the door and almost ran smack into my problem.

44

"Careful," he said, steadying me with his hands on my upper arms. "We don't want you falling down again."

Yanking my arms away, I glared up at him. There was only one way to fight with fire.

"What are you doing sneaking up on me?"

"To find out if you were capable of swimming."

This made me pause. "What?"

"Your sisters mentioned something about falling in. As I've seen your balance issues first hand, I was simply assuring myself you would not drown."

Crossing my arms, I kept my glare on him. "You're not funny, you know."

Mimicking my pose, he leaned against the opposite wall. "I'm a little funny."

"Not to me."

"Charming, then."

"No."

He grinned. "I'll have to work on that. Are you coming back to dinner, or would you prefer staying here with me the rest of the evening?"

"Have they served coffee yet?" I muttered and started down the hall.

"I'll be sure to stand on the opposite side of the room when they do," he answered me as he followed.

"Like that'll stop me."

"Are you this hostile to all guests in your home?"

I spun around and faced him. "Are you always so annoying a guest in other people's homes?"

"I don't think I'm annoying anyone, except perhaps you. Have you asked yourself why that is?"

Struggling against an annoyed huff of air, knowing that I had indeed asked myself that very question, I said, "I don't have to ask. You may think you're charming and sweet to everyone else," I ignored his widening smile, "But you intentionally rile me up. Tell me, do you enjoy enraged women? Because you haven't seen anything yet."

"Until I met you, I hadn't thought I did. I suppose I was wrong."

I was fuming, so much so that I was surprised not to see steam. Taking a calming breath, I spoke slowly and quietly. "Look, just do us both a favor. Stay away from me."

"Why do you think that would be doing me a favor?"

"Because I ruin men," I snapped out before I could censor it.

"You're worried for me. I find that very enduring. Not to worry, though. I assure you, I can handle myself."

Still grinning, he stepped around me and into the living room, leaving me gawking after him. Realizing my mouth was hanging open, I snapped it shut and stomped after him.

My family was mostly gathered in the living room, though there weren't enough seats for everyone. Pearl and Micah lounged on the floor, with a sleeping Kalia in one lap and a sleeping Mikey in another. Emma was perched on Gerry's lap, while children climbed over my parents and Grandpa Stryder. The few older children were outside playing on the old wooden swing set, being supervised by Jack and Amber. Ella climbed into Talon's lap and was being entertained by extremely animated stories. Before I could look away, he glanced up and our eyes met. His were lit with pure joy. I found myself melting just a little inside.

"Auntie Jade!" My hand was tugged on by Suzy. "Color!"

Smiling down at her, I let her lead me across the room where a few crayons were laid out with paper. For the next ten minutes, I watched as she scribbled absolute nonsense on the page and told her how lovely it was when completed.

"For you!" She said happily, holding out her work of art.

"Oh, thank you, Suzy. It's beautiful."

"Momma!" She cried out, spotting Emma nearby. Her attention was easily diverted.

"Come on, sweetie, time to go home."

"I don't wanna!" She screamed, throwing herself at her mother's legs.

Emma threw me a smile and hauled her up. "We'll be back tomorrow. Give everyone a hug and kiss good-bye," she told Suzy.

Crying, she ran to me and threw her arms around me. "Bye, Auntie Jade."

"Bye, sweetie. I'll see you tomorrow."

"'K," she said before running off to find the next victim.

"Kids, time to go," Pearl called out. Immediately, her children began to give hugs. This was always the longest part of the day.

I watched as Ella clung to Talon's neck. She leaned back and looked up into his eyes. "Will you be here next time?" She asked.

"I would love to, but if I'm not, you can come visit me with your mommy. Okay?"

"Okay!" She said, hugging him again.

Pearl glanced over at them and said, "You told her a princess story, she's going to love you for life. Don't be surprised if she does show up on your doorstep."

"She's welcome anytime." Talon told her.

Pearl flashed him a smile and headed out the door, kids in tow. Emma and Amber were next. Talon stood near the door, saying his goodbye's as well.

"Thank you so much for the invitation, Mrs. Callaghan. You have a wonderful family, you must be so proud."

"Oh, how sweet," my mom said, patting his cheek. "You can come back anytime."

"I may just take you up on that," he said with one of those dimple smiles.

"Talon, good to see you again," my dad said, shaking his hand.

"And you. I'll be stopping by this week about that property," he promised.

I shot my dad an inquisitive look but he missed it. "Be sure that you do."

"Mr. Stryder, would you care for a ride home?" He asked my grandpa.

"If it's not too much trouble. That way Isaac won't have to take me."

46

"It'll be my pleasure," Talon told him. Finally, he turned to me. "Good night, Jade. A pleasure, as always."

He held out his hand. Both my parents and grandfather stared at it, waiting for me to move. I sighed, defeated.

"Night," I told him and gave him a quick shake. When I tried to bring my hand back, he held it just a little longer. That was it. No kissing, no shaking, no other words. He just held it. My cheeks went hot. His smile widened.

"I'll see you soon."

There was that threat again. He released my hand and led my grandpa out. We stood at the door, watching them go. My mom fanned herself.

"Well, well. That boy is something else."

"Mom!" I said, disgusted.

She shrugged, unrepentant. "Well, he is."

My dad chuckled, shaking his head. "Come on, dear. I'll take you upstairs before you have a hot flash."

She slapped him half-heartedly on the arm. "Isaac Callaghan, you know perfectly well I don't get hot flashes."

My dad shot me a knowing look. "Of course not, dear. Come on now."

I watched them walk up the stairs together and shook my head. Some things never changed.

CHAPTER 7

The wind rushed past my face as I spurred the stallion into a gallop. There was such freedom in riding, freedom that never grew tiring no matter how often I rode. This wild one was a rich black, with silky hair flying from mane and tail. Work was to be done, but right now it was all about the ride.

Leading him gently West, I headed toward the trading post. The hot desert sky ran clear and blue as far as the eye could see, stopping only at the edge of the mountains surrounding this desolate valley. Inhaling the dust was like inhaling home. There was such beauty in the endless sea of sand, the sparse landscaping dotted with the occasional cacti or creosote. Many animals made this land home, though they were rarely seen.

It was a land, flora and fauna alike, that could protect itself. Plants were covered with spikes, animals carried poison in their skin. Either was ready and willing to act when an enemy approached. It was about survival here.

The horse slowed, unwillingly, as tents rose up. There was a small village settled here until spring, and was our source of information and the occasional supply. So much could be gleamed from the land, trading was almost unnecessary.

But it would upset the elders if we did not comply, so once every moon cycle I rode out to bring information back.

"Greetings, Eagle Talon."

"Greetings, Bear Paw. I have wares to trade."

The exchange was repetitive but necessary. At the other man's nod, I dismounted and gave the command for the stallion to stay. The exchange was done inside the teepee, thick with musk and stink.

Carefully I lay the bag on the ground, kneeling before it. Bear Paw examined each item before speaking.

"A sack of grain, your choice of corn."

"Thank you, Bear Paw."

He sat back then. "There are rumors of pale faces," he told me.

"Pale faces?" I asked, and masked any emotion those words created.

Nodding, he continued. "Our brothers to the East have brought word. They are dangerous, untrusting and murder the land. Any you see should be killed on sight, before they kill you."

These brought a strong twist to my stomach. That's not what is supposed to happen. The pale faces mean great things. Why is there death surrounding this news?

"Thank you, Bear Paw. We will be watchful."

Groaning, I rolled over and shoved my face into my pillow. I hadn't had a decent night sleep since I'd met Talon. These dreams were so odd, leaving nothing with me once I awoke but the vague feeling they were all about him.

Raising my head, I glanced at the clock and read 3:00 AM. With another long-suffering groan, I curled up again but couldn't go back to sleep. Did other people have this problem?

I laid awake for another hour before shuffling off to the shower. I ran it until it went cold.

Downstairs, I brewed the coffee and left it on warm for my mom and dad. Pouring a mug for myself, I sat at my stool and stared out the window. It was still dark, but not from the hour. Clouds were brewing again, and it looked like a nice thunderstorm was on its way. Just as I thought it, a rumbling started in the distance and ended with a satisfying bolt of thunder. As a kid, thunderstorms had always fascinated me. Not much had changed.

I went out to the small porch and snuggled into the cushioned chair. I would be protected here, but there would be no hindrance on the show. Bolts of lightning lit the sky in brilliant streaks. The thunder followed just a few seconds later. A vague memory of a children's book crossed through my mind, something about counting the seconds between the lightning and thunder to tell how far away the storm was. I wasn't sure how true it was, but I counted anyway.

Five. It was getting close. No rain yet, but the wind began to pick up. The trees swayed with the force of it and I took a quick glance around the yard to make sure nothing could become a projectile missile. Everything was clear, so I turned my attention back to the sky.

Another bolt of lightning. Three seconds. Taking a sip of coffee, I watched the clouds approach. The next streak of light had me glancing back to the trees.

My heart jumped. Standing not 20 feet away was a huge, black wolf. Its head was turned towards me as if it was studying me just as intently as I was studying it. Around him, the wind blew and thunder shook the ground. Another bolt of lightning shot down, lighting the forest around him momentarily. Thunder sounded immediately after. It was here.

Neither of us moved, perhaps too awed or frightened to do so. He was larger than any wolf I'd seen in these parts and absolutely magnificent. Even his tail stayed perfectly still, and if it weren't for the consistent streams of lightening I might not have even seen him at all. Ropes of muscle moved subtly beneath his thick fur, emanating his great power. Another thunderclap. He was gone.

I let out a breath I hadn't realized I was holding. Man, oh man, why didn't I have my camera? Though, looking back over the seemingly endless moment, I probably wouldn't have been quick enough to use it.

That had to be the same animal, I realized, that I'd seen running through the trees. No way was there more than one of those running around, not that size and color.

Once the rain started in, I made my way back inside. To my surprise, my mom was bustling around the kitchen making breakfast. Though I wasn't sure why at the time, I made no mention of the incredible moment I'd just had. It felt like a secret that wasn't mine to tell.

"Hi, sweetie. Would you like some eggs before you take off today?"

"Sure. What are you doing up so early?"

"The storm woke me. I actually beat your father today. Imagine that."

I smiled at her unusually cheery mood. She must have downed her first cup of caffeine like a shot to be this perky.

"So," she began and I stifled a groan, "Big date tonight."

"It's not a date," I reiterated. "We're just friends, going out for a drink."

Sliding whipped eggs into a frying pan, she turned and studied me. "Are you happy?"

The question took me by surprise. I started to answer automatically, but she held up a hand. "Think about it before you answer. Really, are you happy?"

"I'm happy to be around family again," I said honestly.

"And?"

"And nothing. That's what I'm here for."

Her eyes looked sad for just a moment before she turned back to the eggs. "I'm happy to have you here, honey. I hope you know that. But there's more to life. We just don't want you to miss out."

Sighing, I rose from the stool and wrapped my arms around her. "Thanks, Mom. But stop worrying about me. I'll be fine."

Leaning back into me, she sighed. "I know. You're my survivor. I just don't want you to survive alone."

Throughout the day, I thought about what my mom had said. No one in my family really knew my true thoughts about relationships. I'd just been against them for so long, that they all believed I still was and needed to be otherwise convinced. The truth was, I wanted to get married and have kids. Living in Florida, I wasn't around kids a lot, and moving back here made me realize how much I missed them. Kids really were awesome. But then I tried to picture myself, in a white dress- or picture myself, with little clones clinging to my legs- and it just didn't fit. Was something wrong with me? Or were my standards too high?

There were men in my past that were great guys. Most of them, by now, were actually married and starting families. When I dated them, every so often I tried to see myself with them in five years, ten years- and all I got was a blank screen. I was at a point now where I'd been single for over a year. That was unheard of for me. Always, since I'd been a teenager, I'd had some fling or another. And now, this voluntary drought.

Shaking myself out of these thoughts, I glanced over to my grandma. Her eyes were half closed, her body beginning to stoop. Quickly I rearranged her bed and got her comfortable for the night. She was sleeping more and more often, which worried me. The doctors assured us that was normal.

Checking my watch, I saw it was later than I realized and I hurried home to change. I was supposed to meet Rick in half an hour. I drove the few blocks home, dashed upstairs and threw on a green, wrap around shirt that tied in the back and a pair of jeans. It wasn't overly dressy, but it was clean. Running a brush quickly through my hair, I grabbed a purse and ran back down the stairs.

"Bye, Mom!" I called out, spotting her in the kitchen on my way out.

"Have fun, honey!" She called back, and the slamming door was her only answer.

The Spade was in the next town over, a 20-minute drive. It had decent food and a couple pool tables, more than most places in town could boast. After work it was packed, but by 8:00, the crowd dwindled down to the serious drinkers and on the weekends or summertime, the younger crowd.

I was only a couple minutes late, but Rick was there with a table staked out. He waved me over and I sat down gratefully.

"What'll you have?" A young, pretty girl with a name tag that identified her as Robin asked just as I settled.

"Spotted Cow," I replied immediately. Rick raised a brow at me.

"What's that?"

"Good old Wisconsin beer," I explained.

He nodded. "Bring me the same," he told her.

When she left, he turned back to me. "Beer, huh?"

I shrugged. "Can't claim to be from here and not drink beer. That'd be like saying I don't like cheese. Practically against the law."

He laughed as the waitress set the beers down. Taking a sip, he grinned. "That's pretty good."

"Of course it is," I told him with an answering smile. "There's a few things we know, and beer is one of them."

"What are the others?" He asked curiously.

"Cheese and football," I responded. He laughed again.

"Hungry?"

"Starved." When he mentioned it, I realized I hadn't eaten since breakfast. Lunchtime somehow managed to pass me by. Again.

"Are you up for some appetizers? I'm curious about some of these," he said, staring at the menu.

"How long have you lived up here?" I asked him, realizing I really didn't know anything about him.

"We moved in the middle of the school year, so just about six months."

"Ever been here?"

"No, just heard about it."

I sighed, shaking my head. "You have much to learn, young one."

When the waitress came back, I ordered fried cheese curds, beer soaked mini brats and onion rings, which were fried in beer batter. Life just didn't get any better.

"If I have a heart attack, promise to get me to a hospital," Rick begged as the waitress went to put in the order.

I laughed. "Promise. These are delicacies here, you know. I hope you enjoy them."

"I've come to the conclusion that anything fried is good. So, you were living down in Florida, right?"

Nodding, I said, "That's right. I still have my house there and plan to go back, eventually."

"You came up here because of your grandma?"

Shifting uncomfortably in my seat, I tried to answer honestly. "Yes. When I realized she was sick, I wanted to be here. Where'd you move from?" I was hoping the subject change wasn't too abrupt.

He seemed to notice, but left it alone. "LA. When my wife died, I wanted to get out of the city and raise my daughter somewhere better."

"I'm so sorry," I said, automatically reaching out and grasping his hand. "When did it happen?"

"Three years ago," he said, giving a small smile. "It took me a while to find this place."

Putting my hand back in my lap, I asked, "How did it happen?"

"A car accident. Happens every day there, just never thought it'd happen to me. Cassie hardly remembers her."

His eyes were sad, and I felt my own tear up. "She's lucky to have you," I said, meaning it. "So how did you come to find Sun Valley?"

Clearing his throat, he seemed grateful for the distraction. "I was a partner in a law firm down in LA, and I put out feelers for a small town that needed a lawyer. This was one of three that popped up, and when I came to visit with Cassie, it just immediately felt like home. So, this is where we stayed."

I remembered Pearl mentioning he was a lawyer, probably the only one in town. I couldn't imagine his work load being too hefty, which probably left plenty of time for him to spend with his daughter.

Our appetizers arrived and I got the pleasure of watching him taste fried cheese curds for the first time. I dug in, making up for lunch, and we ordered actual dinner too.

As I finished off a bacon cheeseburger, I looked up to see Rick watching me with awe. "For a small girl, you sure can eat."

It made me grin. "I'll take that as a compliment. You, on the other hand," I gestured towards his plate with only half the burger gone, "You need some help."

"You're welcome to it," he said jokingly, holding out the plate.

Shaking my head, I patted my stomach. "I'm stuffed. Give me an hour or so."

He leaned back, obviously amused by me. "So," he began, and his tone reminded me of my sisters. "I heard Talon Wolfchild came to dinner last night."

I groaned. Of course he did. "Great. Pearl asked you to sniff out details, didn't she?"

His eyes were lit with a smile. "Of course not. Pearl would never do something so intrusive."

Rolling my eyes, I leaned back in my chair also. "Nothing is going on with us. We've run into each other briefly a couple times, end of story."

He sobered his face and nodded seriously. "I can see that."

My fist tightening, I leaned forward menacingly. "Hey now..."

Stopping me, he held up a hand and leaned towards me. "Seriously, we're friends now, right?"

"Sure," I said, not relaxing my pose.

"Just- just be careful, okay? I've only met him a couple times, and he acted perfectly polite, but there was just something off about him. Something dangerous, almost. I couldn't quite put my finger on it, but sometimes you can just tell, you know?"

I sat back again. I knew. "Acting like a big brother now, Rick?" I asked sweetly, taking the tension from the conversation.

He smiled, but it was reserved. "I've had enough practice. Just promise me you'll be careful."

Crossing my heart, I held up my hand and said, "Scouts honor."

That night, I couldn't sleep. Most of it I stood, staring out the window. The brief conversation with Rick about Talon was disturbing me. Of course I felt that something was off about him. Besides the fact that I seemed utterly obsessed with him, which I shouldn't be, he was definitely a man with secrets. Secrets that, no matter how much I admonished myself, I had to uncover. Unconsciously I looked in the direction of his house. Just what are you hiding, Talon Wolfchild?

CHAPTER 8

I was groggy the next morning, working on my first cup of coffee. For someone who claimed not to be a coffee drinker, I was sure packing in the liquid lately. I blamed my sleepless nights on Talon, his face keeping me from falling into blissful, dreamless oblivion. It had to stop soon or I'd be likely to fall on my face walking out the door.

My mom came into the kitchen looking tired as well. Maybe it was something in the air.

"Fun night?" She asked, giving me a once over.

I shrugged. "Fun enough."

She studied me again. "Hung over?"

I nearly spit out my drink. "No, not hung over. Just trouble sleeping."

She nodded in understanding and grabbed a bagel from the fridge. Holding it out in silent question, she waited until I shook my head to pop it in the toaster. Sitting down, she cradled the mug in her hands and stared blankly at the counter.

"What property is Dad showing Talon?" I asked, remembering the comment Talon made on his way out from dinner.

She glanced over at me, surprised. "I'm not sure. You'll nave to ask your father."

"Ask him what?" We both glanced up at my dad's voice, which sounded more awake than the two of us put together.

"Just wondering about something Talon said to you on Sunday, about looking at a property."

He nodded and snagged a bottle of yogurt out of the fridge. My mom and I both did an involuntary cringe. My dad had gone on a health food kick a few months back, and we didn't share in his enthusiasm.

"Black Bear Lake," he answered me, "The property that lines his now. It's mostly forest, but it has that beautiful lake in the middle. It was government owned, but it's up for sale."

Black Bear Lake. I knew it well- since it was government owned, the land hadn't been touched and was still in its natural state. It was a great place to photograph.

"That means he's planning on staying," I mused. "No one else has tried to snatch it up, build nice cabins on the lake?"

He shook his head this time. "Technically, it's not up for sale yet. It will be at the end of the week. I don't really know how Talon knew about it ahead of time. It hasn't exactly been advertised." Shrugging, he took a bottle of water and planted a kiss on top of my mom's head. "I'll see you ladies later."

My mom gave half a wave and took another gulp from her mug.

Following in my dad's suit, I kissed my mom on the cheek and headed out the door myself. There was a good hour of morning light for photos before I was due at the nursing home, and I wanted to take full advantage of it.

The day went by quickly, with my grandma in a better frame of mind than I'd seen her in the past week. I left late that night, wanting to spend every possible second with her while she was in high spirits. Grandpa Stryder was there most of the day as well, and most of their children stopped by to visit at one time or another. It was close to seven when I left and I was tired, but also elated. For a good hour, Grandma was able to speak, recalling current events as if there was no sickness tearing her body and mind apart.

I knew, from conversations with different doctors, that a lot of times elderly people with cases of Alzheimer's or the like would come back like that, just before death. A gift of sorts for the family. I kept that thought out of my head, and prayed instead for more time.

Pearl was holding a barbecue, which I was talked into going to even though all I wanted to do was go home. The barbeque was well under way when I arrived, a small tribute to the warm summer day. Kids were swimming off dinner in a large blow up pool while adults lounged around drinking a fruit punch concoction.

Greetings were thrown at me from every direction, and I waved in response to them. Just a quick appearance, I told myself, and I could go home.

I perched myself near the food table, a good place to stand to look inconspicuous and busy. The voice at my ear didn't bother me as much as others might have.

"Is there anything normal to drink around here?"

Rick was staring doubtfully into his fruity drink, complete with umbrella. With a quick, appreciative laugh, I leaned in and whispered, "I know where the beer's hidden."

"You would have my undying loyalty," he told me seriously.

Leading him towards the garage, I asked, "How's Cassie?"

"Having the time of her life. Ashton asked her to play Marco-Polo."

"How sweet," I commented, and stopped in front of the fridge inside the garage. "What's your poison?"

"Anything but this," he said, setting the drink aside.

Pulling out the two closest beers, I turned and offered one. "Any new prospects lately?"

Rolling his eyes and taking a large gulp from the bottle, he said, "Sandy Stevens has been none-too-subtly offering me her companionship."

"Ah, Seductress Sandy. She stole Richie Cunningham from me in third grade. Never forgave her for that."

A brow raised. "Really. Maybe I'll give her a shot, after all."

"Auntie Jade!" Eyes bright, Aspen streaked around the corner and into the garage. "Oh, hello Mr. Rick. Auntie Jade! Will you take pictures of our rock concert, please? Pretty please?"

"Rock concert?" I asked. "Sounds exciting. I'd be happy to. But only under one condition."

Aspen looked confused. "What?"

"I get the first autograph, so I can sell it when you're famous."

56

Her lips spread into a huge grin. "Okay!"

She ran off again, probably to spread the news.

"You're awfully good with them," Rick commented. "Sure you don't want any of your own?"

"Not anytime soon," I told him, taking a sip to emphasize. "We'd better get out there, rumors will start."

"You don't sound too excited about that," Rick observed.

Shrugging casually, I answered him, "Just don't feel like being around people today, I guess."

"Want me to leave?"

I looked over at him, realizing he would. "No. One or two I can handle."

We drank in companionable silence for a while, Rick watching the pool out the small window. When he spoke again, our drinks were near empty.

"You have a great family," he told me.

"Thanks. I know it."

Grinning, he grabbed two more and nudged me. "Ready for this?"

"Guess I'll have to be."

We wandered back out, watching the kids swim and the men construct a fire pit for the evening. It had been a long time since I'd sat with a campfire, though I didn't plan on staying that long. With any luck, I'd be sleeping in bed while s'mores were being consumed.

Emma arrived then, struggling under the weight of two kids and a diaper bag that put most suitcases to shame. Brows creasing, I glanced over at Gerry and noticed he was already here, and obviously had been for a while. He was in the supervisor position of the fire pit, a beer in his hand and his cheeks red with the evidence of the many before it.

Poor Emma looked like she was about to tip over, and was shooting her husband threatening looks which were systematically ignored. Before I could act, Rick was at her side, hauling Suzy to one hip and slinging the bag over his shoulder.

"Let me help you with this," he said with a smile.

They stared at each other for a long moment, which started to make even me uncomfortable. Breaking the connection, Emma looked down and mumbled a thanks. As they walked towards me, Suzy held out her hands and flung herself at me. There wasn't much choice but to grab her.

"I'm Rick," he told Emma, extending a hand.

"Emma," she said softly, still not making eye contact.

"You two haven't met?" I asked.

Without looking away, Rick shook his head. "I just met Amber today, too." Finally, he spared me a glance. "I'm sure everyone was at the picnic, but Pearl was pretty set on my itinerary that day."

"Oh!" Emma looked up, surprised. "You're that Rick."

One brow up, he smiled at her. "Good to know I've been talked about."

Emma blushed, something I couldn't remember seeing her do before. Not since high school, at least. "Not like that. Just- we all knew you and Jade were going to hang out."

"Ah, yes, when she tried to give me a heart attack."

This seemed to startle Emma. "What?"

"I've never had so much fried food in one setting. All delicious, of course," he added.

I shrugged, but realized I wasn't really in the conversation anymore.

"Jade's always been able to do that," Emma said, waving her hand towards me in a small acknowledgement. "Eat anything she wants and not gain an ounce. I drink whole milk and gain five pounds."

I started to protest, but Rick beat me to it. "You look perfectly fine to me," he told her.

She blushed again, looking down.

"Hey, honey," Gerry came up then, oblivious to the conversation. "Ron, isn't it?"

"Rick, actually." Rick's expression darkened.

"Right, right. Hey, there's Mikey. Let me have him, I'm gonna show him off a little."

Suzy struggled in my arms, reaching out towards her father. "Daddy!"

"Hey, little girl. You stay here with Mama and Auntie Jade and be a good girl."

Grabbing Mikey out of Emma's arms, he was gone again.

Her arms fluttering uselessly, Emma struggled for something to say. "Oh, um, I should take that bag back from you. Suzy, honey, do you want to go swimming?"

Suzy squirmed anxiously. "Yeah!"

Emma grabbed the bag and Suzy and took off, head down. I stared after her, dumbfounded.

"What was that?" I asked, eyeing Rick.

He was all innocence. "What?"

"I may be out of the game, but I know chemistry when I see it. You were flirting with my sister. My *married* sister."

He shrugged. "Just trying to be helpful."

"Helpful, my butt," I muttered, but it was to deaf ears. He was distracted again.

Turning, I saw why. Emma emerged from the house with Suzy in tow, both sporting swimsuits.

Whacking him on the arm, I whispered, "Tongue in mouth!"

A splash of water hit him on the side of the head and he snapped out of the trance. "Daddy! Watch this!"

He turned immediately and a grin lit up his face. Cassie was swimming across the pool in long strokes. "Nice job, Cassie! Where'd you learn that?"

"Ashton taught me!"

"Pearl takes all the kids to swim lessons," I told him. "There's an indoor pool in the next town over."

58

"I'll have to check that out," Rick said, and I saw his eyes dart towards Emma again.

"Yeesh," I admonished him. "Eyes forward, corporal."

"Yeah, yeah," he grumbled. "A man can appreciate the view at least, can't he?"

"Not when it's my sister." But I smiled at him anyway.

When Emma slid into the pool, toting Suzy around on a blow-up tube, Cassie zeroed in on her immediately. Unlike the silent stares I received, Emma got a huge smile and a greeting.

"Hi!" She said enthusiastically.

Emma smiled serenely. "Hi there."

"Can I help you with the baby?"

Suzy seemed indignant by this remark. "I'm not a baby. I'm 2!"

"I'm Cassie," she smiled.

"Suzy!"

"Want to swim with me, Suzy?"

"Yeah!"

Emma smiled down at her. "Where's your mommy and daddy, Cassie?"

Rick stepped forward, about to interrupt, when Cassie pointed. "That's daddy. Mommy's in heaven."

Emma's eyes, wide and apologetic, shot to Rick's. "I'm so sorry," she said in a low voice.

I watched the pain shoot across Rick's face.

"It's okay," Cassie went on, unfazed. "Daddy says Mommy watches over me and makes sure I'm okay. She had eyes just like yours," she said, looking at Emma.

Emma looked down at her again, emotions swirling on her face. Finally, she decided on a smile. "I bet she was a very special mommy, wasn't she?"

"Yup," Cassie agreed. "Can we swim over there? Ashton's over there."

Rick ran a hand over his heart, staring at his little girl.

I rubbed a hand over his shoulder, trying to soothe. "See," I told him quietly. "She does remember. And she won't forget."

He nodded, and kept staring after Cassie.

The day slowly turned into night, and my plans of leaving early were slowly diminished as the rock concert was set up. A promise was a promise, and I couldn't bear to break one to any of these kids.

Aspen and Cassie took center stage, along with a neighborhood friend named Beth, and after being pampered by Pearl for an hour were knockouts with princess dresses complete with feather boas. Their hair flew out in every which direction and I saw that Pearl had even let them add a little makeup. Ashton, Ewan and Junior were the backup dancers, and Beth's older sister, Liz, accompanied them on a portable keyboard.

59

All the adults and younger kids sat in the grass while I crouched in front, camera poised. Micah had even built a little wooden stage for the kids to perform on. They'd all obviously put quite a bit of work into this.

They sang renditions of popular songs by the latest teenage superstars, only stumbling over the words once. Cassie had an excellent voice, surprising the audience with her range. The boys spun on the floor and threw each other around, and I had a sneaking suspicion it was more improv than practiced. All in all, it turned out beautifully, and I got some wonderful shots.

Somehow, I was talked into staying for the fire directly after the concert. Most of the adults brought their own folding chairs and were circled around the growing flames. Kids sat in laps or on fallen logs, the anticipation for their chocolaty treats growing. I saw Rick sitting with Cassie in his lap, and her new friend Suzy snuggled in there with her. It made me grin. Ella was in my lap tonight and the only one besides Mikey falling asleep. It was well past bedtime for most of the kids, but the excitement was tangible in the air.

The back of my neck tingled and my heart beat sped. Without turning, I knew that Talon had arrived.

"Hope I'm not late," he said quietly, yet his voice carried across the wide circle.

Pearl shot him a wide grin. "Not at all. Here's an extra seat," she pulled one from behind her and hauled it right next to me. "Please, sit down. We're going to make s'mores in a minute."

"Thank you," he said politely and eased himself gracefully into the chair. I watched, enviously. Half the time *normal* people sat in one, they either broke or collapsed, and the other half they looked like a complete klutz. Not with him, of course.

"Good evening," he said amicably.

Ella's eyes shot open and her arms reached out. Talon lifted her easily from my lap to his, where she snuggled in and fell back into sleep.

"I didn't know you were invited," I said.

"Pearl was kind enough to extend an invitation. I would have been here sooner, but I was caught up."

I didn't ask what he was caught up with, though I was curious. Far as I knew, the only work obligations he had were his own house and Amber's kitchen.

Staring back into the fire, I watched as the flames leapt and crackled, shooting sparks high into the sky. It was getting darker, and the first stars were starting to show. Marshmallows and roasting sticks were passed around. Ella's eyes popped open again, and looked hopefully up at Talon.

"Marshmallow?" She asked.

He glanced over at me, a little helplessly.

"I'm afraid I've never done this before. Would you be willing to show me?"

"You've... never had a s'more?"

He shook his head. I shook my own, sadly. "You're missing out. Come on, Ella, let's show him how it's done."

She held on to the roasting stick, a fresh marshmallow perched on the end.

"Now," I began, "I like to burn mine and eat them off layer by layer. However, for the perfect s'more, you want your marshmallow to be golden brown."

I demonstrated, rotating Ella's so it was just above the flame and coated evenly. "The trick is, to get it cooked through without falling off. It's a very fine line."

Judging it to be near done, I instructed Talon to hold out a graham cracker with a piece of chocolate on it. Helping Ella maneuver the marshmallow onto it, I squished the top together and pulled the stick out. Perfection.

"Now," I said, "You eat it."

Ella demonstrated by taking a giant bite, marshmallow oozing out and covering her face. She grinned up at Talon, holding out the sandwich to share.

With a nod from me, he took a small bite and chewed carefully. "Delicious," he announced to Ella's delight. She burrowed back into his warmth and happily finished off the rest.

"It seems you've done this before," Talon said.

"Once or twice," I answered him. "Kind of a summer ritual."

He nodded thoughtfully. Taking a look around the circle of smiling faces, he determined, "It's a good one."

As the kids were beginning to drop off, Rick wound his way towards me, Cassie asleep in his arms.

"Rick," Talon nodded toward him. "Good to see you again."

"You too, Talon. Came to say good night," he held Cassie out in his arms. "Time for bed."

"Night, Rick. We'll have to hang out again soon," I told him.

"Sounds good. Have a good night."

"Drive carefully," Talon said.

Rick walked off, and I noticed the glance in Emma's direction as he went. I shook my head, but kept comments to myself.

"He's a good man," Talon said once he was out of range.

"Yes, I think so."

"He would never act on it," he said quietly.

My sharp glance had him smiling. "I saw the look as well as you did. I must say, I'm a bit relieved."

"Relieved?" I asked, confused.

His smile was sheepish now. "I know Pearl meant for you two to hit it off. Truth be told, I'm relieved it doesn't seem to have worked out that way."

Flushing, I turned my eyes back to the dwindling fire. "I still can't promise you anything," I told him finally.

"I know. I can wait."

The next day, Grandma was back to normal.

That brief window of communication was a gift, and I tried to see it that way when frustration mounted.

On my way home, I drove past Amber's and noticed a string of cars parked. It looked like Pearl and Micah both drove a car, and there was that truck.

I stopped, I told myself, because I was curious as to why Pearl and Micah drove separate cars. The truck had nothing to do with it.

As I got out, I saw a fierce game of tag in the back yard, so I followed the squeals and shouts to find Amber and Pearl standing at the edge of a grove of trees, arms crossed and staring into the woods. Penny, Sandy, Ella and Kalia were the only ones racing around, the other kids and the men missing.

"What's up?" I asked, making my two sisters turn.

Amber rolled her eyes. "Jack decided to let Junior try dirt biking."

"And talked Micah into it, so Ashton, Aspen and Ewan are out with him."

"Dirt biking? By themselves?" My voice rose on the last.

"Yeah. They make kid bikes now. I guess it's a big thing. Anyway, they're all out there now. Tal joined them." Amber watched me for a reaction.

"Oh," I said nonchalantly. "He any good?"

"I'd say so," Pearl commented, more to herself than us.

I glanced up and saw the object of our conversation fly out of the woods, followed further back by a trail of kids and the other two men. The wind whipped through his hair and he had a huge grin pasted on his face.

Spinning in a quick arc, dirt flying, he headed back into the trees. The engine revved and he was gone.

Amber and Pearl waved to the kids as they went by at a much more sedate pace. Junior, the youngest of the bunch, teetered a bit on the turn but held his own. I knew, if my heart was in my throat, Amber and Pearl's must be.

"They have a governor," Amber informed me. "They can only go up to somewhere around 15 or 20 miles an hour."

"The kids, anyway," Pearl said with a grin as Micah tried a maneuver similar to Talon's and almost ate it. "Nice one, honey!" She called out, only to be met with a scowl. "They've been at this for hours," Pearl told me, yawning. "Boys and their toys."

"Looks like fun," I said, watching as snippets of Talon came into view again. He was wearing a white shirt today, making it easy to see through the trees. As he neared us, he slid into a sideways stop.

"Want to ride?" He asked me.

I swallowed. Sure, it looked fun, but I wasn't totally sure I could handle it.

62

"We'll go slow, I promise," he said, holding out a hand patiently.

Ignoring my sister's grins, I walked hesitantly towards him. "Only if I can drive."

Raising a brow, he slid back and balanced the bike with his feet. "Have you been on a dirt bike before?"

"No," I told him, swinging a leg over. "But I've driven a motorcycle. It can't be that different, right?"

"Not at all," he grinned. "Just a little bumpier."

Just as the kids were coming out of the woods, I eased into gear, but gave it a little too much gas. The kids laughed as they went by, making my eyes narrow.

Talon's feet steadying us, he wrapped his arms securely around me and whispered in my ear. "Why don't I help you a bit on this first run?"

"Yeah, yeah," I muttered. "I got it."

His hands eased over mine anyway, and I tried my best to ignore the physical reaction that gave me. His body was warm, as usual, and his touch sent electrical currents up my arms.

"Are you ready?" He asked.

Nodding, I let him carefully get us into gear. The first jolt of speed had me grinning just as widely as he was.

"Just follow the trail," he told me, slowly releasing his hold on my hands and shifting it to my waist. "I'll be here if you need me."

I wound through the narrow trail Jack had made over numerous, similar trips. There wasn't much room for error, as a tree would quickly let you know when you swerved. I took the first trip slow, only needing help on the sharp turn in the thick woods to lead us back towards the house. On the way back, I worked up enough confidence to hit the gas. As long as I concentrated on the trail, there didn't seem to be a problem. We were just coming to the edge when Talon leaned closer again to whisper into my ear.

"Having fun?" He breathed, sending tingles down my spine, and my hands jerked involuntarily on the handles.

The bike shot off the path and veered straight for a tree. Before either of us could react, we slammed into it and went flying.

Somehow, Talon managed to twist around until he was beneath me. We hit the ground hard, and his hands were immediately running over me.

"Are you okay? Are you hurt? Did you hit your head?"

I was shaking, my head buried in his chest.

"Jade? Jade, look at me. Are you all right? Is anything broken, bleeding?"

I tried to shake my head, but found it difficult to move.

"Jade! Honey, look at me."

He gently lifted my face, and I watched as his worried expression turned dangerous. I was in a fit of giggles, trying desperately to hold it in.

"I'm... fine!" I managed, and burst into another round.

Talon shook his head, unbelieving.

"How... are... you?" I gasped between hysterics.

"Perfectly fine," he muttered, shaking his head. "May I inquire as to what is so funny?"

"That... was... so... much... fun!"

He was still holding my face in his hands, staring at me incredulously. Finally, my eyes focused on his again, and my humor quickly faded.

The look in his eyes was no longer incredulous. It looked almost... hungry. Something deep inside me answered that look, but I shoved it back down. We stared at each other for one long moment before I finally cleared my throat.

"We... we should get up," I said quietly.

"Yes," he agreed, but made no move to do so.

My body was lying against his hard mass, and it was impossible to ignore that fact. Slowly, so slowly, he began lowering my face to his. I made no move to protest.

"Jade! Talon!"

Startled by the voices, I jerked up and glanced back towards the trail. Amber and Pearl were rushing towards us, fear on their faces.

"Over here," I called. "We're okay."

I got up quickly, holding out a hand to Talon. With a groan that had nothing to do with the fall, he stood and stayed by my side.

Amber was the first to reach us, inspecting carefully.

"We heard the crash, and thought..." She trailed off, studying my face carefully. She must have realized they interrupted something, because she began babbling. "Well, um, I can see you're all right. Would you like some help with the bike? Maybe some lemonade. I've got fresh in the kitchen."

"We're fine," Talon assured her again. "I'll get the bike, if you help Jade back. I'd like her to sit for a while, just in case."

I shot a look back at him. "You're the one that took the fall," I said.

His smile showed his dimple. "I'm fine, I assure you. I'll join you in a minute."

Nodding, I let Amber lead me away.

CHAPTER 9

The days had been long and guarded. White men were scattered through the territory, wreaking havoc. It saddened me, to see the destruction. This wasn't how it was supposed to be.

We stayed hidden a good deal of the time, knowing a fight was eminent if we crossed them. I had great faith in my skills, and my fathers, but worried for both him and my mother. There were only three of us, after all, and we could die.

So, we stayed hidden, hunting by night and sticking to the caves by day. It was difficult, after so much freedom, to close ourselves off. I craved the wind in my face, and savored the night when we were more free to roam.

We were in the mountains now, the summer heat too oppressive in the valley. It came early this year, the heat, and we moved sooner than normal. Perhaps it was for the best. The white man didn't seem to venture too high into the mountains.

I inhaled the night, letting my senses take over as I prepared for the hunt. There was larger game here, and we were eating well, though we were careful with the smoke from our cook fires. We kept them small and only at night, using the caves to filter out the smoke naturally.

Sensing large game to the West, I set out. Wearing only buckskin pants, the cool night air wrapped silkily along my body. Strapped to my back was my bow, though I rarely used it, and secured along my belt were knives of various sizes. The only other weapon I needed was myself, my senses.

My speed, agility and reflexes were growing daily. Soon, I would reach 25 summers, and my mother would begin the change. I was ready for it, though I knew of its downfalls. I would withstand the pain, because it would lead me to my destiny.

Waking up Monday morning, I made my way down to the nursing home as usual. Emma was there with the kids, as was becoming a Monday ritual. She looked haggard today, large circles under her eyes and a slump to her shoulders that wasn't normally present.

I was holding Mikey, who was awake for once, while Suzy sat patiently with Grandma. It always amazed me how easily children could adapt to any environment.

Leaning close to Emma, I whispered, "You doing okay?"

"Hm? Oh, yes, fine. Mikey was just up crying last night, that's all. I think a tooth is coming in."

Her reason was plausible, but she didn't look me in the eye as she gave it. "Anything else?" I asked.

Shaking her head, she stared over at Suzy. I dropped it, for now.

Grandma really seemed to respond to the kids. She smiled at them, and helped Suzy play with a few of the toys Emma had brought with. It raised my spirits to see.

65

That night, Grandma went to bed early and I set off towards home. As I drove, I was in such a good mood that I decided I didn't want to go home. There was still a faint light in the sky as I drove out to Fish Lake, which was technically a pond, and an old running path that surrounded it. It was such a lovely night, I figured a walk would do me good.

The moon was still three quarters full, plenty of light to make my way around as the sky darkened. Ducks and geese swam lazily in the water while fireflies danced happily in the humid air. Surprisingly, the night was warm as the sun sank into the western sky. For the first time in a long time, I felt content.

After one trip around the pond, I sat down in a favored spot from my younger days. A smile played around my lips as I remembered stopping here and getting my first kiss from Bobby Lane. It was a summer romance, and we were 13. If only things were still so simple.

I lay back and let my gaze roam across the sky. Stars began peeking out across the navy backdrop. Venus, if I wasn't mistaken, hung close to the moon and winked out at the world from so many miles away. The sky never seemed to lose its appeal, though I stared it at almost every night for my entire life.

I was so comfortable, and so content, that my eyes slid closed and sleep overtook me. What felt like only minutes later, I was startled awake by a noise that I couldn't quite place in my half dream state.

Slowly I opened my eyes, surprised to see the complete darkness surrounding me. Even the moon was gone, enclosed by the endless clouds that plagued the Midwest. I sat up carefully, attempting to sort out the noise that awoke me.

A howl sounded, and to my dismay I realized it wasn't in the distance as normal. My heart sped up, remembering the sight of the giant black wolf that I'd seen just earlier this week. An animal that size could eat me for a snack.

Looking around warily, I judged my way back to my car doable and rose to my feet. My heart kept pounding a steady rhythm, fear running through me in streams. Ridiculous, I tried to tell myself, but I was beyond reasoning. Perhaps with even the small light from the moon I would have been fine, but the weather had other ideas.

The wind picked up, blowing eerily through the trees. I quickened my pace, wanting to be back in my car with the windows up and doors locked. Just as I reached the edge of the woods, mere feet from the road, a voice called out from behind me.

"Jade?"

I spun around, a hand on my heart and a scream on my lips. Immediately, I recognized the figure but made no move to relax my position.

"What are you doing here?" I squeaked out, too terrified still to care that my voice gave me away.

"Walking," he responded, keeping his distance. Those black eyes were focused on me, unwavering.

With great effort, I slid my hand to my side and took a gulp of air. "You have strange habits," I commented, slightly more composed. He grinned, his perfect white teeth visible in the night.

"As do you. Come here," he extended his hand, expecting me to take it.

"Why?" I asked, more curiosity than hostility in my tone now.

"I want to show you something."

He made no move towards me, just stood patiently waiting. This fact alone made me take the step towards him to clasp his hand. "Wait!" I said, suddenly remembering the reason for my fear. "I heard a wolf howling, we probably shouldn't..."

"We'll be fine," he said, his voice implacable. I found myself following him without resistance.

As I allowed myself to focus, I realized he was, at least, wearing a t-shirt and jeans. Should have been very non-threatening. His hand that wrapped so easily around mine was hot and immovable. Instead of feeling captured, I felt safe.

We walked side by side, though he was leading me. The silence continued in the dark night, but all fear dissipated in his presence. That was something I would evaluate later.

He stepped through the thick vegetation and into a clearing, similar to the one I'd first met him in. It was small, perhaps only six feet across, and ringed by trees. It looked too perfect to be natural, and too natural to be so perfect. The clouds shifting above let out a stream of light, leaving the clearing bathed in moonlight.

"It's beautiful," I commented.

"Come," he said simply, leading me into the center and releasing my hand. He stood facing me, watching me. I wasn't sure what I was supposed to do.

"Do you feel it?" He asked, his voice soft and compelling.

I stared back at him, baffled. His look betrayed no sense of humor, so I opened my senses to what he could possibly mean.

The moment I relaxed, I felt it. My head fell back, absorbing the soft light on my face. From my sides, my arms rose of their own accord and reached up towards the heavens. I don't know how long I stood there, or what exactly was flowing through me, but it felt invigorating. Eventually, I dropped my arms and my head fell back into place. When my eyes opened, they were looking directly into his.

"Talon," I whispered, still under the mysterious trance. My hands rose once again, but this time they rested gently on his chest. A spark, an electric shock pulsed between us. Leaning in, I pressed my lips softly against his.

He made no move, leaving his own hands against his sides and allowing me to lead the kiss. The same energy that flowed through me just moments before was now a gentle hum, fusing us together. Slowly I pulled away and just stared up at him.

"What... was that?" I finally managed to ask, dazed.

My hands began to slide back down, but they were held in place by his. The heat seared through me, warming my suddenly cold body. "I told you I would show you how the earth called to me. I always keep my promises."

"I'm starving," Pearl commented, plopping into a chair across from me. She'd called me early that morning, talking me into meeting her for lunch at the Log Cabin, the only sit-down restaurant in town.

"Where are the kids?" I asked, stifling a yawn.

"Liz, the girl next door, is watching them."

"All five?" I asked, my brow raised. "Isn't she only 12?"

"Fifteen," Pearl said absently, looking over the menu. "She absolutely adores them, and vice versa. Besides, it's nap time, so only Ashton is awake."

For the first time, she glanced up and really studied me. It made me uncomfortable, realizing how I must look.

"You look awful," she affirmed. "What have you been up to?"

I shrugged. Last night had been like a dream, hazy and unbelievable. I still wasn't quite sure what had happened. But I got home after midnight, and was up at 4:00. My sleeping patterns were getting ridiculous.

"Not sleeping well," I decided on as an excuse, not wanting to delve too deeply into my other explanations.

"Whatever you say," she said, but kept watching me.

A waitress approached our table, and when I glanced up I had to stop myself from gasping aloud. It wasn't often that I was blown away by good looks, but this woman- or was she just a girl?- was gorgeous. She had copper skin, which reminded me immediately of Talon, and long, straight black hair. Her face was oval with a pointed chin and held big, dark eyes.

Oddly, she gave me the same shocked look that I gave to her. We stared at each other for what felt like hours. Finally, she broke and smiled over at Pearl.

"What can I get you ladies today?" She asked in a voice that was soft, but sounded years older than she looked.

"I'll have the chicken wrap and a lemonade," Pearl said, giving me the eye. I was still staring at the woman. "You're new here, aren't you? I'm Pearl, so nice to meet you," she chattered on, holding out her hand.

They shook and the woman answered, "I'm Lani. It's a pleasure."

They both looked at me. I blinked. "I'm Jade," I managed.

She smiled, and her eyes looked suddenly sad. "Jade. Nice to meet you, too. What will you be having today?"

"Um..." I scanned the menu and picked the first thing. "A BLT. And a coke, thanks."

68

She nodded, a smile still on her lips, and walked away. Finally, I met Pearl's inquisitive gaze.

"What?" I asked her.

"What yourself. You were ogling our waitress."

It made me laugh. "No, I wasn't. It's just- wow, she's gorgeous. I mean, I realize that sounds close to lesbian, but wow."

Pearl laughed. "I agree. I've heard about her," of course she had, "but there's not much going around yet. Lots of speculation. I think she moved from somewhere back East. She lives alone, no boyfriend or kids."

Lani came back then with our drinks, leaving without a word. I sipped my coke gratefully, desperately needing the caffeine boost. As the sugar rushed through me, I looked again at Pearl.

"So, what'd you want to talk about?" I asked.

She pouted a little. "Can't I want to have lunch with my big sister without wanting something?"

I merely stared at her, one brow slightly lifted.

"Okay, okay. I wanted to find out about your night with Rick. He was totally closed mouthed yesterday about it."

I laughed. He probably told her all about it, but since there were no juicy details, Pearl considered that closed mouthed. "It was fun, Pearl. We had dinner, a couple drinks. We talked. I think we could be friends."

She sat back, looking disappointed. Then, a small grin lit her face. "So, what about Tal?"

I closed my eyes briefly. Just the subject I'd been trying to avoid all day. "What about him?"

"Come on, Jade. Something has to be going on there," she urged.

Studying her for a long while, I made a decision. I needed someone to talk to about this, and while Pearl loved to gossip, when it came to something serious, she was completely trustworthy.

"I don't know, Pearl. I just don't know. I've never felt like this before."

Her eyes lit up. I went on, "Please, please promise me this is just between us, okay? I just really need a sounding board."

She nodded, settling herself into her seat to listen. I sighed and continued. "Whenever I'm around him, emotions come out stronger than I've ever felt. Not just attraction, that I could handle. He riles me up, calms me down, makes me want to scream or cry, and all the while I want to run away, but there's some kind of pull that keeps me going back."

I slumped in my chair, aggravated. Pearl sighed happily. "You're in love."

My eyes snapped up. "What?"

"You're in love, silly. That's how it feels."

"No. No, no, no. No. I don't think so, no."

69

She laughed. "Okay, maybe you can't admit it yet, but I'm telling you, that's where you're headed."

I fiddled with my napkin, and decided to spill completely. "Something... strange happened last night," I finally blurted out.

Her brows knit together. "Strange?"

I nodded. "I went for a walk around Fish Lake after I left Grandma, and I fell asleep. When I woke up, I was walking back to my car when he just sort of appeared out of nowhere." I watched Pearl's brows crease further, trying to decipher where this was headed.

"Did he hurt you?"

"Oh, no! Of course not. Scared the crap out of me, but once I settled, we went for a walk. He led me to this clearing..." I trailed off, realizing how crazy the next part was going to sound.

Lani appeared then with our lunch. "Can I get you anything else?" She asked, smiling pleasantly.

"No, thank you," Pearl told her brightly. Before she left, Lani gave me a worried glance.

I didn't have time to read into it, because Pearl was pressing for more. "So, what happened in the clearing?" She asked, biting into her wrap.

Clearing my throat, I decided to continue. Let her think I was crazy. I was pretty sure I was, anyway. "The moon came out, so it was light. He led me into the center, and as I relaxed, I felt..." I trailed off again, trying to come up with the right words to convey the feeling. Pearl was watching me, completely still. "I felt energy washing through me. Power. It was incredible, like nothing I've ever felt before. And then I kissed him."

On the opposite side of the room, a clatter of dishes sounded and we both glanced over. Lani was bent over, scooping up the mess. I glanced back to Pearl, and she was beaming.

"How was it?"

I rolled my eyes. She would focus on that. "Not the point, Pearl. What the hell happened in that clearing?"

She thought about it, chewing on a fry. "A lot of times, our minds do funny things in extreme circumstances. It was dark, you were in a mystical clearing with moonlight shining down and an extremely attractive man with you. Maybe you just imagined it."

"Maybe," I conceded, but I knew it was doubtful.

That night, my mind drifted back to the clearing. After the kiss, Talon had simply led me back to my car and, as was becoming custom, disappeared into the night. That was it. No explanations, no words at all. Well, I wouldn't go through another sleepless night wondering.

I turned towards his house and followed the dirt drive around. It was dusk again, that strange hour between day and night. His truck sat before the garage, and I suddenly realized that didn't mean he was home. I hoped he was, just so I could get some answers out of him.

Stepping out of my car, I started around back, not even thinking about trying the front door. The house was dark, dropping my optimism a few points, but I knocked anyway. Standing around, feeling slightly idiotic now, I ventured down the steps and started towards a building I guessed was his workshop. Sure enough, he walked around the side of the building just as I approached.

He never seemed surprised to see me, and his smile was easy in greeting.

"Good evening, Jade," he said.

"Hi." It was all I could come up with.

"Would you like to come inside?" He asked, holding a hand out towards his house.

"Sure," I said, and led the way. When I reached the door, he reached around to pull the door open for me. "Thanks," I murmured, and strode inside. I chose the kitchen for our talk.

I slid onto a countertop, comfortable in the beautiful space. He leaned back against the center island, facing me. "Would you like something to drink?" He asked.

"No, thanks."

He stayed unmoving, waiting for me to speak. It was obvious I had something on my mind.

"What happened last night?"

He looked confused. "Which part of last night?"

I fixed him in a stare. "Let's start with the clearing."

Crossing his arms, he gazed at me, amused. "The earth spoke to you."

My mouth opened, and immediately snapped shut. How did you answer something like that?

"And then you kissed me," he continued, just as serenely.

"I..." I couldn't argue with that. I decided to back track. "What do you mean, the earth spoke to me? That just doesn't happen."

"Perhaps not in your world, Jade, but it does in mine."

"You're talking in circles. Can you please, pretty please just give me a straight answer?"

"Would you believe me if I did?"

He had me there. "I'll try," I answered honestly.

Seeming to think before he answered, he explained slowly, "My culture, my beliefs, are very old. Do you know where I was raised?"

I shook my head.

"On an Indian reservation in the southwest," he answered. "Part of the Apache people. Of course, most reservations now flow into society quite easily, but my parents raised me differently. We lived off the land and migrated into the high mountains during the summer, and into the valley during the winter. I was taught much of what most recent generations have forgotten. To be one with the land."

He paused then, watching me for my reaction. I gave him none, though I suddenly got a strange sense of Deja-vu, so he kept talking.

"If you let it, the earth will speak to you. With today's technology, people have forgotten that. So, when I say the earth spoke to you, that's what I mean. You opened yourself up to it. You seemed to be natural at it."

For a moment, he looked thoughtful, but he quickly turned his attention back to me.

His words hit me hard. He was absolutely right. Wasn't I the one in school who pored over Native American literature, fascinated by the culture before the Europeans so hastily ruined it? Wasn't I the one to travel into the southwest, a place that I foolishly thought would still be similar to those days, only to be extremely disappointed at what I found? An amazing culture of people ruined by 'modernizing.'

I cleared my throat but found I had nothing to say. Instead, I blurted out the first thing that popped into my head.

"What were you doing at Fish Lake?"

My question seemed to take him by surprise. "Out walking."

"Right," I answered, "One of your strange habits."

"And yours. There's something else you want to ask."

It wasn't a question. For some reason, he could read me better than even my family.

"How did you know the wolf wouldn't be a problem?"

He shifted, looking uncomfortable for the first time since I'd met him. "Wildlife is closely attuned to nature. I grew up with wild animals and," he stopped, studied me for a moment and went on, "and I can communicate with them."

I stared in stunned silence. Was he being serious? The look on his face told me yes, indeed he was. I swallowed, hard. "Like with the earth?" I asked stupidly.

"Yes. Similar."

Nodding, I tried to sound as normal as possible. "I see."

He studied me again, his eyes glittering in the light. "Do you?"

Shrugging, I dropped to the floor. "Look, Talon, I'll admit this is way over my head and comprehension. But I believe you."

He continued to stare at me, incredulous. "You believe me," he repeated slowly.

"Sure. What happened last night, that wasn't normal for me. You're not normal. It sort of goes together. So, unless some other explanation pops up, yes, I believe you."

He was stock still, unblinking.

"Well, I should be getting home. I'd really like to get a full night's sleep."

This seemed to snap him back. "You aren't sleeping well?" He eyes looked worried.

"Not really. No big deal. I figure it's just stress."

I hoped the casual dismissal in my voice soothed him. The look in his eyes was making my stomach tie up in knots.

"Well, goodnight, then." I started for the door.

"Jade."

His tone made me turn more than the single syllable of my name.

"Thank you."

I nodded once, sharply, and headed out the door.

Driving home, I felt a weight lift off me. I wasn't completely sure what caused it. The seriously odd conversation or my sudden acceptance of his words. Either way, I realized something, and having realized it I was no longer afraid. Pearl was right.

I was in love with him.

CHAPTER 10

That night, I lay down and fell immediately to sleep. The last thing I remember was hearing Talon's velvety voice in my subconscious before I succumbed to unconsciousness.

When I woke the next morning, the sun was shining brightly in the sky. With a cursory glance at the clock, I shot out of bed and into the shower. It was 8:00, later than I'd slept since I'd been back.

Flying downstairs, I skipped the coffee and grabbed a granola bar on the way out. Both my parents were gone, so I wasn't sidetracked by conversation. Hopping in my car, I made it to the nursing home in record time.

Breakfast was just closing down as I arrived, so I slid into the seat beside Grandma and gave her a huge grin. She stared at me, then turned back to her meal. It was a slow morning, interrupted only by a visit from Emma.

"Two times in one week," I commented.

She shrugged. "I'm able to be here, so I figure why not?"

Emma did flight reservations from home, a perk with two young children to watch after. This left her schedule a little more flexible than Amber, who taught third grade at the school. The school was tiny by any means, servicing three towns and still the largest class consisted of possibly 50 children. All grades went to the same school, and it was a bus ride for all of them. This year, Amber's class held 34 children, the only third grade class.

Pearl was a full-time mommy, which was, to me, the most difficult job. Like everything else she did, though, she was amazing at it.

"What's up with you today?" Emma asked, studying me. I looked up from my hand of cards and feigned ignorance.

"What do you mean?"

I knew what she meant. There was a little smile that couldn't be wiped from my face. Suzy sat in my lap, grabbing the cards out of my hand and attempting to rip them apart. Mikey slept in a carrier, peacefully oblivious to the world. Grandma was having an okay day, playing cards but non-responsive otherwise.

"You seem... different. Is there a man I should know about?"

I struggled to regain my composure. "I just got a really good night's sleep, that's all. I feel good today."

She didn't buy it for an instant. "Is it Tal? I knew it. What happened? Are you two dating?"

I gave in to an eye roll. "We're not dating." Were we? "We've just... come to terms."

Her brows rose straight to her hairline. "Come to... terms?"

I grinned. "Yup."

Shaking her head, she laid down a group of twos. "Grandma, you've got a wild child for a granddaughter over here."

It could have been just me, but I'm pretty sure she smiled.

I left the nursing home earlier in the evening than normal. Two of my mom's sisters were there, seeing to Grandma's needs, so I didn't feel the guilt I normally would have. As I made my way to my car, an all too familiar voice stopped me.

"Hello."

It was velvet, and I wrapped myself in it.

Turning, I met him with a casual look. "Hello," I answered.

He smiled, but seemed more nervous than usual. "Do you have plans this evening?"

My eyes narrowed. "How did you know I'd leave early?"

He shrugged, but didn't answer.

I sighed. "Not really."

"Good. Come with me."

I glanced around, looking for his truck. It was nowhere in sight. "Are we walking?"

His grin widening, he shook his head. As he had before, he held out a hand, waiting for me to grasp it.

This time I did immediately, needing no thought. He led me to the side of the building and up to a sleek, black car.

Halting in my tracks, I stared in astonishment. "Is that," I paused, collecting the drool that was forming, "A Porsche?"

He grinned, boyish. "911 Carrera. You like it?"

My mouth was hanging open. I nodded dumbly. While I didn't know a whole lot about the mechanics of vehicles, I knew this one cost somewhere in the six figures.

"How?" I trailed off as he led me around to the passenger side. When he opened the door, I stood staring, afraid to touch it.

"It's easier to drive when you're actually sitting *in* the car," he commented, amused by me once again.

"I know, but... jeez, a Porsche."

He laughed, the sound ringing out into the night. "Get in."

I did, fervently rubbing my hands along the black dash and leather seat. It looked as if no expense were spared on the details.

He slid in beside me, smooth as could be. Amazing, I thought. He managed to look completely at home in his beat-up truck and in this sports car.

"Would you like the top down?" He asked, his eyes lit with humor.

"Would I ever," I breathed. It slid back flawlessly, letting the evening rays of sun reflect off my golden hair.

"Seat belt, please," he admonished, and as soon as it clicked, he was off.

It was absolutely exhilarating. Laughing, I stuck my hands out to catch the wind. When I glanced over at his speed, my eyes bugged out at the number. My expression just made him laugh, and I joined in. Something inside me trusted him, so I followed my instinct.

We sped along the open road, watching the sun sink slowly towards the horizon. There was no conversation, just a sharing of pure enjoyment. Eventually, he slowed down and looked over at me.

"Hungry?"

"Yes, actually."

Nodding, he got back up to speed and made our way to the nearest town. With a jolt, I realized we'd gone nearly two hundred miles in a little over an hour. Luckily, no cops had pulled us over. That, or they weren't able to catch us.

We were in Madison, the capitol and party town, thanks to the college, of Wisconsin. I hadn't spent much time here, and I found the city beautiful. Talon pulled up alongside an old, white farmhouse that had been converted into a restaurant.

When he parked, Talon came around to open my door and took my hand. Glancing down at myself, suddenly self-conscious, I realized I was only wearing jeans and a blouse.

"When you pull up in a car like this," Talon whispered in my ear, "No one cares what you're wearing. They will merely think us eccentric."

I laughed, following him inside. "Without money, you're crazy. With money, you're eccentric. I like that."

"Good evening," a friendly hostess said as we entered. "Welcome to Otto's. Do you have a reservation with us tonight?"

Talon smiled at her, but didn't seem to notice the effect it had. "Wolfchild," he said in his smooth voice.

"Of course," she smiled and led us immediately upstairs and outside.

On the deck, there was soft jazz playing from a live band and candles lit on the tables. We sat facing West, affording us a view of the terrific sunset.

"Wow," I said as the hostess left us.

"Glad you like it," he said, and smiled again. "Hope you don't mind, but I already ordered."

My gaze switched from the view to him, sharpening. "You planned this a bit ahead of time, didn't you?"

His smile was unrepentant.

"How did you know I'd be free?"

Shrugging, he responded, "I took my chances. Guess I was lucky."

After studying him for a moment, I was interrupted by a sommelier, who approached with a bottle of wine. I watched as he displayed the label, uncorked and poured a tester into Talon's glass. At Talon's nod, he finished pouring the glass and set to work on mine. He talked about the vintage and the flavors in it all the while.

"Cakebread," Talon said, holding up his glass for a toast. "I was told it would go well with dinner."

"Cheers, then," I said, and took a sip. It went down smooth and slightly sweet. "I like it. How did you find this place?"

"It was recommended."

I could tell I wouldn't be getting any further response from him. "Just full of surprises, aren't you?" I mused.

"Let's hope so."

Our waiter appeared then with a platter of appetizers. "Mushroom caps, prosciutto and basil wrapped shrimp and bruschetta," he announced, gesturing towards each item. "Can I bring you anything else at the moment?"

Talon glanced at me, and I shook my head. "No, thank you."

"Very good, sir," the waiter said and left.

"What'd you do, bribe everyone here?" I asked and picked up a mushroom.

"Of course not. I merely offered sexual favors."

I choked. From his tone, it was hard for a minute to tell if he was kidding. But his eyes were alight with amusement I was beginning to recognize.

"Whatever gets the job done," I said when I got my voice back.

The food was delicious. I found myself relaxing again, though I had a million questions zooming through my mind.

"What is it?" He asked, seeming to read my thoughts.

"I don't think what I want to ask is appropriate dinner conversation."

He raised a brow and I felt myself blush. "Not like that. It's just..."

"Yes?"

"A Porsche, for crying out loud?"

He grinned again, his dimple apparent. "You're wondering why, if I have all this money, I bought a dump like the old Wilson house."

I floundered a bit. "Well, no, not exactly. I mean, you're doing beautiful work on it, but... yeah."

His laugh rang out again, causing people at nearby tables to glance over. "My," he paused here, just long enough for me to notice, "family was wealthy, through different business ventures. The work was passed on to me, and I excelled at it. Now," he moved his shoulders restlessly, "I'm taking a break. That's why I bought the house. I enjoy working with my hands."

"And Black Bear Lake?"

He glanced up, seeming surprised.

"It's a small town, remember? So, you're planning on sticking around?"

He paused to deliberate before answering. "I like my space while I'm here. I have no immediate plans."

I studied him again, and he looked right back. While he seemed to be answering my questions, he wasn't saying much at all.

Something clicked then, and I was annoyed with myself for not putting two and two together. "You told me you were raised on the land," I began. His brows knit together, but he nodded the confirmation. "What was the family business then?"

78

He paused just briefly. "We had a gemstone business."

This brought me up short. "Gemstone?"

He nodded, watching me carefully. "It was easy for us to find gemstones in the earth. We would then sell them to local jewelers. Though we didn't need much money, I've always found having it makes certain things simpler."

My mouth stayed closed as the waiter appeared. The appetizer plate was cleared and salads were brought out. I chewed thoughtfully, enjoying the tangy raspberry flavor in the dressing.

"You're keeping something from me," I thought aloud. "Something big. I just wonder..."

His gaze was on mine again, frowning. "Wonder what?"

"I wonder when you'll trust me enough to tell me."

"Trusting you is not the issue."

"What is?"

"You trusting me."

His answer surprised me, to say the least. What did that mean?

"I do trust you."

He shook his head, smiling wryly. "No, you don't."

"What do you mean? I just got into a car with you going well over a hundred miles. I'd say that's pretty trusting."

"There are different types of trust," he replied cryptically.

"Did you really want ice water on your jeans?" I asked sweetly.

It worked. My statement made the hard edge to his jaw relax. "You could try, but I don't believe you would enjoy my retaliation in such a public place."

Color stole up my neck at his words. Retaliation. So, that's what he called it.

Salad plates were removed and two platters were set down before us. The waiter hovered nearby.

"Which would you prefer?" Talon asked me, gesturing towards the table.

Before me sat two delicious looking dishes, one salmon with a variety of vegetables and potatoes on the side, and one that looked to be chicken stuffed with some kind of cheese and a similar assortment.

"They both look delicious," I said, and Talon smiled.

"I was hoping you'd say that." With a slight nod at the waiter, the dishes were picked up and set down again a few minutes later, with each platter holding half and half.

"Good idea," I complimented him. The waiter disappeared again, and I wondered idly how detailed Talon's instructions had been for the evening.

As we dug into our meal, I thought about the last few weeks as a whole. Isolating just the events that involved Talon left me dizzy. My own emotions, more than anything he did, kept me on a roller coaster.

"What are you thinking about?" Talon asked, his gaze on me.

"You," I answered before I could censor.

A slow smile lit his face. "What about me?"

I shook my head slowly, glancing around the dimly lit deck. The music was still going, unobtrusively in the background. The sun still hadn't quite reached the horizon, but with a few clouds was shooting pinks and oranges across the sky. Light conversation buzzed around us, mostly couples enjoying the atmosphere.

"Every time I'm with you, it's," I hesitated, trying to come up with the proper explanation. "Unbelievable. I mean, who meets someone in the middle of the forest, in the middle of the night? And going from that to this," I gestured around, encompassing the restaurant, the car, the impeccable service he undoubtedly put some effort into, "It's a lot to take in."

His expression turned worried, his brows knitting together. I hated knowing I put it there. "Would you prefer I left you alone?"

With his eyes steady on mine, I shook my head decisively. "No."

"Would you rather I be predictable?"

This time a smirk twisted my mouth. "No."

His expression relaxed, just slightly. "Would you like dessert?"

The smirk turned into a laugh. "Yes."

His teeth flashed and he held out a hand. "Dance with me first."

Bewilderment crossed my face. "What?"

He didn't answer, just continued holding out his hand.

"There isn't a dance floor."

"And?"

We held a staring contest which I quickly lost. With a sigh, I placed my hand in his.

He pulled me to my feet and swung me into his arms right next to the table. The band members, along with every occupant of the restaurant, glanced over at us. Most of them with smiles.

"Everyone's staring," I hissed.

"Were there other people here?" He asked innocently.

Rolling my eyes, I allowed him to lead me in a circle. To my surprise, couples all along the deck rose and joined in, swaying to the slow tune. Closing my eyes, I relaxed against his frame, allowing him to lead me. His heat penetrated through my clothes, and even as a cool wind came in, I stayed perfectly warm.

After a delicious chocolate cake dessert, we walked to the car and I didn't object when he slipped his hand around mine. He stopped in front of the car and glanced at me from the corner of his eye.

"Would you like to drive?"

My jaw dropped as I faced him. "Are you kidding?"

"No."

"Hell yes, I do!" Yanking the keys out of his hand, I slid into the driver's side and let out a contented sigh. He got into the passenger seat, chuckling softly.

"Go as fast as you want," he told me, "But you have to promise if I say to slow down, you will do so immediately."

I gave him a sideways glance, but decided against asking questions. "I can do that."

Buckling his seat belt, watching me until mine was secure, he settled back to enjoy the ride.

Even if I had tried, I wouldn't have been able to stop the look of pure enjoyment on my face. When I risked the occasional look over, I saw Talon with his eyes halfway closed and a small smile on his lips. He never yelled, or freaked out, even when I initially hit the accelerator and wasn't ready for the immediate jolt of power. His posture stayed the same, serene, through the entire trip.

Only once it changed, as we neared a small town about fifty miles outside home.

"Slow down to the speed limit," he said quietly.

I did so immediately. After a couple miles, we passed a cop on the side of the road. My eyes narrowed on him, but I didn't ask.

"Okay," he told me after we were clear, "Have fun."

We made it to the edge of town and I noted, pleased, that my journey was quicker than his.

"Put the top up," Talon murmured.

He must have seen the question, and slight disappointment, in my face, so he explained, "This car is a little conspicuous for this town. With the tinted windows, no one will know who is in it."

"Okay," I agreed immediately. No one knew better than I how fast word spread. With the top up and the sun down, the interior was lit solely by the red lights of the dash. The few people that were still outside stopped and stared as we rolled by, and I laughed joyfully.

I took the long way to his drive, on a deserted road to stay out of sight. As I neared his house, he pushed a hidden button to open the garage, and I rolled inside. Getting out of the car, a huge grin still present on my face, I glanced around and noticed another shiny black vehicle.

"How in the world did you sneak these into town without being noticed?" I asked, examining a Harley Sportster sitting regally in its own lane of the garage.

"I have my ways," he said, making me laugh. "Would you like to come inside for a while?"

I looked over at him, alerted by his suddenly nervous tone. Now what did he have up his sleeve?

"All right," I said, following him.

"I've finished a couple more things," he said as we walked inside. "I'd like you to see them."

He led me into the front living room, where before a single couch had sat. Now, the walls were painted a pale peach, which set off the lighter colors of the smooth, hard wood floor. The same couch, a brilliant white, sat against one wall, facing a picture window looking out into the woods. Beneath the window was a low, white settee with no back, and between the two on one end was a big, overstuffed white chair and on the opposite end, a gorgeous rock fireplace. Huge, fluffy pillows were piled high on each piece of furniture and a low coffee table held a single vase with peach roses, practically matching the walls.

One painting hung above the couch, a beautiful portrayal of a desert landscape. From the ceiling hung a low chandelier, a rustic black with six spokes topped with flower shaped glass. I took a swift breath in.

"Talon, it's gorgeous," I told him.

"Thank you. Come, there's more."

I followed him back down the hall, passing room after room that was stripped bare. He led me up a winding staircase, which had also been stripped of the carpet, and down a long hall towards the front of the house. At the end was the master bedroom.

He led me straight into the master bath, though I tried to look around the bedroom first. I only caught mere glimpses of beauty before I was astonished.

From what I could tell, he knocked down a wall between the original bath and another room, possibly what was a small bedroom. Front and center sat a whirlpool tub with water cascading sides. A long, his and her sink lined one wall while a separate, open shower filled another corner. Ornately carved doors led to what I believed was the closet, and a separate room housed the toilet.

Directly over the tub hung another chandelier, which I could hardly picture putting in a grand ballroom, never mind a bathroom. A fireplace, which was two sided and could be seen from the bedroom, sat in view of the tub.

"Talon," I breathed, unable to say anything more.

"Come," he said again, tugging on my hand to lead me back into the master bedroom.

The fireplace was opposite the bed with two big, easy chairs before it. My eyes took in the bed next, a huge, four poster deal, and made it no further. Hanging prominently against that wall was a photograph that made my heart skip a beat.

It was in the woods, the light streaming through the thick foliage haphazardly. Standing in the center was a huge gray wolf, its body turned away but looking back, directly at me.

I was still, unable to breathe, for endless minutes. Talon said nothing, standing beside me, waiting for my reaction.

Humiliating tears sprung to my eyes. Of all the reactions Talon must have expected, it probably wasn't this one.

"How did you get this?" There was more anger in my words than even I expected.

"I purchased it."

82

My gaze shot to his, stunned. This photograph, larger than life in his bedroom, was the first I'd ever sold.

"I have to go."

Spinning on my heel, I made my way to the door, not slowing as I flew down the stairs. It didn't surprise me when I heard his voice so close.

"Jade, wait," he pleaded, but I was already out the door. "You don't have a car. Let me drive you."

"I'll walk," I answered him, not looking back. Anywhere in town was less than a 15-minute walk. I'd be fine.

"Take one of my vehicles, then. I won't drive you."

"I'm fine."

I charged down his driveway, restraining my hand from wiping at my face. I couldn't explain the tears to myself, nonetheless to him right now. Over and over I prayed for him to let me go.

He did. There were no footsteps, though I doubted I'd be able to hear them anyway, and no more words. I kept up my pace until I was sure I was out of sight, then paused to let the tears come. I only gave them a couple minutes before taking a deep breath and wiping them away. Then, head thrown back, I continued on my way.

I only made it half a mile before being stopped. That didn't surprise me. It was very rare to walk through town without running into someone I knew, even as the evening approached darkness. The person that stopped me, however, took me by surprise.

"Jade, isn't it?" The soft, slightly accented voice gave me pause. Turning, I caught sight of Lani, the waitress from the Log Cabin, walking towards me.

"Yes. Hi. Lani, right?"

I noticed her slight pause as she caught sight of my face, and I wondered how much of my crying jag was still in evidence.

"That's right. Are you okay?"

She was near me now, standing close and waiting for my answer.

"Of course. I was just taking a walk, that's all."

"You've been crying."

Her statement surprised me for the bluntness of it.

"It's nothing."

She stared at me, her gaze worried. "Have a drink with me."

I was surprised again, first by her statement and then by my easy acquiescence. I followed her into the nearest bar, which sat ten at capacity.

There was one man in there, staring into his mug of beer. We sat at the opposite end, farthest from the door. The bartender, a woman somewhere in her forties whom I vaguely recognized, came over.

"Two glasses of wine," Lani said without specifying. In this place, there was only one type of wine; house.

She waited until the glasses were set down and the bartender made herself busy at the other end before turning to me.

"I hope you don't think I'm crazy," she asked, with a tight smile.

"No more so than I am," I assured her.

Her expression stayed the same, though slightly more relaxed. "I fear you're in danger," she admitted softly, her eyes flicking towards the door and back.

I cleared my throat. Then I blinked. "What?"

She smiled again, still tight lipped, her eyes flicking constantly between the door, me and back again. "The man you were with tonight." She leaned toward me, and though I'm pretty sure I imagined it, she seemed to sniff me. Before I could blink again, she was sitting back in her chair, her eyes on the move. "He's dangerous."

"Talon?" I squeaked out, then took a sip of my wine. I had a feeling I'd need it.

"If that's who you were with just recently, yes."

My eyes narrowed on hers. "How do you know, if you don't even know who he is?"

She exhaled and studied me. "You know, too. You've felt it."

"No," I shook my head in denial. "Something off maybe, but not dangerous."

Her brows knit, obviously hearing the honesty in my voice. One smooth hand reached out and rested upon my arm in a soothing gesture. My arm flinched back involuntarily.

It was hot, just like Talon's was. As if they were both running a low-grade fever. She pulled her hand into her lap, her eyes downcast. "I'm sorry."

"Who are you?" I asked quietly.

Her eyes flicked again, to the door and back.

"Not who, Jade. What."

I stared at her, incredulous. A bubble of laughter exploded before I could stop it. Her wide eyes shot to mine, clearly baffled.

"I'm sorry," I said, but couldn't suppress another burst of laughter. "You just sound so ominous."

Her gaze was steady on mine, clearly not understanding the joke. I sobered immediately.

"You're serious, aren't you?"

She nodded.

"You really think he's dangerous?"

"I know he is."

"How?"

Her eyes flicked. "It's difficult to explain."

"Try, please."

She shook her head. "You wouldn't believe me if I told you."

"So just what, exactly, do you want me to do?"

"Stay away from him."

This time I shook my head. "I can't do that."

"Please." Her eyes were on mine again, steady and pleading.

"I can't do that unless I know why."

She was torn, struggling with some hidden battle. I watched as she took a breath and let it out again. "He's going to kill you."

CHAPTER 11

My eyes were wide and my breathing was stopped. Her words reverberated around my head before finally sinking in.

"Kill me?"

She nodded gravely.

"Kill me."

She nodded again.

"*Kill me.*"

Her eyes watched me, seeing the shock register on my face.

"Why would you say that?"

"It's the truth."

"You couldn't possibly know that. You don't even know him." I felt the anger bubbling up and battle with fear.

"I've seen his kind before. I know what they do. He'll lure you, doing whatever is necessary, and when you're completely comfortable with him, he'll take your life."

With wide eyes and erratic breathing, I stumbled to my feet and went for the door. She was there immediately, steadying me with a hand on my arm and another at my back. Walking quickly, she rounded a corner and sat me down on a park bench.

My head was spinning. How could I fall in love for the first time just to find out he was a murderer? But then again, I didn't know this woman. I trusted her instinctively, which was odd for me, but I really didn't know her. Maybe she was just crazy and enjoyed watching other people suffer.

"Why are you doing this to me?" I whispered.

"I'm sorry, Jade, I really am. But you have to know. You have to be safe from him."

My head was shaking, though I wasn't sure what I was trying to deny. "Even if what you're saying is true, how would I do that?"

"You have to leave. Immediately. Somewhere he won't be able to find you."

This time I knew the reason of my denial. "My family is here. I couldn't leave even if I wanted to. My grandma's sick, and if what you're saying is true, the rest of my family could be in danger."

She thought about this for a brief moment before answering. "Allow me to help you."

I looked up at her then, my head clearing. "Lani," I paused, considering my words. "I trust you. I don't know why, but I do. But I also trust Talon. Again, I'm not sure why, but I really don't sense anything bad in him." Her look was becoming reserved, so I rushed on. "I've never been wrong before, about people. I can read them rather quickly. This pull," I paused again, holding a palm out, "I know you feel it too. The first day we met, you saw something in me. I feel that same pull to him."

Lani sat back, her expression worried again. Her brows knit together while she thought this through. She closed her eyes briefly before answering. "I feel it too. To you," she clarified. "Which means to me that I need to help you. The fact that you feel it," she trailed off, mulling it over. "That throws me for a bit of a curve."

We sat silently for a while, each sifting through our own thoughts. "Promise me something," she finally said.

"I'll try," I told her.

She smiled faintly. "Think over what I've said tonight. Don't see him again until I see you."

I nodded. "I don't think that'll be a problem."

"Where's your car?"

"At the nursing home."

"Let me give you a ride," she said. "It would make me feel better," she added when I hesitated.

"All right."

We rode in silence, and as I stepped out, she stopped me. "Jade."

I turned, looking back at her. "Yes?"

She started to stay something but changed her mind. "Be safe."

I nodded once and walked over to my car. The drive home was short, too short, and I sat in the driveway to calm down before I went in under scrutiny of my parents.

How did the day go so completely haywire? This morning, I had stars in my eyes. Then, the amazing and spontaneous trip to Madison. And now...

Stepping out of the car, I made it to the steps before I heard my name.

"Jade."

The voice was quiet, hesitant. My heart raced, but it wasn't in fear.

Looks like I wasn't going to be able to keep my promise to Lani.

Turning slowly, I focused on the face that had become so familiar to me in so short a time.

"Talon."

He approached carefully, reminding me of our first two meetings. Stopping a few feet away, he said, "I apologize."

"For what?"

He seemed as baffled as I did. "For whatever I did to upset you."

I laughed, only slightly hysterical. "No, Talon, I'm sorry. I overreacted and I'm not even sure why." Shaking my head, I leaned against the step railing. "I feel like my emotions run amuck whenever I'm around you."

I surprised myself by speaking and acting so normally. While he stood there, unmoving, I took my time studying his features. His eyes drew me the most, dark and endless, framed by those long lashes. Though, his smile in full bloom rivaled for attention easily. Then there were his strong, masculine features in the shape of his jaw and nose.

When I allowed myself to roam farther, his body made me want things I hadn't allowed myself in a very long time.

Standing here under the moonlight, Lani's warnings were laughable. How could someone who spoke of nature the way he did be plotting my downfall?

"Is that a normal thing for you? Your emotions running amuck?"

He took a step closer, and I stayed perfectly still. I was a step up, which made us closer in height. Of course, midget I was, I still had to look up to meet his eye.

"Not at all. That's why I don't have the ability to handle them."

Slowly his hand rose and cupped the side of my face. "There was something I wanted to do tonight, but I didn't get the chance."

His voice was a whisper and I felt myself sinking into him. As if he had all the time in the world, he moved in slow, deliberately. When his lips met mine, I felt my entire body reaching for him.

Resisting the urge, I kept my hands at my sides and savored the soft pressure as it lasted.

When he pulled away, his face stayed close to mine. My entire vision was filled with his face.

"Are you upset that I have your photo?"

"No," I shook my head slightly. "Just surprised, I think. That was the first one I sold. It was taken here."

He smiled. "I know. By Black Bear Lake, if I'm not mistaken."

My eyes widened. "That's right," my voice came out in a whisper. The photo had been taken on an early morning voyage, just a few weeks before I left for Florida. After getting the job with James Royce, it was the most exciting day of my life when it sold. "Is that," I began, but realized how foolish it sounded.

"Is what?" He prompted, his eyes glittering at me.

"Is that why you're buying that property?" As soon as it came out, I felt color steal up my neck. People just didn't buy huge parcels of land because of a picture.

"Yes." His answer was immediate and unmistakably sincere.

"Oh." It was all I could come up with. Clearing my throat, I tried again. "You're insane."

His lips turned up at the edges. I was amusing him again. All this time he still hadn't moved, and though the night was turning cool, I stayed toasty warm.

"It can be argued so." His eyes peered into mine, sharpening on something he saw. "What's wrong?"

"Nothing," I lied.

"There's a part of you closed off. Did something happen after you left?"

I was silent for a few moments. How in the world could he tell that?

"Is your grandmother okay?" He asked.

"Oh, yes, she's fine."

89

"Then what is it?"

Sighing, I edged away from him. "You're still hiding something from me, Talon. I need to know what that is."

His eyes tightened as if under stress. For the first time, I saw a little bit of menace in him.

"Can you accept me for who I am, without knowing?"

I thought about that before answering. "I already have," I answered. "Now it's your turn."

Turning, I opened the door and stepped inside, not waiting for his answer. Not certain I would get one.

Evading my parents, I went immediately to my room and laid down, though I knew sleep would not come. My head was too full.

How do I get myself into these fixes? Why couldn't I just like someone like Rick, or even that guy with puppies? Or any other perfectly normal men my sisters and aunts and extended relatives tried to set me up with? What was wrong with me?

Forcing myself to be honest, I could answer that question. Because I wouldn't be happy with someone like Rick, or guy with puppies, or any others. Fate led me to Talon, and Talon was who I wanted.

But what if he *was* trying to kill me? I shook my head at that. It couldn't be. He wasn't a whack job. And I didn't fall for lunatics.

Correction. I didn't fall for anyone.

Sighing, I shoved a pillow over my head. A pulse was beating against the front of my head, and the pressure helped. I wanted to scream, but didn't want to alert my parents to anything being wrong. I wanted to cry, but I'd already done that tonight. Instead, regardless of my thoughts and headache, I slept.

When I woke, it was with a start. I couldn't be sure if my subconscious dredged up memories while I slept, or if I'd just come to terms with the bizarre conversations the night before, but something finally clicked.

Not who, but what.

Lani said those words to me, and she wasn't speaking of Talon. At least not just of Talon. I thought through their similarities. Physically, they were both beautiful. Dark hair and skin, they could be related. Then there was the heat. It wasn't normal.

I didn't know enough about Lani to categorize more similarities, except the knack to evade questions they seemed to share. And, maybe, the way they spoke. It wasn't in modern slang, which made sense when I thought about the way Talon grew up. I couldn't imagine there were many children around when he was living off the earth with his parents. Lani, though, I didn't know.

Something was off about both of them. The odd moment where Lani sniffed me had me pausing. I didn't imagine that, I was sure of it.

So now I had pieces of a puzzle, but no edges to begin fitting them together. I sighed, and glanced at my clock. 3:00 AM. Great.

I lay in bed until I fell back asleep. When I woke again, two hours later, the face of the big black wolf was hovering in my subconscious. What a strange thing to dream about. Maybe seeing my photo hanging at Talon's brought on the memory.

I trudged through the next couple days, exhausted more by my mind than by my lack of sleep. Sticking to my usual routine at the nursing home, I managed to get through the days unscathed. Friday night, I needed a change of pace.

Whenever I was down, I visited Pearl. With five endless bundles of energy running around, it was difficult to not be caught up in the high spirits. Pearl handled motherhood so well, too. There were so many times I'd seen frazzled mothers at their wit's end with just one or two kids to look after. Pearl managed it all beautifully.

It helped, I supposed, to have such a supportive husband. With those frazzled moms usually came an uncaring father, expecting dinner cooked, laundry folded and children perfect examples of discipline- all without lifting a finger. My sisters were lucky to find such exceptional men, all within such a small town. Of my sisters, though, Pearl's life just seemed that much smoother, that much happier.

That's why I visited her tonight, instead of my other two siblings. Even knowing I would have to listen to her latest gossip and her ragging, I chose her house to uplift my spirits.

After a cursory knock, I shoved open the door and called out a greeting. I stepped into the oddly quiet living room and glanced down the hallway, but there was no commotion. Both cars were parked in the driveway, and the lights were on, so I was pretty sure they were home.

"Hello!" I called out again, wandering towards the stairs. One set led up to the three bedrooms and one led down to the basement. Partway up the stairs, I heard conversation float up and reversed my direction.

"Hello," I called again, now in hearing distance.

"Jade, is that you?"

Pearl came into view as I rounded the corner, holding Kalia in one arm and holding onto Ella's hand with the other. The three older children were studying an unfinished wall intently with their dad.

"What's up?" I asked, and noted the markings on the wall under scrutiny.

"We're finally going to finish the basement," Pearl said happily. "We're thinking a playroom, one for the kids and one for the adults, a bathroom and a guest bedroom."

"That'll be great," I told her. As of now, the basement was one giant, empty concrete room. Truth be told, it sort of gave me the creeps. A single bulb hung down in the middle of the room, barely casting enough light into the dark corners to chase away the shadows. In one corner the water softener and furnace rumbled eerily.

Unconsciously I rubbed my palms over my arms, soothing the goosebumps that appeared. That's odd. I'd never been claustrophobic before.

91

"Micah found a pool table," Pearl was going on, "down at Larry's Furniture. It's used, but it's a great deal and still in really good shape. Then I was thinking we could build a nice bar along one wall. The bedroom will probably end up being Ashton's eventually, or maybe Ashton and Ewan could share so the girls could split up a little more. Maybe make room for a new baby room," she added with a sly smile at her husband.

"Pearl won't be happy until we're bursting at the seams," Micah grinned, obviously okay with the thought. "Maybe we should just split this into four or five bedrooms, instead."

Pearl's eyes lit up. "Could we?"

Shaking his head, Micah turned back to his measuring. "Shouldn't have given her the idea," he muttered.

"He'll come around to it," Pearl whispered conspiratorially to me. "Come on kids, let's go entertain auntie Jade upstairs.

"Aw, mom, can I stay down here with Dad?" Ashton complained.

"Only if you help me mark," Micah told him, snagging him in a headlock.

"All right, everyone else then," Pearl said and was immediately obeyed.

As she turned to head up, Micah grabbed her around the waist and planted a loud kiss on her lips. "I'll be up soon," he promised.

Slightly dazed, she led me back up the stairs, Kalia still in her arms. I followed, shaking my head. Five children and still like teenagers.

"Mama, can I watch Aladdin?" Aspen asked, now the leader of the pack with Ashton occupied.

"Sure, but just until bedtime. Jade, would you like something to drink?"

The kids marched into the living room and settled, and I went with Pearl into the kitchen. "Whatever you have cold would be great."

"Iced tea?" She asked, and poured out two glasses when I nodded.

"So, you guys are thinking pretty seriously about having another?" I asked, settling onto a worn kitchen chair.

"Pretty seriously, yes," Pearl responded. Her tone had me studying her face.

"Are you...?"

"Yes! We were going to wait to tell everyone, but I'm just bursting I'm so excited!"

Jumping up, I pulled her into a hug. "That's wonderful! How far along are you?"

"Only five weeks," she told me, and pressed a hand to her stomach. "That's why we wanted to wait a few more weeks, so you have to promise to keep it quiet."

"Of course, I will. Oh, man, I can't believe it. Auntie of 11."

"You know, you could try it out for yourself sometime," Pearl said.

"Yeah, yeah," I waved her off. "One day. For now, I'll just live vicariously through you."

She grinned. She couldn't help it. "I'm happy to oblige you."

CHAPTER 12

As Saturday hit, I had the sudden urge to get more questions answered.

Getting done at the nursing home, I hopped into my car and decided to go to the Log Cabin. I needed to eat anyway, since I'd skipped lunch, and that way I would have a chance to talk to Lani.

She spotted me immediately when I entered, giving me a small smile and a wave. I sat at a side table, out of the way of the crowd. I watched Lani as she moved to each table, a stab of jealousy sneaking in as she moved with complete grace and little effort. A low-cut pair of jeans showed a line of her skin before a red halter covered it up, and she wore her hair up in a black biker's cap. It was the type of outfit that I would have loved to have the confidence to wear, but never would.

Within minutes she was at my table, sliding in across from me.

"I'm so glad to see you," she said pleasantly. "Are you eating?"

"Thought I might," I shrugged. "Haven't had much today."

She nodded, studied my face and asked, "What'll you have?"

I ordered a soda and a burger and sat back, enjoying the time to myself. While I sat there, I spotted two tables full of relatives, which waved at me from across the room. I waved back, but made no move to go visit. I just couldn't work up the effort.

Lani brought out my drink and food in record time. "I'm off in half an hour, can you stick around that long?" She asked.

"Sure," I replied. What else did I have to do?

I ate slowly, stretching the time out and watching as the place slowly shut down. There seemed to be an hour that was completely packed, and otherwise it was the luck of the draw.

When I couldn't sit still any longer, I went up to the front to pay and grabbed a seat at the bar. This section was more full than the restaurant now, the nightly drinkers coming out. After only a couple minutes, Lani saddled up next to me.

"Let's go for a walk," she said, and I followed her out. The night was clear and warm, though I wore a jacket anyway. Lani had slid on a jean jacket matching her pants as we walked out, though I couldn't imagine her being cold.

"I am sorry for the way I acted the other night," Lani began, heading North through town. "It was uncalled for."

With a sideways glance, I replied, "That's okay."

She laughed. "Sure, some crazy lady telling you the man you're dating wants to kill you. No big deal."

"Well, when you put it that way," I grinned, then stopped. "What do you mean, man I'm dating?"

"Jade, I don't have to remind you it's a small town. Rumors have a tendency to fly. Besides that, I could see in your expression how you care for him."

I noticed she refused to use his name, and wondered why that was. "Do you believe what you told me?"

She sighed, and I could tell this had bothered her. "In a way, yes. Jade," she paused, halting her movement and facing me. We were on the outskirts of town already, the woods rising up on either side of us. "My people," she stopped again, paced away and back, "I don't know much of my childhood. There are many traditions and legends that I'm not familiar with. I only know what I've seen, and what I've seen has been violence."

"You do know I have no idea what you're talking about," I reminded her.

She smiled wryly. "I know." She sighed again. "I've just... I've never explained this to anyone before. It must have been ingrained in me since birth to protect this secret, since it's one of the few things I remember."

Her eyes were flashing in every direction again, which I took to be a normal thing for her. Whatever she'd gone through, her life obviously had not been easy.

"Lani, I..." The thought stuck in my throat as huge shadows passed over us.

Lani's head whipped around, facing into the trees. She ducked into a low crouch, a guttural sound emanating from her throat. "Run," she growled at me.

"Wha-"

"Run!" She pointed the opposite direction, but took off into the woods.

My head flipped behind me and back again, unsure. Then I followed her.

Though I was running at full speed, I caught no trace of her. She was gone. I stopped and turned, heading back towards the road to see if I could find another path she might have taken. As I was about to approach the road, I noticed a scrap of material laying off to the side. Curious, I walked over to it and found Lani's shirt. Laying in a neat pile were the rest of her clothes and hat.

I stared at it, dumbfounded. Was she running through the woods... naked?

A low growl snapped me back to attention, and I spun around to face the interior of the woods. My pounding heart told me I wasn't alone, though I couldn't make out any figures. I stood silent, still gripping the article of clothing in my hand.

At once, two figures appeared coming towards me at angles. My heart stopped beating and leaped, instead, into my throat.

Huge, black panthers, their eyes shining brightly, stalked me. The look in their eyes was unmistakable. Lunch.

I didn't move. Couldn't move. Fear and fascination kept me firmly in place, simply waiting for the end. Even if I ran, they could catch me. There was no way for me, small as I was, to fight off one of these cats. Forget two.

I waited. It was all I could do.

They were close now; one leap could put either of them on top of me. The one to my left crouched low, preparing for the attack. I squeezed my eyes shut tight.

But the hit didn't come. My eyes shot open, looking quickly around. A sound like a freight train hitting a brick wall sounded, and I saw a blur of movement as another figure flew

94

out of the foliage and took the cat to my left tumbling. The one on my right was momentarily distracted, so I took the advantage. I ran.

It didn't get me far. The cat beat me to the road, blocking my path. I was stuck again, frozen in place. A deep rumble resonated from its throat, and it crouched.

The figure, the same as earlier, hit the cat sideways and they went tumbling. This time, I caught a look at it. If I wasn't mistaken, it was a leopard.

That was insane. Leopards weren't in Wisconsin. Neither were panthers, for that matter. Maybe the occasional mountain lion or cougar, but even that was rare.

But I couldn't discount the sight before my eyes. The two cats circled each other, the black panther favoring a front paw from the original attack. I was frozen to the spot, realizing any movement by me now could potentially turn both cats on me.

The panther lunged, swiping out with a claw. Lithely, the leopard evaded the attack and came back with one of its own. It hit home, and the panther let out a hiss that had all the little hairs on my neck standing on end.

The circling was done. They went in, a tangle of muscular bodies whipping in every direction, attempting to get the upper hand. When they came apart again, the leopard was limping, and I could clearly see blood on its side.

My sympathies reached out to the animal, though it was irrational. It could just as easily turn on me as the panthers. But it had come to my rescue, whether it knew it or not.

The panther was stalking the leopard again, on the prowl. He crouched, going in for the kill, when a fourth figure flew in from the side. They rolled out of sight, and I glanced helplessly at the leopard lying so still on the ground.

From the foliage, there was one strangled howl and then silence. Cautiously, I made my way towards the leopard. I wasn't thinking, but felt as if I could help. I had to try.

As I approached, a black form leapt through the trees and into my path. My heart jumped again, my movements frozen as I thought it was the panther come back for revenge. Then, as fear allowed my eyes to adjust, I realized the form was not a cat. It was a wolf. *The* wolf.

It stared at me, much as it had in my parent's back yard. I knew it had to be the same one, an animal that size wasn't normal. A low, keening whine came from the leopard and we both turned to stare.

The wolf trotted over, nuzzling at the leopard's neck. An angry hiss was the response, and the wolf backed away, looking up at me again. Without coherent thought, I walked closer.

The wolf stayed back, out of sight of the cat but close enough to intrude. Cautiously, and slowly as possible, I knelt beside the wounded animal. Its giant head shifted towards me, and I gasped aloud.

Without a doubt, I knew I was looking into Lani's eyes.

The red shirt, pressed tightly into the leopard's side, was now soaked with blood. I murmured soothing nonsense while I tried to inspect the damage.

"She needs blood," a voice came out of the darkness, making me jump nearly out of my skin.

Keeping my hands firmly in place, I turned to see Talon standing a few feet away, the wolf gone. I shifted that information to the back of my mind and focused on the problem at hand.

"She needs a doctor," I retorted, but he shook his head.

"There is no doctor here that can treat her. Is your car near?"

I nodded, grasping his plan. Shifting so one hand could press firmly down on the wound, I dug into my pocket and tossed him the key. "It's in front of the Log Cabin. Hurry."

As I waited, I looked down at Lani's form with tears in my eyes. She'd told me to run, and then fought when she was outnumbered. She'd saved me.

And Talon saved her.

The thought came out of nowhere, but immediately I saw the truth in it. He was the wolf.

For the time being, I decided to let all logic fly out the window. Logic obviously was not part of this world. For tonight, I would help Lani. Tomorrow, I would ask questions.

In mere minutes the car was there, as close to the trees as Talon could manage it. It was a ten-minute walk for us, and about a three-minute drive with normal speed limits, but I was pretty sure it had been less than two that Talon was standing next to me.

He was at my side again, and this time Lani remained silent. I glanced at her, nervous by her lack of response. Her eyes were closed and her body still, though I could still feel a slight heartbeat.

My eyes met Talon's, pleading silently. "She needs to shift back," he said softly.

I swallowed hard. "Shift back? How does she do that?"

"You need to talk to her, coax her into it. It will be painful and she needs to know you're with her."

Nodding, I glanced back at the still form. "Lani?" I said softly. "It's Jade. I'm going to make sure you're okay, but I need you to shift back."

The words felt ridiculous, but Talon nodded in encouragement. He knelt with the rest of her clothes in his arms. I didn't even notice he'd left.

"I've got your clothes here, Lani. Shift back and I can help you into them."

Glancing at Talon, I raised my brows. "I don't know if trying to wiggle her into jeans will be best. I think I have a blanket and probably some extra clothes somewhere in the car. Would you check?"

He nodded and was gone. Just like that, even though my eyes were on him, he disappeared.

Giving my head a hard shake, I glanced back down at Lani and stroked a hand through her thick fur. "It'll be okay, Lani, I promise." The blanket was held out to me, and I laid it gently across her body. Looking up at Talon, I asked, "Could you stand a little way back? You make her nervous."

He complied without question. "Lani," I said again. "You're all covered up. Shift back now, so I can help your wounds."

As I watched, chewing on my lower lip, her form shimmered, almost transparent, and changed into the human one I was used to. A gasp stuck in my throat and for a few long seconds I stared, wide-eyed.

Later, I reminded myself.

"That's it. Now I'll get you somewhere I can help you." Crouching on my feet, I slipped my hands beneath her and gently lifted her. She was taller than I was, though probably weighed less than I did. After carrying around multiple nieces and nephews for the last few months, I was hoping I had it in me.

Talon approached, about to interfere. "No," I told him sternly. "She trusts me. I can do this." I kept my gaze steady on his until he nodded once and backed away again.

Carefully, trying to avoid her injuries and knowing I didn't succeed, I lifted her into my arms, her legs draped over one arm and her back resting against the other. Thank goodness, the car was only feet away.

Talon was there before me, opening the back door and helping me leverage her into a comfortable position, touching her as little as possible. Closing the door gently, he faced me.

"Are you okay to drive?" He asked, his hands on my upper arms and his eyes studying my face.

I nodded.

"Take her to my home. If you need to, leave her in the car until you get her blood."

My face paled when he said that. I was hoping I'd made that up earlier.

He searched my face anxiously, so I carefully composed it and nodded again.

"In the master bedroom, go into the closet. On the right-hand side, there is a panel hidden behind the second piece of wood. 6374. Can you remember that?"

"6374," I repeated dutifully.

"That's the code to get into the chamber. Inside is a refrigerator unit with bags of blood. Take two and give them to her."

I paled again. "With a needle?"

His mouth tightened, but he answered. "Orally."

I felt my stomach drop, and I fought revulsion. I nodded again, afraid to speak. He studied me for a moment longer, then pressed his lips against mine in a hard, almost desperate kiss.

"I will be there shortly. After she has the blood, wait a few minutes and she should be able to walk with your help. There's a bed in the second room on the left, at the top of the stairs. Put her in there until I return."

"Where are you...?"

97

"I have to take care of the bodies," he said simply, and was gone again.

I felt hysterics threatening to come on, but then I glanced into the back seat. Lani's fragile, helpless form lay there, so I took in three quick breaths and rushed around to the driver's side.

The drive seemed to take forever. I was pushing the speed limits, but the roads were not the smoothest and I was forced to slow down to avoid jostling Lani too much. Finally, I made it to his drive, and started the trek up.

The entire time I reassured Lani, telling her everything was going to be fine. She didn't respond, and I feared the worst. But when I parked, I saw her shoulders moving up and down, her breath coming slow, too slow.

It spurred me into action. I ran across the small expanse of lawn and into the house, charging straight up the stairs. In the master closet, I fumbled with the board until I was able to pry it out of place and found a keypad. Blood smeared as I typed in the code. *6374*, I repeated to myself and watched in amazement as the entire wall shifted and slid, noiselessly, to expose a small room.

The room was perhaps three feet deep and six feet wide, but it was packed. Weapons of every kind lined the free walls. Most of them looked illegal. A refrigerator unit took up the opposite wall, as promised. Without a second look at the arsenal, I opened the fridge and took two packets out, shutting it and rushing back downstairs. I didn't bother closing the wall, partly because I wasn't sure how, and partly because I knew Talon would when he got back. Lani needed my help, and that was uppermost in my mind.

Opening the back door of the car, I stared at the packets in my hand, and back to Lani. Just how, exactly, was I supposed to get her unconscious body to drink blood? And how was I supposed to open the packets?

My eyes shot around the car and landed on my key ring. It worked for clothing tags, I concluded, so it should work for this. Taking the largest key I had, I poked a hole in the bag and tore across. Blood sloshed out, but I ignored it. The blanket and myself were already covered in blood, dried blood, so a little more didn't matter.

Squatting in the small area between the back of the driver seat and where Lani lay, I lifted her head into the crook of my arm and forced her mouth open. Slowly, and sloppily, I poured the contents in. Her throat convulsively swallowed, to my relief, and the bag was soon gone. Using my makeshift knife, I slit open the next bag and repeated the process.

When it was gone, I lay her head back gently on the seat and waited. Somewhere, far in the back of my head, I was freaking out. I shoved that part farther back and rubbed my hands together impatiently.

"Jade."

The voice was soft and not far away. When I looked up, a grateful smile was on my face, but it soon disappeared. "Can we get her inside?" I asked.

He nodded and pulled me out of the car. "I'm going to carry her," he said. "Stay with me, hold her hand and talk to her, in case she comes out of it."

Without waiting for my approval, he easily pulled her out of the car and into his arms. I did as he asked, holding her hand and walking beside them until we were upstairs. Talon laid her gently on the bed and looked at me.

"How are you doing?"

I shook my head. "Don't ask me that yet."

A tight smile appeared briefly. "I'll be right back."

When he came back, his arms were full of blankets and clothes.

"Help her get dressed, and pile her with blankets."

"But what about her injury?" I asked.

"It's healing. When she's dressed, I'll come in and put a bandage on, and give her more blood."

I nodded and braced myself. Carefully, I lifted her arms and slid a huge t-shirt over her head, sliding it down to cover the injury. It fell nearly to her knees.

Talon had also brought in a pair of drawstring pants, which I slipped up and left lower on her hips so they wouldn't rub against the scratch. Lifting the shirt up to expose the three long marks marring her skin, I was surprised. They looked hours old, not minutes.

Talon appeared then with sutures and worked quickly. As he was finishing, Lani's eyes slid open.

"Jade?" She said hoarsely.

I was sitting on the side of the bed and grabbed her hand automatically. "I'm here."

"Are you okay?"

I laughed softly. "Yes, thanks to you." Taking the cup Talon handed me, trying very hard not to look inside, I held it to Lani's lips.

"Drink this," I told her.

Her eyes widened, but she complied. She drank it quickly and closed her eyes again.

"She needs to rest," Talon said softly. "Come out when you're ready."

I nodded, staring down at Lani's face. Piling the blankets on top of her, I made sure she was comfortable before quietly walking out of the room, closing the door behind me.

A soft light was on in the master bedroom, and I approached cautiously. With nothing more to do, my thoughts were threatening to spill and I knew there were questions I had that I really didn't want to know the answers to quite yet.

Talon was standing at a window, staring out into the night. With just the lamp light, he was shadowed and dangerous looking. I took in a swift breath for confidence and stepped inside.

He turned immediately, silently. Neither of us moved for a long minute, measuring the other. Finally, I stepped towards him and he held out his arms.

Falling into him, I held on tightly around his waist, my face pressed against his chest. Tears sprang to my eyes and I let them fall, unashamed.

"I almost lost you," he whispered into my hair, pressing kisses along my temple.

"You saved me," I said reverently. "You saved Lani."

We stood there, clinging to each other as if nothing else mattered. Right then, nothing else did.

Finally, with great reluctance, I pulled away. "I have to make a phone call," I told him.

Nodding, he gestured towards the night stand where a phone sat. He did have a phone, I thought dumbly. Another mystery solved.

Picking it up, I hesitated on the dials. My first thought was to call my parents, so they wouldn't worry. There was no way I was going home and leaving Lani here alone. But what would I tell them? My mom would surely hear the shakiness in my voice and ask questions.

I typed in a number and waited for the rings. Glancing at the clock, I was surprised to realize it was just after 8:00. It felt like midnight.

"Hello!" Answered a cheery voice.

"Hey, Pearl," I tried to sound normal.

"Jade! I was just going to call you. I talked to Rick today, and he mentioned he's going on a date with Sandy Stevens, you remember her from school? Big nose, big boobs, big gossip? Well, I just wanted to make sure that you were okay with that, otherwise I'll call him right now and stop him from making a mistake."

I closed my eyes, a small smile playing on my lips. Leave it to Pearl to bring me back to earth. "No, Pearl, that's fine. Really, I'm not interested in him more than a friend. Listen," I continued before she could get into another rant. "Can you do me a favor?"

"Sure. What do you need?"

My tone must have finally gotten through, because she was instantly on alert. "Can you call Mom and Dad and just tell them I'm staying with you? Come up with something good, okay?"

"Absolutely! What are you really doing? Oh, it's Tal, isn't it? Way to go, Jade!"

Closing my eyes again, I rubbed against my forehead with my palm. "I'll tell you all about it tomorrow, Pearl, I promise. Thanks."

"Yes, tomorrow, of course. I want all the details."

"Sure thing. I have to go now. Thank you."

"Oh, right. Sorry," she giggled. "See you tomorrow."

I hung up and waited a moment before turning. I couldn't quite read the expression in Talon's eyes, but it was more humorous than I liked.

"The old 'pretend to be sleeping at a friend's while you're really up to no good' routine," he smiled.

I smiled back, but it didn't quite reach my eyes. "It will be easier this way. My mom would hear my voice and know something's wrong. Pearl hears it and thinks I'm having some hot, passionate affair. This way, no one worries."

100

But when I met his gaze again, I realized that wasn't true. His smile had disappeared and his eyes were tight. "I don't want you to lie to your family," he said softly.

I sighed. "And just what am I supposed to tell them? The truth?" I laughed, but it came out bitter. "Right. That'll happen."

"I'm sorry," he said, turning away. "I should have left you alone."

Shaking my head, I walked up to him and laid a hand on his arm. He turned and stared down at it.

"No, you shouldn't have," I said firmly.

His eyes shot back to mine, and a hint of a smile was in them. "Here you are, comforting me, when it should be the other way around."

"I decided not to think about anything that happened tonight until tomorrow."

"Can you really do that?" He asked, eyes narrowed.

"I'd really, really like to," I said honestly. "I don't know if I can take any more tonight."

"Are you afraid?" He asked, his eyes guarded again.

I studied him for a long while before responding. "Of you? No."

He sighed. "Are you tired?"

"A little," I admitted. "But I don't think I can sleep."

"Come here," he said, holding out his hand. He led me into the bathroom and sat me on the edge of the tub. With infinite patience and tenderness, he washed the blood from my arms and face. His touch was soothing, and I was surprised by how much blood was on me. After he was finished, he led me into the closet and picked out another t-shirt and pant combination, handing them to me.

"Change," he ordered, "And then come lay down."

He left me inside the closet, which was almost larger than my room at home. Thankfully, I noticed, the secret room was hidden once again.

The clothes were gigantic on me, so I rolled them best I could and made my way back to the room. A fire was lit, and Talon was standing before it, staring down. He took my hand and led me to the bed, lifting me gently up.

I slid under the covers, sinking into the soft feel of them. The bed was the most comfortable thing I'd ever laid on, and my body instantly felt relaxed. Talon lay beside me, above the covers, and gently stroked my hair.

"This is a wonderful bed," I muttered, more tired than I realized.

"Good," he smiled wholly. "I picked it out for you."

I sent him a harsh look, but let my eyes slide close right away. "You're insane," I told him again.

He laughed gently. "I know."

The dark was closing in, and I surrendered gratefully to it.

"Sleep," I heard a whispered voice urge me. "Sleep, little one, until I wish for you to wake."

CHAPTER 13

When I woke, it was with complete disorientation. The bed was too soft, the sheets too silky. Even the sun was piercing my eyes from the wrong direction.

Opening them slowly, the night's events rushed back to me immediately. I was in Talon's bedroom, and he was some kind of mythical being.

"Good morning," I heard him say, and I had to look around before I spotted him. He was standing in the archway between the bedroom and bathroom, wearing only a pair of jeans. My heart raced involuntarily.

"Morning," I replied.

"Did you sleep well?" He didn't move, as if he was afraid to get too close.

Stretching my arms out, I answered, "Yes, actually. Thanks."

The clock on the bedside read just after 6:00. "How's Lani?" I asked.

"Fine. Still sleeping, but I believe she'll wake soon. I think she'd prefer it if you were there instead of me."

Nodding, I slid out of bed with a little reluctance. It really was very comfortable.

I paused in front of him. He was still studying me, obviously expecting me to have a break down and scream or go into shock or something terrifyingly girly. I just stared back.

"I um," he paused, looking flustered for the first time since I'd met him. "I have some clothes for you."

Raising my eyebrows, I waited patiently for him to finish.

"They should fit," he continued, and finally gave up and moved aside. "They're in the closet, on the bench. You can shower and use anything in the bathroom that you need."

"Thank you," I told him and walked inside. Behind me, a door slid closed, leaving me with total privacy.

Stepping into the shower, I allowed the searing hot water to soothe my muscles and wash away all the grit from the night before. I stayed in longer than normal, enjoying the multiple shower heads and the smell of Talon's soap.

I would have stayed longer, just like the bed, but Lani was waiting for me. And Talon was right, she would not be happy waking up to him.

Inside the closet, there was a pile of clothes, as promised. They were brand new, and I only shook my head and wondered how he pulled that off. They fit perfectly, of course, a pair of khakis and a white shirt. Deftly I pulled my wet hair into a braid, knotting the end for it to stay. It would last a little while, anyway.

Talon was in the bedroom, fully dressed. He examined me again, but spoke easier than earlier. "You look better."

"Thanks. For the clothes, and everything."

"Hm," he murmured, examining me again. "I would have preferred a dress, but this suits you."

I blushed and looked down, not completely sure why. Whether it was simply his words or the look in his eye when he said them.

"Is Lani awake yet?" I asked, trying to distract us both.

"Not yet. If you want to go in, I'll make you both something to eat."

My stomach flipped at the thought of food, reminded of what was stored just a few feet from where I stood.

"I'm not that hungry," I said.

His teeth flashed in a smile. "Eggs and toast," he assured me. "Purely human food."

I flinched at the phrase, but covered it by turning to walk down the hall. When I reached her door, I opened it quietly and peeked in. She was still in the same position I'd left her in, covered by blankets.

Her head turned towards me as I entered, and I thought I caught a glimpse of shame in her eyes. It cleared with a soft smile, but her eyes remained guarded.

"Good morning," her voice was hoarse, but no worse than last night.

"Morning," I said brightly, sitting beside her. There was a pile of clothes on an old wooden chair under the window, and I didn't have to look to know they were also new and more than likely would fit Lani to a T.

"I'm," she stopped to clear her throat, "I'm so sorry."

"No big deal," I answered. "Happens all the time."

She let out a short laugh. It was obviously painful, and I fluttered my hands uselessly.

"This should help," Talon's voice said quietly from the doorway. He held a tray in his hands, complete with a pot of tea.

I glanced at Lani, worried about her reaction to Talon's presence. Her eyes were wary but accepting, I saw with relief.

Talon approached me with the tray, careful to stay some distance from Lani. She struggled momentarily to sit up, and I reached out automatically to help. Sending me a small smile, she focused back on Talon.

"Thank you for your help." I could see the distaste she felt at the words and felt a surge of sympathy rush through me.

"You're welcome," Talon said politely, busying himself with arranging the tray. I poured a cup of tea and handed it to Lani before pouring one for myself.

"So," I began conversationally. "Who wants to explain the panthers' appearance in Wisconsin?"

Talon and Lani exchanged a glance. I waited patiently, taking a sip from the cup.

"Jade," Talon knelt before me and took hold of my free hand. His eyes were dark and reserved, focused entirely on me. "I was hoping to break this to you a better way, but it seems fate has decided otherwise."

"What do you mean, break this to her?" Lani's voice was sharp and disbelieving.

104

"She is my mate," Talon said simply, never looking away from me. I felt a rush of color steal up my neck at his words. Lani gave a disbelieving grunt but remained silent. "We are a race of people known as many names."

"Species, more like," Lani muttered.

"Nevertheless, we are different than regular humans."

His words brought a small spark of hope. "Regular humans? You mean you *are* human, just... different?"

"That's correct. We have many abilities, many special gifts. One, as you saw last night, is the ability to shape shift. But with great power comes great weakness."

"The blood," I blurted out, swallowing hard.

"Yes, that's right. We don't have the ability to reproduce our blood cells, as you do."

I thought this over a minute. "So, you're a vampire."

His teeth flashed without humor. "Not precisely."

"But..."

He moved my hand to his chest, pressing it against his heart. "Feel that?" He asked softly. "I am not undead. My heart beats, my blood is hot."

Too hot. His skin seemed to burn through the thin layer of his shirt.

"Okay," I said slowly. "What else?"

"We can eat," he gestured towards the plate of food, "Go out in the sun," he gestured towards the window, "And have children."

"Really?" That threw me off.

"Yes. And some of us have some extra abilities." He looked to Lani now.

She looked down, embarrassed. "I can speak to animals."

"What do you mean?" I felt completely out of my element. The only way I was still in the room, having such a calm conversation about such extraordinary things, was because it was still pushed back in my mind, in the 'review later' file.

"Telepathically," she explained.

"Oh," I said, and turned back to Talon. "And you?"

He shook his head, disbelieving. "How are you handling this so calmly?"

"I'm not. It just hasn't sunk in yet. You may as well get it all out in the open now."

"All of us are able to manipulate the elements. Fire, water, earth, wind. That is where our name comes from. The Elementals." He waited, expecting some kind of reaction from me. I didn't give him one. "It's not a commonly known name, obviously, but I assume many of the old legends come from our people."

"Vampires, werewolves, witches" I nodded, thinking it over. "You've pretty much got it covered."

"Yes," he grinned, "we do."

"There's more," I said, "Isn't there?"

He glanced at Lani again and quickly back to me. "We don't sleep often," he confided.

"Unless we're injured," Lani added. "Sleep heals us."

I looked at her curiously. She nodded, understanding, and pulled back the blankets. Lifting up her shirt, she showed me the spot that had been gushing blood not 12 hours ago; it was perfectly smooth.

I gasped and stared, unable to look away. Finally, Lani covered up again and I switched my gaze to her face. "Incredible," I breathed.

"Jade," Talon drew my attention back. "Eat for me."

I accepted the plate, feeling odd doing something as mundane as eating when I'd just witnessed a miracle.

"You too," he commanded, handing a plate to Lani.

She sniffed it before taking a bite. I heard a low hiss come from Talon. "I didn't poison it."

To my surprise, Lani grinned. "Just checking."

There was silence while we ate, and I kept switching my fascinated gaze from one to the other. I felt like I was in a room with two celebrities; a fact that made me feel both inferior and awed. Talon kept his eyes on me, probably watching for some kind of sign of a nervous breakdown. Truth be told, that should have been my reaction. It was logical, normal, to be freaked out when faced with such out of this world truths.

But I wasn't freaked out, or afraid. I was... curious. Intrigued. Well, I'd questioned my sanity before. At least that wasn't new.

"Please tell me what you're thinking," Talon begged, lifting the empty plate from my lap and setting it back on the tray.

"Oh, um," I stalled, not sure what to say. "You mean you can't read minds?"

"No, *I* can't." The way he said it seemed to imply others could.

"I was thinking it makes sense," I finally told him. "You know, all these legends must have come from somewhere. People just aren't that creative. Look at Hollywood. Every other movie has the same story line."

My little rant awarded me two raised eyebrows, one from each. I went on, undaunted. "I'm just saying, I think it's neat that there are people who can do the things you do."

"Neat." Talon looked incredulous.

"Yes," I reiterated. "Neat." Glancing over at Lani, I thought of another line of questioning that got me off the hook. "Would you like to explain some things?"

She seemed to understand what I was getting at. "Well," she began, and sent a nervous look at Talon. "I've lived my life basically alone. I don't remember my childhood. One morning I woke up in a forest, alone. I knew what I was," she emphasized with her hands, "That must be ingrained in us as children, but everything else was blank. I've been wandering, picking up odd jobs here and there. I found out, the hard way, that if I stay in one place too long, they find me."

Talon's eyes narrowed. "Who finds you?"

"The others. Like you. I've never met another female of my kind, though I'm assuming some exist. The ones I've run across have been men." Her eyes drifted down again, picking at a piece of lint on the blanket. "They've always been evil," she continued softly. "I've seen them kill, torture."

"What do you normally do?" Talon asked.

"Run. Except on rare occurrences like last night, when I fight."

Rising, Talon cursed under his breath and paced to the door and back. I hung my head, ashamed.

"You only had to fight because I was stupid. I should have run."

"No," they said in unison, and Lani finished the thought. "They would have gone after you anyway. You did nothing wrong." She waited until I looked back at her. "I would have done the same."

"How often?" Talon asked.

"How often what?"

"How often do you have to move?"

Lani thought about this. "I'd say every few months. This is the fastest I've been found."

Talon looked at me, his eyes dark. "They sense you. Both of you. You are unclaimed and a strong lure."

Lani and I exchanged a glance.

"Unclaimed?" Lani spat out.

"A lure?" I exclaimed simultaneously. "Talon, my family-"

"Are safe. I promise."

"How can you know that? Even if they were under your personal protection, you can't be everywhere at once!"

"They would be only interested in you," he persisted.

"Why? And if that's true, they could use my family to get to me. Or worse, you."

His hard stare found me. "How is that worse?"

I blushed, realizing my words. "They're both bad, okay? And now Lani's in danger, because of me? Why? What's different now than the 18 years I lived here? Or the seven years I lived in Florida?"

With a sigh, Talon sank down in front of me again.

"I have a theory, but, mind you, it's only a theory. When Elementals have children, they don't fully develop until their mid-twenties. Twenty-five, to be exact."

I took that in. "But I'm not an Elemental."

"Right. There is another group of humans, however, who are gifted."

"Gifted?" I choked out. "What does that mean?"

Lani butt in this time. "Those who are gifted can be turned," she explained. Talon shot her a glare. "What?" She shrugged. "She'd find out sooner or later."

"You think I'm... gifted?" I tested the word out.

107

"Since you are my mate, yes, I believe you are," Talon replied gently.

"Wouldn't I know?" Looking between the two, I knew confusion was plain on my face.

His mouth turned down at the edges, his brow creasing. "Nothing odd has happened to you lately?"

At my bland stare, his teeth flashed in a grin. "Besides me, that is."

"No."

Talon and Lani exchanged another glance, but I couldn't understand their concern. I was normal. Well, normal as far as I knew existed until last night. No magical powers, no inner animal. Just me.

"Let's not worry about this now. We should get you home." Talon stood and extended his hand to me.

"Home?" I asked numbly.

"Yes. Home, where you live. Your parents will be worried if you don't show up eventually."

"Right," I muttered, and glanced over at Lani. "Need a ride?"

"Sure," she answered, sending Talon a nervous glance.

"There are clothes for your use," Talon gestured towards the chair. "I will leave you now so you can get dressed."

Taking hold of my hand, he led me downstairs, balancing the tray in the other hand. When we were in the kitchen, he studied me again. "Are you positive you're all right?"

"Sure," I shrugged. "Why wouldn't I be?"

Shaking his head in disbelief, he grabbed me in a sudden hug. "Amazing," he murmured into my hair. "Absolutely amazing."

There was a delicate clearing of a throat at the doorway, making us break apart guiltily.

"Enough of that," Lani said sternly.

She was wearing the new clothes, and, sure enough, they fit perfectly. She cleared her throat again, but this time it was nervously. "Um," she began, diverting her eyes from Talon. "Thanks again for everything. I'd like to talk to you, if you don't mind later, about our people."

"Anytime," Talon answered immediately.

Lani flashed him a smile and looked at me. "Ready when you are," I assured her.

Nodding, she stepped outside. I followed, with Talon at my heels.

"Oh, no," I groaned.

"What is it?" Talon was at my side, a worried expression on his face.

"My car has blood all over it," I explained.

He shook his head. "I took care of it."

I stared at him, then turned to walk to my car. I kept staring at the shiny outside and the like-new inside. With a quick shake of my own head, I opened the door. "Thank you," I told Talon, watching him over the door.

"No problem. I didn't want it to raise any questions."

"Right."

Lani smirked and got into the passenger side.

"I'll see you tonight," Talon said.

"What?"

"Dinner tonight. I am invited, aren't I?"

I stared at him again, baffled. "Dinner?"

He laughed. "It's Sunday. And even if you're not going to invite me, I believe I was invited by Ella. I very well couldn't disappoint her."

Rolling my eyes, I dropped into my car. "Five o'clock," I told him. "Don't be late."

CHAPTER 14

At 4:55, the doorbell rang. Most of the family was already gathered, children running amuck and dinner about to come out of the oven. Tonight, it was meatloaf, green bean casserole, scalloped potatoes and rhubarb pie for dessert.

As of yet, I'd managed to avoid being alone with Pearl. She tried, extremely hard, but I had a few moves of my own. When the doorbell rang, I felt as if the battering ram that had been banging against my stomach all day went into overtime. Why I was so nervous, I wasn't completely sure. So many things had been running around in my mind all day, and yet only a few stuck out.

She's my mate.

Those words were easily forgotten in the bizarre conversation this morning, but they were said. And they were now foremost on my mind.

Mate. What an odd word to use. Not that odd, I supposed, considering the fact that he could turn into an animal. But still, he was human. Humans just didn't run around saying things like mate.

"I'll get it!" Pearl announced before I could rev myself into action. She was gone before I could tell her no.

I glanced around the dining room at my other two sisters, who were helping me set the table. Both of them grinned at me, knowing all too well that I was sunk.

Pearl walked in, an arm looped through Talon's. The battering ram reversed directions once before slamming again. Man, he was gorgeous.

I managed half a smile before sliding off into the kitchen. Behind me, I could hear my sisters greeting our guest with voices pitched higher than was natural. Breathe, I ordered myself. Last night I handled much worse than this.

The door swung open and I spun, my stomach jumping into my throat. No, I realized. Last night was easy compared to this. Last night I was in shock. Now, I was fully functioning. I'd had time today to think things through. And all of that brought me to this point.

"Hello," Talon said in his velvet voice. He was on guard again, standing well away from me.

"Hey," I responded, pretty normally I thought.

"I've been sent in here to help," he gestured towards the stove.

"Oh, right, sure," I spun around again and grabbed oven mitts out of the drawer.

"Are you all right?" His voice was lower, and closer.

Without turning, I nodded my head. "Sure. Just fine."

"Are you angry with me?"

"No."

"Are you afraid of me?"

111

I let out a sharp laugh, verging on hysteria. "No." Not afraid of him. Afraid of the way I felt for him, maybe. But not afraid of him.

"All right," his voice sounded relieved but strained still.

Taking in a deep breath, I turned and faced him. "What did you mean when you said I was your mate?"

His face relaxed. "Is that what is bothering you?"

I moved my shoulders restlessly. "More or less."

"Perhaps my wording was off when I said that. I did not mean to upset you."

I sighed. "Well, what *did* you mean?"

The door opened and I looked up, annoyed. It was Amber, and she looked as uncomfortable as I did unhappy.

"Uh- the kids are getting anxious. Mom wanted me to see what the holdup was."

"Yeah, yeah, we're coming," I told her, and turned back to the oven again. "Grab a couple oven mitts, would you?" I said to Talon, and held out the meatloaf pan for him to take. As he was about to turn around, I told him under my breath, "You will explain later."

"Of course," he answered, and left to bring the dish out.

Since Amber was there, I handed her the potatoes and took the green beans myself. Not surprisingly, the chair open for me was next to Talon.

This week, at least, my sisters seemed to be more contained around him. They still giggled, and stared, and bat their lashes, but it wasn't as bad. Dinner actually was going very smoothly, to my great relief and surprise. Until dessert.

"When are you two getting married?" Grandpa Stryder aimed a look at Talon and shot the entire table into silence.

My mouth opened but no words came out.

"Well, sir," Talon grinned, "I'm just trying to get your granddaughter to date me first."

"Yes, yes," he waved this away as inconsequential. "But I'm getting on in years, and I'd like to dance at Jade's wedding."

I started to say something then, but Talon placed a hand on my knee and prevented it. "I'll work even harder on it."

"Are you going to take care of her?" Grandpa Stryder went on.

"Yes, of course I will."

"A woman has needs, you know. Physically, emotionally, sexually."

A strangled gasp that gurgled in my throat was the only response at the table.

Pearl glanced at me and once around the silent table.

"I'm pregnant!" She blurted out.

All eyes turned from my red face to her. After three extremely long seconds of silence, pandemonium broke out. Amid the congratulations and questions, Pearl sent me a wink that coaxed out half a smile from my frozen face. Talon applied pressure to my knee and leaned in, unnoticed in the unexpected turn of events.

"Don't worry," he soothed. "Your grandfather just wants to see you happy."

I managed to nod, not trusting my voice just yet.

"And, for future reference, I can and will take care of *all* your needs."

This time when my face turned red, no one but Talon witnessed it.

The next morning I was in a daze. When Emma came in to visit Grandma with Suzy and Mikey, she noticed.

"Jade, what's going on?"

When I started to deny anything, I stopped myself and simply shook my head.

"No offense, but you look awful. Maybe you should take a break today, go do something fun. I have the morning free, and I think Pearl was planning on stopping by later today. Grandma won't be alone."

I studied my sister's face, saw the dark circles under her own eyes, but more than that, the worry for me. Sticking around would only increase that worry and I couldn't handle any questions.

"All right," I finally agreed. She seemed relieved. "But I'll probably stop by back for dinner. I don't want to be gone all day."

"Okay," Emma agreed. "Call me if you need to talk."

I nodded, gathered up my things and walked out.

When I got into my car, there was only one place I could think of to go. One place I wanted to go. Talon's.

There was unfinished business between us, on so many levels. He left the night before without a chance to answer my question from the kitchen. Plus, with the revelations from the night previous that, I knew we had to have a long talk anyway.

Of course, I could chicken out and go see Lani instead. When I thought about that, I knew it wasn't what I wanted. I would check on her, of course, later today or tomorrow, but the person I wanted to see was Talon.

Turning the keys in my engine, I began driving towards his house when I realized he might very well be at Amber's. The kitchen was almost complete, and it was a workday. Her house was on the way anyway- might as well check by there first.

Sure enough, his truck was outside. I got out slowly and let myself in the door. The sound of electric tools greeted me.

"Hey," I said when the buzzing paused for a moment. I couldn't see him, squatted behind the island as he was. At my voice, he peered over and a slow smile lit his face.

"Hi," he responded. Just as slow as his smile, he rose to his feet, watching me.

We stood staring at each other, my stomach twisted into those now familiar knots.

With my eyes on his, I made my way around the island to stand before him. With steady hands that belied how my insides felt, I ran my palms over his chest to rest on his shoulders. His hands automatically moved to my hips, burning hotly through my clothes. He still smelled like campfires and evergreens, with the not entirely unpleasant odor of sawdust mixed in.

113

Our heads moved inexorably closer. I couldn't have stopped it if I wanted to. And I didn't want to.

When our lips met, it was soft. Then the fire caught, held, and I went up in flames.

My hands secured around his neck, dragging him closer. His hands tightened around my hips, wrapping in the material there to hold me against him. Our bodies moved restlessly, unable to get enough, be close enough.

This was not what I had planned when coming to see him. This was something else, something... *elemental*.

In a smooth turn, my body was pressed against the counter and one leg wrapped itself around him. My hands were moving now, roaming, exploring, memorizing. His did the same, one finding its way to my hair, securing there to hold my head still for his exploration.

It was hot and crazy and all I could think was... *more*.

I wanted more. Then, with a sudden gasp, I pulled my head away. There was just a scant few inches between us and I stared at him, willing the blood that had rushed to my head back to the rest of my body.

"We're in my sister's kitchen," I said, a little breathlessly.

He nodded, looking as frustrated and on fire as I felt.

"This is not appropriate behavior for the work place."

I couldn't help it. I laughed, hard. Carefully, he put more space between us without relinquishing his entire hold on me. "Perhaps we could go back to my house," he began, and added at the look on my face, "I imagine you have some more questions for me. I just have a couple things to wrap up here, if you don't mind waiting a few minutes."

I shook my head. "That's fine."

He took a deep breath, and I found inexplicable satisfaction in the fact that he was as affected by me as I was by him.

Bending back to his task, I didn't bother to pretend I was doing anything but watching him. The electrical hum resumed, and I waited patiently for him to finish. When he did, he carefully packed his tools and lifted the box.

"Ready?" He asked.

At my nod, he took my hand and headed for the door. I closed it behind me and walked with him to the back of his truck. After setting the toolbox in the bed, he walked me to my driver's door and opened it. He pressed his lips to mine once, and quirked a smile.

"Drive safe."

I grinned at him. "You too."

Less than five minutes later, we were standing in his kitchen. It felt safer than, say, the bedroom, but after the explosive moment in my sister's kitchen, maybe it wasn't.

"Something to drink?" He asked.

"Sure," I told him. It would give my hands something to do.

114

He poured us both glasses of lemonade and leaned against one counter. I hopped up opposite him, legs dangling.

"So..." I began, not sure where to go from there.

"What did you want to know more about, now that you've had time to process?"

I lifted my hands, palms up. "Everything. But, let's start with you. You can... shift..." I wasn't sure precisely how to put it. "Into a wolf? What else can you do?"

He crossed his arms and watched me carefully. "I can shift into any form. The wolf is what is known as my natural form, the form I was able to shift into without thought. Over time, with practice, I was able to take on any other."

I processed that. "Were your parents..."

"The same? Yes and no. My mother was fully Elemental. She had her own powers, was an amazing woman. My father was fully human. He had no powers, was not gifted and therefore could not be converted, but he loved my mother like no other I've seen."

"What could your mother do?" I asked, curious. I wasn't sure what he meant by being converted, but would get back to that.

"She was able to foresee events."

"Tell the future?" I asked, my brow raising.

"Yes. She saw you."

"Me?" I squeaked out.

"Yes." He lips quirked into a smile. "You."

"But... how..."

He took the couple steps to close the distance between us and rested his hands on my upper arms. "Breathe, Jade. You're doing exceptionally well with all the information that has been placed before you. Just keep breathing."

Nodding, I took in a deep, shaky breath. "Okay," I said. "Okay. Your mom saw me. Did you know I'd be here? Is that why you moved here?"

"That's not as easily answered. I didn't know when, or where, I would find you. Your photograph, the one hanging in the bedroom, spoke to me. I didn't know what it meant, why I felt so compelled by it. I didn't know J. Callaghan was actually you, my other half."

One hand slid down my arm and brought my hand up to cover his heart. I felt the strong beat, steady, as he stared into my eyes.

"That's what you are, Jade. My other half. I know you feel it too."

I'd forgotten to breathe again, and I wasn't admitting anything just yet. Coming to the conclusion that I'd fallen in love with him was hard enough. Being his other half was a whole other ball game I wasn't ready for.

Clearing my throat delicately, I said, "Tell me more. About you, your family."

He backed up against the counter again. The sudden loss of heat sent a shiver through me.

"I told you before that I grew up differently. I learned the old ways, the ways of the earth. My mother never hid what she was from me, or my father. He knew everything and did

115

his best to raise me in both worlds. We didn't have a lot of contact to the outside world. Most of the time, it was just the three of us."

Some forgotten memory- or was it a dream? Flirted with the edges of my conscious. Desert sky, the smell of a horse after a run. Sand, small villages. Teepees.

My head spun and my vision blurred. Both hands gripped the edge of the counter, trying desperately to stay in control. Images, too many images, swirled through my mind.

"Jade, honey, what's wrong?"

I felt his arms wrapped around me again, but his voice was far away. I was *not* going to faint again. With every ounce of effort I could muster, I willed my head to stop spinning and managed to lift my eyes to his.

"You... I saw you... I *was* you..."

I knew I wasn't making sense. Talon captured my face between his hands, looking into my eyes. "Tell me."

"I... I had dreams. Of you. I mean, it's like I *was* you. I saw your mom, your dad. On a hunt, going to villages. They weren't dreams, were they? They were memories. *Your* memories."

He seemed taken aback.

"That can't be," I murmured, "How can that be?"

"I'm not sure," Talon began. "I've not dealt with mated Elementals in my time. From the old stories, I know there is a strong connection. A very strong connection between two that are meant to be together. Perhaps, somehow, as you slept, you connected to my memories."

I focused on him again, feeling clear. "Your memories. Talon, all those dreams took place in the desert. But not like the desert is now. There were wild horses, and... teepees, for crying out loud. If I didn't know better, I would say this happened hundreds of years ago."

He stayed quiet, completely focused on me, his hands still framing my face. The color drained from it.

"Talon, how old are you?" I asked quietly.

"I think you already know that answer."

My eyes searched his face, waiting for him to tell me it was all a big joke. *Ha-ha, Jade, you should have seen your expression.* No such luck.

"This is crazy," I whispered.

"Yet you believe it."

I looked at him helplessly. "Yes."

He stayed silent, watching me carefully. He was waiting, whether for me to break down or to ask more questions, I wasn't sure. Truth was, I didn't know which way it would go either.

Slowly I took a sip of lemonade then cleared my throat.

"Um," I began, then stopped. There was more I wanted to ask, but I couldn't get the latest revelation out of my head. Finally, I decided on something he'd said earlier. "What's a conversion?"

His eyes tightened. "We do not have to discuss this now."

That made my heart speed up. "Why? How bad is it?"

Looking down, he seemed to struggle with himself for a few moments before making the decision to answer.

"It is not... pleasant. I went through it myself, my mother converted me fully into her world."

He didn't say what I now knew. *For me.* He converted to live long enough to meet me.

And I thank him by throwing iced tea in his lap.

Taking a deep breath, knowing I had to handle it, somehow, I said, "Please, Talon. Tell me. I promise I won't faint."

This brought out the smallest smile. "You have to exchange blood with one that is fully Elemental. The person converting has to possess special gifts, talents, in order for the conversion to take hold."

"And what if the person doesn't possess these special gifts?" I asked, fearing the answer.

"They would die."

Though I was expecting it, the answer still made me wince. "Have you thought about converting me?"

"No." He said it sharply, then softened his tone. "Even if you possess the gifts, which I'm not sure right now if you do, I would not wish to put you through such pain."

"But... that means... while I grow old and die, you stay this young?"

He shifted uncomfortably again. "Not necessarily. If I choose to give up my gifts, such as shifting, just stop using them altogether, I would lose my longevity."

"You would give up immortality... for me?" My heart squeezed tightly.

"Yes. Jade, immortality would mean nothing without you to spend it with."

Not sure how to respond, I lifted a hand to his face and let it rest there. "You are an amazing man, Talon Wolfchild."

He smiled, fully this time. "I'm glad you think so, Jade Callaghan."

Dropping the hand, I sighed. "You know, all this talk of the supernatural makes me hungry."

He laughed. "I would be delighted to fix you brunch."

My stomach rumbled in response. I laughed too. "No complaints here."

Knocking softly at the door, I glanced sideways at Talon. "Maybe you should wait outside," I mused aloud. After lunch, I'd decided we needed to check on Lani.

117

He glanced at me sharply. "She has questions I am able to answer. It is time she realizes not all men are evil."

Turning back to the door to hide the smile, I heard locks being turned and Lani appeared in the doorway. She smiled tentatively at me before looking at Talon. There was a brief hesitation before she stepped back to allow us entry.

"Please, come in," she said, gesturing with her hand.

"How are you feeling?" I asked immediately, walking past her into the cozy living room.

"Much better, thank you," Lani followed me in to the room. "Thank both of you. I apologize, this is very odd for me."

Sitting on the couch, I grabbed Talon's hand and pulled him down beside me, hoping he would look less intimidating. He squeezed my hand, raising a brow at me as if reading my thoughts.

"Believe me, I've had my fill of strange lately," I grinned at her.

She smiled appreciatively back before focusing on Talon. "I have so many questions I'm not really sure where to begin."

"Why don't you tell me a little about yourself," Talon began. "What do you remember of your childhood?"

Lani shook her head while she answered. "I don't. I woke up one evening, in the middle of the forests of South America with no memory of how I got there or who I was. I'm not sure how old I was- I was fully grown, but as we age differently, that didn't mean much."

"Oh, Lani, you must have been terrified," I felt my heart reach out to her. "What did you do?"

"Wander," she answered. "At first I thought I'd come across someone that knew me, could tell me who I was or who my family was. After many years, it became obvious I would not find such a person. When I stayed too long in one place, the shadow men would find me."

Talon stiffened, obviously distressed that Lani had been alone to defend herself against these creatures.

"The first time they found me, I was so afraid, struggling wildly. My hands turned to claws, raking across their faces and bodies. That realization only made me more afraid. Not only did I not know who I was, but *what* I was. I managed to escape, and did not stop running for a very long time."

"How long are you typically in one place before they find you?" Talon asked.

Lani paused, thinking about her answer. "It depends. I usually try to blend in, find a job waitressing and live as normally as I can. When I use my power, it seems to draw them in. I try not to shift or use any magic unless it's absolutely necessary. The longest I've stayed in one place was about a year. As I mentioned earlier, this is the fastest I've been found."

Talon's hand tightened on mine again, and I knew our thoughts went the same direction.

"Because of me," I said quietly.

Talon gripped my chin with his fingers, forcing my gaze to him. "Do not take blame for the depraved actions of these foul beings."

"It really doesn't matter why they found us," Lani added. "What matters is how we handle it."

"You'll stay?" I asked.

She stared at her hands for a moment, lying still in her lap. When her eyes met mine again, they were steady. "Yes. I will stay to ensure your safety."

"You must have more questions," Talon prompted.

Lani nodded. "There are times where I will get a flash of a memory, but nothing concrete. After wandering for so long, not being able to trust anyone, it is not an easy thing now."

She took a deep breath, and I silently encouraged her to speak her mind.

"I have family somewhere. I know I do, but I'd given up on ever finding them. Do you know anyone who might be able to help me?"

Lani's look was so hopeful, I felt a vice squeeze my chest, knowing Talon's history and that he didn't know any others like himself.

With bated breath, I waited for his response.

"I did not grow up with others like us," Talon finally explained quietly. "However, I have done considerable research into different legends. It seems you would have better luck with certain cultures. As I've told Jade," here he squeezed my hand, "The Irish have a long history of magic in their veins. My people, as connected to the earth as we are, would also be a good place to research. I've also come across many stories from Australia, with their shaman, the gods of Egypt, Paganists all across Europe. It is a good bet that we could find other Elementals within these groups."

Lani nodded, seeming to absorb the information.

"It was always my plan, once I found Jade, to seek out others," Talon spoke again, looking at me. "If you're up for it, we can go with Lani."

"Yes!" I exclaimed happily.

"Oh, Jade, you don't have to," Lani began, but I cut her right off again.

"Of course, we will come with you!" I told her again. "Safety in numbers, and all that."

Lani rolled her eyes. "It doesn't have to be right away," she emphasized. "And you don't have to stay with me forever. But, I suppose, some company for a little while might do me some good."

Beaming at Talon, an idea struck. "We need to do something fun."

"What?" They asked me in unison.

"F-U-N," I spelled out. "All this evil shadow men – new species – being alone business is depressing." A lightbulb lit. "Fourth of July is this weekend!"

119

They were both still staring at me. I could see I would be in charge of entertainment.

"It's a big deal around here. What do you say, Lani?"

"Maybe not something quite so big, Jade. But, you're right. We do need some fun. Let's just start small, okay?"

"Talon?" I asked, heart in my eyes.

"How could I deny you?"

Grinning with triumph, I looked back at Lani. "What do you like to do?"

She looked around, seeming at a loss. "I'm not really sure."

Jaw dropping, I stared at her. "We really need to fix this."

"She could come to dinner at your parents," Talon murmured mischievously in my ear. "Once your sisters get a hold of her, she'll be set up with more dates than she'll know what to do with."

"Yeah!" I thought the idea was great.

"No," Lani spoke simultaneously, her face paling.

"Okay, fine. How about dinner? Just the three of us."

Lani looked from my face to Talon's, considering. Finally, she nodded tightly. "That is acceptable."

Rolling my eyes, I stood, pulling Talon with me. "Next week," I told her. "After the 4th."

She agreed, and Talon and I left. I'd pull Lani out of her shell if it was the last thing I did.

120

CHAPTER 15

"Come on," I called out to Talon. "I'm driving."

He came downstairs, sporting a dark blue, American flag shirt and jeans. "Is this appropriate enough?" He asked, a brow raised.

I gave him a once over and shrugged. "You'll do."

Before I could read his intention, I was trapped between two very strong arms. "I'll do?" He growled, and pressed his mouth to mine.

It was a good thing he held on to me so tight, because my knees went weak. I wasn't sure that I'd ever get used to that.

His head rose, just far enough to look down at me.

"Um," I began, attempting to clear my head. The satisfied gleam in his eye had me narrowing mine. "Like I said, you'll do."

"If you were not forcing me to go to this inferno event, I would gladly prove you otherwise."

"Too bad. We're going. It's tradition, and besides, you've never been to a parade. I'd say it's time you went."

His hand slid into mine as I turned to leave. "As long as I'm with you, I suppose it doesn't matter."

Rolling my eyes, ignoring the flip in my chest at his words, I sighed, "Smooth words are not getting you out of it, or the fireworks."

He opened my door and grinned down at me. "I'm beginning to see the appeal of fireworks. Darkness, warm blanket- it has its possibilities."

I slammed the door shut on him.

Chuckling, he walked around and slid into the passenger side. At least he was in a good mood. I couldn't be angry with that.

I drove the 20 minutes to the next town, where the annual event was held. This year was special, because the 4th of July actually fell on a Saturday, so all the festivities weren't a week early or a week late, as usual.

The streets were already lined with cars, though we were almost an hour early. There was a car show and vendors set up along the parade route, selling everything from jewelry to cheese curds to beer. I already knew we'd be making a stop for funnel cake at some point in the day.

Expertly, I maneuvered through the crowd and into one of the parking lots set up for the event. Our meeting point was only a block away, and I had no doubt there were already family there, staking out our spot.

"Ashton's in the parade this year, you know," I told Talon.

"So I heard. Boy Scouts, right?"

"That's right. That means we get extra candy."

He took my hand again as we headed down the street, a gesture I was slowly getting accustomed to. At times like this, walking down the bright street with flags streaming and children laughing, everything else in Talon's life seemed a little surreal.

"Auntie Jade! Talon!" More than one little voice called out to us as we neared the spot. Ella ran up to Talon, lifting her arms up. Talon lifted her with one hand, keeping the other securely around mine.

"Do you like my pretty?" Ella asked Talon, looking up at him with her heart in her eyes.

"Let me see," Talon said, and Ella obligingly swung her head around to show off the red, white and blue ribbon tied securely to her pony tail.

"I sure do. Think I could have one just like it?"

She giggled with delight. "No, these are for girls."

"Guess I'll stick with the basic black, then."

I smiled over at my parents, already staked out in their chairs with a cooler between them, and all my sisters. Rick joined us as well, Cassie running around with Suzy as was becoming usual. The other kids joined them as well, excitement tangible in the air.

"Did you show Talon your pretty, Ella?" Pearl asked.

"Yeah," she giggled again. "He wanted one too, but I told him it's just for girls."

"I'm sure we could have made an exception," Pearl winked at us. "Grab a seat," she told us, "We've got extras. Want a drink?"

"I'm good for now," I told her, and Talon declined as well.

Ella got down to run with the other kids while we waited for the parade to start. When Talon got into a deep conversation about dirt biking with Jack, I wandered over to Emma.

"What's up?" I asked, stretching out on the curb beside her.

Mikey slept in her arms, a two-kid stroller sitting beside her. "Oh, not much," she answered. "Just waiting for the fire trucks to come by and scare the bejeezus out of Mikey."

She smiled over at me, but it was reserved.

"Where's Gerry at?" I asked.

She shrugged. "Didn't want to come today. He'll be at the fireworks tonight, though."

That had been happening quite a bit lately, and I wondered idly what the change was. I'd have to talk to Amber about it later, she was the most observant of us.

We sat quietly, watching the havoc wreak around us while everyone got antsy to begin. I glanced back once, noticing Rick and Micah had joined the intense conversation with Talon and Jack. Talon glanced at me, shot me a smile and focused back on the topic. I felt my heart jump and couldn't stop the silly grin from forming.

It seemed that whatever Rick's reservations had been about Talon were now gone. That was a relief, since I had a feeling Rick was going to be a large part of my life in one way or another. I glanced at Emma again, who was staring down at Mikey with a little smile only a mother could have for a child.

The first wail of a siren brought the kids front and center, poised for candy retrieval. Talon sat next to me, his arm sliding around my shoulders.

"It's time," he said darkly, making me laugh.

"Just wait," I told him. "You'll love it."

The police car was first, heading up the festivities, followed by three fire trucks. These were the first to throw candy, and the kids went nuts.

"Most parades aren't allowed to throw candy anymore," I told Talon. "Something about kids running into the street being dangerous."

"What do they do?"

"They have to walk around the side and hand it out. Takes all the fun out of it."

He raised a brow, turning towards me. "I can see when we have children, I will be in charge of discipline and safety."

"Children?" I squeaked out, staring. A blast from an old car's horn made me jump nearly out of my skin.

Talon's laughter rang out, and even though I squirmed, he pulled me close. "Yes," he murmured into my hair. "Lots and lots of children."

"Talon! Talon!" Ella's cry had us both turning our heads, though Talon didn't relinquish his hold. "There's candy stuck out there, and a car's gonna run it over!"

Her look of desperation had Talon loosening his hold and standing. "Let's go rescue it."

He held out his hand, which she took immediately. Together they ventured into the street, timing their movements with the cars passing. Ella nabbed the candy and they rushed back, laughing.

"We got it, Auntie Jade!"

"Nice job, Ella."

"You better stay by me," Talon told her. "Just in case any more need rescuing."

She nodded solemnly, waiting for him to sit by me before perching on his lap.

"Don't think that just because she's here I forgive you."

He looked over at me, pure innocence on his face. "Are you accusing me as using a child as a buffer?"

"That's exactly what I'm accusing."

His smile was unrepentant, and I couldn't stop my answering one.

Despite his best efforts not to, Talon enjoyed himself. In such a tight knit community, it was difficult not to feel part of the camaraderie. As the parade came to an end, I watched as Rick helped Emma load a sleepy Suzy and already sleeping Mikey into the stroller. Cassie walked alongside Emma, reaching out to take her hand while Rick pushed the stroller towards the concessions.

123

"They make quite a picture, don't they?" Talon murmured in my ear. For the moment, we were alone and following the group at a slow pace.

"Yeah," I answered absently. I had warring feelings about that. "Which reminds me," I continued, looking up at him.

He smiled down at me, and it was difficult to keep up even a facade of angry. I sighed. "Don't get me wrong. I love children. I'm just not ready yet."

"No worries," he soothed. "We have plenty of time."

When he said it, I almost believed him.

I spent the afternoon dragging him from booth to booth, sampling such delicacies as mini donuts, funnel cake and a dozen of other things deep fried. By the end of the day, my stomach was so full I was afraid I might expand in the sun and explode.

Dusk came slowly, and though it was past all their bedtimes, the kids ran rampant. We made our way towards the ball field where the fireworks would be set off and reserved our spot.

While the sun sank slowly in the sky, they held races for the kids and a variety of other contests. This had always been my favorite part as a kid, though I'd never actually won anything. I applauded ecstatically when Penny, in the 2-year-old division, won the race by being the only one to run in the correct direction. Suzy had run straight for her mom, on the sidelines, while Kalia stood frozen at the start. The other kids had similar reactions, and Penny took home the jar of jelly beans.

Aspen came in second in the 5-year-old race, and looked incredibly upset by the fact. Talon took her aside, and whatever he told her put a wide smile on her face. At my questioning look after, he only smiled and took my hand again. Sometimes he could be so annoying.

Gerry showed up just after the races, about an hour to sundown. He had a beer in his hand and from the red cheeks, I could tell it wasn't his first.

It bothered me, this new Gerry that I'd never witnessed before. We'd never been close, like my other brother-in-law's, and unlike them, I'd always gotten a slightly uneasy feeling in the pit of my stomach around him. Mostly I ignored it, playing it off as something else, anything else. But now, watching him joke with a group of guys set up next to us, yelling rudely at anyone in the vicinity, I knew it was something more.

Talon felt me stiffen and slipped an arm around my shoulders. "It's not our fight," he whispered.

My jaw clenched, and I didn't even notice he said 'our'. "Emma deserves better."

"I agree. But she has to make her own decisions."

I nodded, still stiff, and glanced at the rest of my family. My mom was looking worriedly between Emma and Gerry, which shouldn't have surprised me. She was sharp when she wanted to be. Pearl was gathering her children closer, under the ruse of the impending show, but flicked uneasy glances towards Gerry and his friends occasionally. Rick sat with them, his face a hard mask, obviously unhappy with the situation.

Talon pulled me down to the blanket that was spread out. "Relax," he whispered again. "The shows about to start."

He was right. The sun had set and the darkness was fast approaching. I snuggled into him as a light breeze blew cool against my skin, letting his heat envelop me. As the fireworks began, even the loudest group quieted down, and the continuous boom overhead drowned out those that didn't.

I let myself relax. as Talon has requested, and watched as the silhouettes lit and ran, lit and ran, a tenuous dance with the highly explosive materials. Bright colors lit the sky again and again. Some kids laughed, some cried. And through it all, Talon never loosened his grip on me. I felt oddly at ease, comforted. As the finale came to its end, Talon took my chin in his hot hand and met his lips to mine. I let myself sink into the kiss, uncaring that family and friends were scattered within viewing range.

He pulled back, too soon, and looked into my eyes. I felt my heart skitter and stop before starting a frantic beating.

"Thank you," he said so quietly only I could hear it.

"You're welcome," I answered. "For what?"

He chuckled and released his hold on my chin. "For today. I enjoyed myself immensely."

I grinned, triumphant. "Told you so."

He rose, still amused, and held out a hand to lift me to my feet. In the ball field, a DJ set his lights to strobe and started the first music of the traditional street dance after the show. Only the youngest kids were beginning to droop, but they all bounced excitedly. "Can we go, can we please?"

They begged their respective parents and were given the okay. Talon and I followed at a much more sedate pace, watching the sheer joy chase across their faces.

Immediately they began bouncing around, more enthusiasm than rhythm in the group.

At the first slow song, Ella ran over and stood in front of Talon, looking shyly up at him. I watched in amusement as Talon knelt before her.

"May I have this dance?" He asked, holding his hand out.

Ella giggled and took it. Talon rose, giving me a sly smile. "You're next."

As he twirled Ella around, I felt something shift inside me. I'd already admitted to myself that I loved him. Now, I realized, I never wanted to be without him.

When the song ended and he returned to my side, I knew my heart was in my eyes, but it couldn't be helped. He held his hand out, patiently, and I laughed.

"This isn't a slow song."

"In my mind, it is," he responded.

Shaking my head, I took his hand. He pulled me in close, his heat enveloping me once again. The electricity between us was shooting off sparks to rival the show we just witnessed.

Our bodies were close, but my eyes remained steady on his. Though no words were exchanged, a decision was made.

"Talon," I whispered, knowing he could hear me just fine. "Take me home."

-

CHAPTER 16

We walked into the nursing home together, and I was surprisingly nervous. Talon could tell.

"Relax, Jade. I promise not to bite."

"Ha, ha," I responded, giving a small wave to Janet as we passed the nurses station. She gave me a thumbs up behind Talon's back.

I'd decided, now that Talon and I were officially together, that it was time he met my grandma.

When we walked into her room, she was sitting up in bed, the television turned on low. With a big smile, I walked up beside her. "Morning, Grandma," I said, giving her a hug before turning to Talon. "There's someone I want you to meet. This is Talon."

She grinned huge, holding out her hands for him to take. Her mouth trembled, and not for the first time I wished I could understand her.

I was concentrating so much on my Grandma's reaction to Talon, I hadn't notice his reaction to her. Glancing up at him, seeing an expression that could only be categorized as shock, my eyes widened.

"Talon?" I spoke hesitantly.

His eyes met mine in amazement. "She knows who I am." Before I could respond to that, he began speaking to her. "Yes, Jade is my other half. I knew it the moment we met."

My grandma nodded, her eyes closing with a satisfied smile on her face. As for me, my mouth was hanging open, not quite understanding what was going on.

"You knew?" Talon began, "You knew that Jade was gifted?"

"I'm what?!" I exclaimed louder than I meant to.

My grandma's eyes popped open again, her mouth quivering in answer. It finally dawned on me that although the thread of sound was too quiet for me to pick up on, it would be no trouble for Talon. Suddenly my whole body was tense with anticipation. I could have a conversation with my grandma again.

Then I snapped back to the conversation already going on, and tried to make some sense of it.

"That's amazing," Talon was intently listening, and I waited impatiently to be let in on the information.

Finally, Talon turned to me, excitement in his eyes. "Your grandmother is gifted. She has the sight."

"What? The what?" My eyes shot between the two of them.

"The gifted gene runs in your family. Not surprising, with your strong Irish roots. Magic is a large part of their history."

Talon seemed to be going off on a tangent so I straightened his path. "What does it mean that she has 'the sight'?"

"It is similar to what my mother did," Talon began. "Your grandmother would have dreams of outcomes. She could also read people through touch."

I glanced at her hands still wrapped around Talon's, and tried to process this. "Grandma, this is incredible."

Her lips began moving again, and I waited for Talon to translate. He stiffened, as if he received an electric shock. Meeting my gaze again, he studied me for a moment.

"You are an empath," he finally spoke.

I paused. "A what?"

"It's such a subtle gift, it's no wonder I missed it." Turning back to my grandma, he asked, "What of Madeleine, and your other children and grandchildren?"

She answered, and I waited with baited breath. Was my whole family gifted?

"Interesting," Talon finally spoke. He turned to me. "Both of her grandparents, who immigrated here from Ireland, were gifted, as were their children. Her mother, your great-grandmother, could make things grow. What an exceptional gift. But her husband, your great-grandfather, was not gifted, and so it has become a watered-down gene, for lack of better way to explain it. She says your mother has a strong sixth sense, as do your sisters, but you are the only one of her children or grandchildren to truly be gifted."

"The dreams," I murmured. "Where I connect with your memories. That's my gift?" My grandma looked interested in this. She asked a question.

"Yes," Talon told her. "She connected to my memories, and even took on my sleeping habits." He looked at me again. "You care so much about others, putting them before yourself, I thought it was your personality. I had no idea it was something more. Perhaps I should have, but I thought we only connected like that because we are mated."

Wincing at his use of that word, I glanced at my grandma but she didn't seem bothered by it.

Though I needed some time to process everything we'd just talked about, I didn't want to let this opportunity go to waste. Talon and I stayed the rest of the morning, with Talon translating my grandma's answers and asking questions of her own. She'd missed out on so much the last few months, it was wonderful to be able to communicate again.

We stayed with her during lunch, but she was tired after and asked to lay down. Squashing the disappointment, we acquiesced, helping her into a comfortable position. Kissing her on the forehead, I promised I'd be back for dinner.

Talon and I walked out, hand in hand, and I felt lighter than I had in a long time.

"Hungry?" Talon asked as we started out of the parking lot.

"Absolutely," I told him.

"I can make something at home, and then we can talk. I'm sure you have more questions."

Nodding, I said, "Yeah, I've had a little time to process now. You know, I'm looking at my childhood with my grandma a bit differently now."

"How do you mean?" he asked.

"My grandma used to always get feelings when something was wrong. Grandpa Stryder let it slip once that she'd have nightmares, but the thing was, she was always right. It became sort of a family joke, and I never thought any more of it."

"You were close with her, growing up," Talon stated.

"I was. More so than my sisters. I always helped her in the garden, though I didn't have as much interest in that. Although, my mom and sisters all have thriving gardens. I wonder..." I trailed off, thinking it through. "You said my great-grandmother could make things grow. Do you think that's what was passed down? My mom always has had a sixth sense about the exact right time to plant. It's uncanny."

"It's a distinct possibility," Talon agreed. "I'm sorry I cannot give you more answers. Remember, I grew up with just my parents, and have not met any of my own kind in the years since. This is somewhat new territory for me, as well."

My heart went out to him. "I'm so sorry," I told him, reaching over to squeeze his hand.

He grinned at me. "There's that empathy again."

Rolling my eyes, I realized we were at his house already. Once we were inside, I settled on a counter to watch Talon work. I offered to help, but he refused. That suited me fine. Watching him was one of my favorite things.

Setting out a tossed salad and some homemade soup he'd warmed up from a container in the freezer, Talon began speculating. "We should see how far your gifts go," he told me.

"What do you mean?" I asked, curious.

"As far as I understand it, there are those that are gifted- like you, and your grandmother- and it is because of that gene that you are able to be converted fully into an Elemental, as I am now. As an Elemental, you gain many strengths, but they all boil down to having control over the elements."

"Manipulating earth, air, fire, water?" I asked.

"Precisely. Shifting into other forms, even, is a manipulation of the cells and energy that already exist."

"Does this mean that you are thinking positively about changing me?"

His lips thinned. "No. I would not put you through that."

"What if I wanted it?" I asked quietly.

He looked at me for a long time, studying my face. Finally, he shook his head. "You would be giving up so much for me. What about your family?"

"What about them?"

"They would continue to age. You would not." This hit me hard. "Also, you would have to drink blood."

Making a face, I scooped up some of the beef soup. "I could get used to that."

He squeezed my hand gently. "You will not have to."

"It's difficult for me, to think about asking you to give up your extraordinary abilities, because of me." My eyes stayed on my meal, not wanting to meet his searching gaze again, and I pressed on. "I'm not asking you to make a decision right now, I'm just asking you to keep both options open. It should be something we decide together."

He sighed, and I knew I'd won this small battle. "You're correct. I cannot make this decision for you. But," he held up a finger in warning, "That does not mean I won't argue my side, fair or not."

I grinned. "You've never played fair. Why start now?"

Talon came with me to the nursing home that evening for dinner, and my grandpa Stryder was there also. It was nice to see him, but it also meant I couldn't talk as freely with Grandma as I had that morning. I did notice her lips trembling as we were leaving, and Talon only smiled in response.

When we were in the car, I asked him what she'd said. "She asked me to take care of you," Talon told me. "And that she approved."

He grinned wide, and I felt something inside me shift. In so short a time, this man had become my whole world.

"Take me home, Talon," I told him. "I want to stay with you tonight."

There was no argument there.

A ringing woke me, shrill and annoying. I was snuggled in a warm cocoon, unwilling to move. An arm tightened across my middle before reaching across to lift the phone from the side table. It was shoved in front of my face, and I squinted at the screen in the darkness.

My mom. I sat up, my heart quickening.

"Mom?" I answered, panic in my voice.

"Jade," I could hear the tears. "Come to the nursing home as quickly as you can."

"Is she-?"

"She's close," my mom said.

Hanging up the phone, I jumped out of bed and pulled on my clothes from the night before, which were scattered on the floor. Talon was up also, pulling on his own. I knew he would have overheard the conversation.

Throwing my hair up in a pony, Talon and I ran downstairs and to my car. Though I initially headed to the driver's side, Talon stopped me, opening the passenger door and relieving me of my keys. Normally that would have annoyed me, but not today. I wasn't focused enough to drive.

As we drove, I had a sinking feeling in the pit of my stomach. My hand clenched into a fist and my breath came in short gasps.

"Breathe, my love. You need to breathe."

Talon's warm hand wrapped around mine, coaxing it out of the tight fist and interlocking with his. I took a deep breath, counting to ten in my head, but refused to speak. Tears were brimming and I feared if I spoke, they would spill over and there would be no stopping them.

As if he understood my need, Talon remained silent and drove steady. When we arrived in the parking lot, I remained silent, staring at the building before us.

"She's gone," I whispered. "I can feel it."

Reaching across to cup my cheek, Talon pulled my face around to his. "We will get through this, together."

For several long seconds, I stared into his eyes, borrowing his strength. Finally, I nodded, and stepped out of the car.

Immediately he was at my side, his arm wrapped around my back. He led me inside, and it didn't take long to run into a family member. My parents were in the lobby and my mom enveloped me in a tight hug. As I passed my dad, he squeezed my hand gently before clapping Talon on the back.

We walked to the room together, and she lay on the bed, but I knew her spirit was gone. Grandpa Stryder stood beside her, gazing down with tears in his eyes. It was too much for me.

Eyes filled to the brim, I spun around and raced for the door, turning away from the main lobby where most of my family waited. Everything was a blur as I sped down the hall. All I could think of was that I needed air. Now.

Slamming against the bar of the exit door, I pushed my way outside and full out sprinted towards the wooded area surrounding the nursing home. With my vision obscured, I stumbled across the first root and caught myself on my hands and knees, immediately falling to the side and curling into a ball. My heart felt as if it had been ripped out.

"Baby," came a voice tight with emotion. Strong hands guided me gently off the ground until I was curled up on a warm lap, arms wrapped securely around me. I buried my face into his neck and sobbed.

We stayed like that for several long minutes until the heaviness began to lift, slowly being replaced by Talon's soothing voice.

"You are breaking my heart, Jade," Talon murmured, stroking my hair softly away from my face.

Lifting my tear streaked face to his, I carefully brought one hand to his face, reveling in the beautiful masculinity that had become as necessary to me as breathing. Our eyes met, each searching the others for an infinite amount of time. There was something that I knew down in my soul, something I'd been fighting since the moment I'd met Talon in the forest. Something he needed to hear, though I was sure he already knew.

"I love you," I said quietly, yet with more conviction than I'd ever felt.

The look in his eyes softened and a heat spread through me, moving along my insides, warming the cold places and healing each piece that had felt broken only moments ago.

"As I love you," he answered before pressing his lips to mine. There was no fire in this kiss, just more of the same warmth that had now extended through all my limbs.

Pulling a handkerchief from his pocket, Talon carefully wiped my face before standing, with me still wrapped in his arms. He held me like that a moment more, watching my face, before setting me on my feet.

"Are you ready to return?"

Nodding, I turned towards the building, gripped his hand in mine, and walked back.

The family was gathering at my parent's house, so Talon brought me to the grocery store to pick up sandwich supplies. It felt good to do something productive.

We arrived at the house first and began creating a buffet style spread on the kitchen island. As I was setting out the condiments, family members started trickling in.

There were more hugs and watery smiles, as I knew there would be for a while to come. My mom and her siblings stayed in the kitchen, while my sisters entertained the kids. I hovered between the kids playing and replenishing the food. Talon stayed by my side, being my rock without the need for words. I appreciated that more than he could ever know.

The days went by in a blur, shuffling from one family gathering to another. A few days after the funeral, I sat staring listlessly in my mom's garden. The sticky heat of summer had finally arrived, and my only movement was to swat at the ever-present mosquitos.

As always, I felt Talon's presence before seeing him. He sat beside me, and though I could feel his worried stare, I continued to gaze straight ahead.

"Jade," he finally said.

I turned to look at him and saw the concern prevalent on his face.

"Baby," he began again, cupping my cheek. "Talk to me."

Shaking my head, I turned away again, a single tear running down my cheek.

"Please, Jade," Talon seemed at his wit's end. "Your tears are my undoing. What can I do?"

"Nothing," I answered. "What am I doing here, Talon? I don't live here. My home, my job is in Miami. I have no purpose anymore."

Talon moved in front of me, crouching to force my eye contact.

"Of course you have a purpose. You are grieving, and that's allowed. But don't stop living."

He moved closer to me, his lips just a hairsbreadth from mine. My breath hitched.

"If you would like to return to Miami, we will go. If you would like to stay here, we will stay. If you would like to go somewhere else altogether, that is fine. You and I are a team now. You will not be rid of me so easily."

His voice sent tendrils of fire racing through my blood. It was the first real sensation I'd felt since the day my grandma died. Not wanting it to end, I leaned forward, closing that small distance between us. My knees hit the ground and I wrapped my arms around him, trying to get as close as possible. In that moment, I wanted nothing between us.

Talon broke the kiss and I groaned in frustration. "Are you trying to rip my clothes off in your parent's yard?"

Surprised, I looked down at my handiwork and realized I'd ripped his shirt off and had been working on his belt.

"Bring me upstairs. Now."

It was nothing short of a demand. Easily lifting me, I wrapped my legs around his waist and turned my entire focus on kissing all of his exposed skin.

He ran at supernatural speed until I found myself laid on my bed, his body covering mine with the same hunger that had been awoken in me. Clothes flew, and I was quickly running out of patience to feel all of him.

As we lay entangled in my sheets, my head rested on his chest, I felt whole for the first time in weeks. His steady heartbeat was a beacon, leading me out of the darkness.

"I could stay like this forever," I told him, tracing lazy circles over his stomach with the tip of my finger.

"That would be agreeable," he responded.

Grinning up at him, I asked, "Oh it would, would it?"

We lay quietly a long time, Talon gently stroking my back. Eventually, I raised my head again. "My parents will be home soon," I reminded him.

Nodding, he released me from his grip and allowed me to stand up. I stretched, enjoying the faint soreness in my limbs. When I glanced over at Talon, relaxed on the bed, all I wanted to do was join him again.

He smirked at me as if reading my mind, and let his eyes trail up and down my body. I blushed, unused to the attention but enjoying it from him. Busying myself looking for my clothes, I found my shirt and held it up, bemused.

"I don't remember this happening," I told him, holding out the torn shirt.

"You were in a bit of a hurry," he purred, satisfied.

"Hm," I murmured, searching for my pants while throwing the ruined garment in the closet. I found Talon's pants, throwing them his direction, then pulled on my own before digging through my drawers to find a new top.

I watched as Talon dressed, pulling his shirt over his broad shoulders. There was a small rip near the bottom, which he covered up by tucking it into his pants.

"All fixed," he grinned at me.

Rolling my eyes, I smoothed down my hair and checked my makeup in the mirror. "Would you like to stay for dinner?" I asked, swiping under my eye to clear the mascara that had escaped there.

Talon approached me from behind, wrapping his arms around my middle and nuzzling my neck. "Of course."

Leaning into him, I closed my eyes, just breathing in his scent. "We better go downstairs before I make your shirt completely unusable."

With a wicked laugh, he kissed my neck, and just as I was starting to melt, he pulled away and opened the door.

"After you, love."

Not one to give up so easily, I paused in the doorway, my back tight against him, and leaned forward slowly to adjust my pant leg.

To my satisfaction, he let out a deep groan, to which I responded by straightening and tossing him a sultry smile over my shoulder.

"You will pay for that," Talon promised.

I couldn't wait.

CHAPTER 17

In the kitchen, I began pulling out ingredients for fried chicken and potato salad. Talon and I worked in tandem, and it surprised me again at how seamlessly we seemed to fit together.

Just as the first batch came out of the oil, my parents walked in. My mom had been helping at the office today, so they'd driven together.

"Smells wonderful," my mom commented, giving me a one-armed hug while I stirred the salad.

She hugged Talon next, whispered "Thank you," and went to put her things away.

I raised a brow at him, but he merely shrugged.

My dad also gave me a hug, and clapped Talon on the back before gathering plates and forks to set the table. Once my mom joined him, I noticed the looks they kept trying to sneak in my direction, and I realized just how distant I'd been lately. It made me feel horrible. No wonder my mom had thanked Talon. He'd brought me back to life.

The salad done, I turned towards Talon, wrapping my arms around him. "I love you," I told him.

With a quick grin, his lips met mine. "I love you, too."

Releasing him, I lifted the bowl to bring to the table. Talon followed not long after with the chicken, and we sat to eat with my parents.

"How was work today?" I asked them.

"Pretty uneventful," my dad replied. "The old gas station is up for sale. What have you two been up to?"

Before I could prevent it, a blush started to creep up my neck to nestle in my cheeks. Luckily, Talon diverted the attention away from me.

"Actually, Jade and I have been speaking about our living arrangements, and she's agreed to move in with me."

Wrong time to take a sip of water. It sprayed out in a huff and I stared at Talon, eyes wide, water dripping down my chin. "What?"

I heard my mom chuckle, rising to get paper towels, but I was frozen to the spot.

Talon leaned in close. "Told you I'd get you back," he taunted with a wink.

My glare was useless, but I employed it anyway.

"That's great news!" My dad burst out. "Your mom and I were hoping you'd decide to stay, Jade, but you hadn't mentioned you were leaning towards it."

"I wasn't," I grumbled, annoyed and knowing it wouldn't last long. Accepting the paper towel from my mom, I began wiping up my mess.

"We haven't worked out the details yet," Talon hedged. "As Jade's job can take her anywhere, and I am able to pick up work wherever I am, we will likely travel often. But," he looked at me, and I couldn't help but get lost in his eyes. "I would like to make this our home base. In addition to your entire family being here, I also have come to think of it as home."

135

Irrational tears began welling up, and I blinked them away. He would pay for this later, but for now, I was overwhelmed at his statement. Giving his hand a squeeze, I turned towards my parents.

"Talon's almost finished with remodeling the house. Maybe in the next few weeks, we could host Sunday night dinner." There. Take that, wolf boy.

My mom's face lit up. "That would be lovely!"

"How soon would you be moving in, Jade? You really don't have much here, anyway," my dad asked.

"Perhaps we could bring a couple bags over tonight," Talon began, and I spun back to him, terror on my face.

Yet, when my eyes met his, I could see the fire in them and it began to warm me all over again. Would I ever get enough of this man?

"That sounds good," I whispered, distracted by my overactive hormones.

He smirked, knowing the effect he had on me, and that he'd just won. Jerk.

Upstairs, I pulled open each drawer and emptied its contents into the duffel bags I'd brought with me. My dad was right; I really didn't have much here.

Once the bags were full, I carefully packed my camera bag. The only things I really had left were a couple of winter coats that I wouldn't need for at least another month, and my developing equipment. Talon was perched on the bed, watching me. I turned to him with a mischievous smile.

"That empty room on the second floor next to the bathroom," I began, "Do you have plans for it yet?"

"No," he told me. "What would you like to use it for?"

"A dark room," I smiled winningly at him. "I know it's old fashioned, but…"

"So am I," Talon interrupted. "Of course, we will create a dark room for you."

Leaning down to kiss him, meaning it to only be a quick peck, I found my arms wrapping around him and my legs straddling his hips. We teetered precariously on the edge of the bed, but I trusted him not to let me fall.

Too quickly he pulled away, clearing his throat. "Jade?"

"Hm?" I answered, rubbing my lips along his jaw line.

"Your parents are downstairs."

"Hm," I answered again, following the line of his neck.

"Perhaps we could continue this… in our home."

I jerked back, narrowing my eyes at him. "That reminds me," I began. "How could you bulldoze me like that?"

He shrugged, unashamed. "It seems to be the only way to get you to agree to what I want."

Trailing my eyes down his chest and back, my lips quirked. "Don't worry. I'll think of a few ways for you to make it up to me."

We drove together to the house, since Talon had walked to my parents that afternoon. Before we reached the turn off, Talon suddenly straightened, his body on full alert.

"Stop the car," he demanded quietly.

"Talon, what is it?" I braked as he'd asked.

"Stay here," was all he said before sliding out of the car.

I watched, terrified, as he sprinted into the woods. Though every part of me screamed to go after him, I'd learned my lesson with Lani and stayed put.

After about a minute, a large shadow passed over the car. Looking up, I saw nothing but the sky at dusk, not even a wisp of a cloud. Heart in my throat, I opened the door and looked around.

"Good evening," came a grating voice from behind me. I spun around, coming face to face with a large, dark man.

His eyes were dark as pitch, yet seemed to glow as he assessed me. Long hair was tied at the nape of his neck and he wore loose fitting black clothing. Just looking at him made me feel like oil was creeping along my skin.

"Who are you?" I asked with more bravado than I felt.

He bowed, a gesture so out of place with the situation I almost laughed. "My name is Frances. And you are?"

Shaking my head, I glanced towards the trees where Talon had disappeared.

"Your... *friend*," he spat out the word like it was poison, "is currently detained."

"What do you want from me?"

Surprising me, Frances threw back his head and laughed, the sound echoing down the street. "Oh, my dear, you will soon find out."

The hair on my arms was raised, as if I needed more warning that this guy was a creep. Every inch of me was on alert, waiting for him to make his move.

Suddenly, he cocked his head to the side, and if he could look annoyed, this was it.

"Well, it seems it will not be as soon as I had hoped. I *will* be seeing you again," Frances said, and before I could process what he meant, he disappeared into smoke and I watched as the large shadow I'd seen earlier passed over me again. It made me shiver, but not from cold.

Talon emerged seconds later, racing towards me, no longer wearing a shirt. Immediately he enveloped me in his arms, murmuring my name over and over as I shook.

"It was a trap," he finally explained, pressing my face to his hot chest. "Are you all right?"

I nodded. "Let's go home," I said.

Talon drove the short distance, his hand gripping mine. If I could have managed to be in his lap, I would have.

We parked, Talon gripping my bags in one hand and leading me to the house with the other. Once I was inside, Talon kissed me quickly and told me he'd be back.

Before I could argue, he was gone.

With nothing to do but wait, I brought my bags upstairs and found empty drawers to throw my clothes in. By the time I was done, Talon was back.

"I put extra security in place," he explained. "Tell me what happened while I was gone."

"At first I stayed in the car, like you asked. But then, a big shadow crossed over, so I got out to look around, and there was a man standing behind the car. He told me his name was Frances. I asked him what he wanted and he told me I'd soon find out."

My eyes met Talon's and I processed his expression. "These are the men Lani talked about, aren't they?"

Barely concealed rage hovered just beneath the surface as Talon answered. "I believe so."

Nodding, I sank down onto the bed. "What happened to you?

"I could hear a woman calling for help," Talon began, and I flinched. His casual mention of his special abilities still shocked me. "It was a trap. There was no woman, and when I ran into the forest, I found myself in the middle of a magic circle. This Frances must have special gifts for conjuring."

"How did you escape?" I asked, looking him over again for any injuries.

Talon sighed, sinking into a crouch before me. "I reversed his spell, effectively closing the magic circle."

Taking his hands in mine, I said, "I didn't know you could do that."

His lips quirked into a smile. "There are many things I can do."

"I suppose that shouldn't surprise me," I grinned back. "Are we safe here?"

"Yes," he told me. "I've put a protection spell on the border. But I'll have to go back out and search for Frances. He cannot be allowed to terrorize you or anyone else."

My heart sank. "Lani. I need to call her."

Talon nodded. "Go ahead."

Grabbing my phone from my bag, I waited while it rang. There was no answer, and I looked worriedly at Talon.

"I will find her first," Talon assured me. "She can do a run with me. I will let you know when I find her."

Wrapping my arms around him, I laid my head against his chest, drawing strength from the steady beat of his heart. "Be safe."

"I won't be long," he promised. "After all, this is our first night living together. We will have to celebrate."

Agreeing, I released him. "Call me as soon as you find Lani," I emphasized.

"You have my word," he answered, and then he was gone.

That would take a long time for me to get used to.

While I waited, I decided to distract myself. Calling Amber, I got ready to have a conversation I'd been dreading.

"Hello."

Amber's strict somberness helped to ground me.

"Hey, Amber. You busy?"

"Not really. Jack has the kids outside. What can I do for you?"

Sighing, I dived right in. "I was wondering if you've noticed anything strange with Gerry."

She paused before answering. "I think we all noticed his behavior at 4th of July."

"Beyond that," I coaxed her. "I'm concerned about Emma."

I could hear Amber take a deep breath. "It's been going on for some time. I got Emma to admit to me that they've been fighting a lot at night, that she hasn't been sleeping. Gerry's been out drinking a lot. I've been worried, but Emma asked me not to do anything. I have to respect her wishes."

While I'd been listening, I realized my hand had clenched into a tight fist. One by one, I relaxed my fingers, leaving an indent in my palm.

"Okay, Amber, thanks for letting me know. I'm worried about her too."

We hung up, and I waited for Talon to get a hold of me. After several minutes, a text beeped in.

Found Lani. Running a circuit now. Stay inside.

I rolled my eyes at his demand, but relief flooded through me that he'd found Lani.

Keeping myself busy until they returned, I finished my unpacking and headed down to the kitchen to make tea. I was just pouring the first cup when Talon returned, so I poured a cup for him also. Lani hadn't come with.

Handing him a cup, I raised a brow.

Sighing, Talon answered my unspoken question. "We didn't find anything."

"Nothing?"

"No trace. No smell, nothing. Frances is obviously experienced with spells."

Fantastic.

CHAPTER 18

"We can't let these evil men run our lives," I squared off with Talon, hands on hips. Softening my tone, I stepped close to him, resting my hands on his chest. "I was avoiding life after my grandma died. You made me realize that, made me realize that no matter what, we have to keep living."

We'd been living together officially for three days, and I was ready to uphold my promise to Lani from weeks before.

He succumbed with a sigh. "One dinner."

"We owe Lani. I've ignored her the last few weeks."

Talon nodded briskly. There was a buzz as my cell phone lit up, and I smirked at the name that popped up. "I'm going to invite Rick."

"Jade," Talon began warningly.

"It will make us keep the conversation light," I argued. "And it's not like I'm trying to set them up. I know it wouldn't work out, anyway."

Texting the details to both Rick and Lani, I set the phone down with a satisfied nod. "This will be good for all of us."

We decided to meet at The Spade, for lack of other options. As we drove, I was bouncing in my seat. Talon placed a calming hand on my lap.

"What is it, my love?"

Shrugging, I cast him a quick glance. "I don't know. Excited to go out, I guess. Nervous about the complete lack of evidence of Frances being around."

"We will find him," Talon promised with a growl. "For tonight, I would like you to have   fun."

"I know, I know, this was my idea, remember?"

We shared a smile as he pulled into the parking lot. It was a quiet night for The Spade, and I thought that might be for the best.

"Looks like we beat them both," I commented, scoping out a booth by the windows. I knew Talon would like to see any activity outside.

I scooted in, leaving Talon the aisle seat. The jittery energy was still prevalent, and when the waitress stopped I ordered a beer. Maybe that would help calm my nerves.

"Jade," Talon said my name sternly. His hands trapped my face, and suddenly my body was tense for another reason. His lips met mine, and my blood began to boil. We'd just had three days nonstop together, yet my entire body still came alive when he touched me.

"Ahem," said an amused voice. "There'll be none of that tonight."

Breaking apart like guilty teenagers, I grinned up at Rick. "How's it going?"

"Not too bad," he answered, shaking Talon's hand while he slid in across from me. Lani appeared in the doorway then, looking around nervously. I waved her over.

Rick groaned. "This isn't a setup, is it?"

"No," I rolled my eyes. "Just friends, desperately needing a night out."

141

Lani approached then, a shaky smile on her lips. "Lani, Rick," I introduced the two. They shook hands, and she sat at the edge of the booth, raising a brow at me.

The waitress approached, and I made sure both Rick and Lani ordered alcoholic drinks. We set in talking about everything from the weather to the construction on the highway. I had to do something about this.

"Shots all around!" I ordered the next time the waitress appeared. "Make them doubles!"

Before anyone could protest, she left to place the order. I knew I could hold my own, though I had no idea what alcohol actually did to Lani and Talon. The way they seemed to always be running a fever, I wondered if the alcohol just burned off.

The shots appeared, and I grinned, making sure everyone held theirs up in a cheer. Then, I crawled over Talon's lap, giving him a little wiggle as I did, and grabbed Lani's hand.

"Come on, we're picking out some music."

There was still an old-fashioned jukebox in the corner, one where five dollars would secure enough music to last the whole night. There was a lot of 60's and 70's in the selections, so I picked several at random.

"What's your favorite music?" I asked Lani.

She shrugged. "I don't really have any."

Mouth gaping at her, I decided to help with that. "All right, I've picked a little bit of everything. By the end of tonight, you will have a favorite type of music."

She seemed disbelieving, but allowed me to drag her into the middle of the floor near the pool table and start dancing. We spun around, and I felt more carefree than I had in a long time. Talon and Rick joined us, and we started having a contest on who could dance the goofiest. Rick pulled out the robot, while I tried the running man. Lani looked completely lost, and while Talon was more of a ballroom kind of dancer, he surprised me with a sporty rendition of the chicken dance.

It got warm pretty quickly, since most of this region didn't believe in air conditioners, so eventually we took a break outside on the small patio used during the day for eating, and at night for smokers. The evening was still warm, but at least there was somewhat of a breeze.

Someone had ordered a pizza, and the waitress left it on one of the tables for us.

"Well, I am seeing a new side of you, Talon," Rick said, taking a slice.

"As I am with you," Talon acknowledged. "You will have to teach me those moves."

"How do you not know the robot?" Rick seemed offended. "We've gotta be about the same age, don't we?"

I choked on my drink. "Hey, what about my running man?" I said to divert the subject. Talon smirked at me.

Rick shrugged. "You could do better."

Smacking his arm with the back of my hand, my eyes caught the reflection of something across the small baseball field the bar used to host softball games. There, at the start of the woods, another flicker of movement.

Talon noticed my gaze, as did Lani.

"Rick," Lani said, moving closer to Rick, getting him to turn away from the woods. "You might have to teach me how to dance."

"What do you mean?" Rick asked. "You've got some moves."

"I do not know these fancy moves you have. I was homeschooled," she added by way of explanation.

"Ah," Rick understood completely.

I tuned them out, approaching Talon. "What is it?" I asked quietly.

"I don't know," he answered. There was a layer of frustration beneath those words, and I suddenly understood.

"Frances."

"He is toying with us. Jade…"

"I'm on it," I answered him.

Flicking my beer into the grass, I grabbed Rick's arm. "Come on, I need another drink. Escort me inside, would you?"

"Of course!" Rick answered. He was clearly not holding his liquor well. All the better, depending what happened next.

Talon had already disappeared, and Lani shot me one last warning look before she, too, faded into the night.

My heart was in my throat, but I knew I had to get Rick to safety first.

Dragging Rick inside, I sat him at the bar and stared nervously out the window. He ordered us another round of drinks, and I tried to rip my eyes away from the woods in order to appear normal.

"Cheers!" Rick clinked his glass to mine and took a deep drink. I discreetly paid the tab, knowing we would not be staying long.

Just minutes later, Talon and Lani reappeared and I sighed in relief. Wrapping his arm around me, Talon spoke to Rick.

"I apologize, but we must leave. You are in no condition to drive, so you are welcome to stay with us tonight and I will get you back to your car tomorrow."

"Sure, buddy," Rick agreed easily. "Cassie's staying overnight at her friend's house."

As we walked outside, I cast nervous glances behind me every few seconds. Lani had already taken off, I could only imagine to where.

A large shadow passed over us, which meant Frances was near. I stiffened, waiting for Rick's reaction. He paused with me, a brow raised.

"Everything all right?"

"You… you didn't see that?"

"See what?"

Exchanging a glance with Talon, I shook my head. "Nothing. I'm seeing things."

Rick shrugged amicably and followed me to the car. Bundling him into the backseat, I slid in front and shared a worried look with Talon. Perhaps having a night out wasn't the best idea I'd ever had.

When we arrived at Talon's, I waited until Rick was set up before asking the burning questions I had.

"Is he out there right now? What happened? Why couldn't Rick see the shadow?"

Talon took a breath, leading me to our bedroom. I curled up in one of the comfortable chairs in front of the fireplace, wrapping my arms around my legs. Though it was too warm for a fire, it would have been nice to stare into.

"He's not going to stop, is he?" I asked quietly.

Talon sat on the edge of the other chair, his hand hot on my arm. "No, I'm afraid not. He was gone by the time Lani and I reached the woods. I can only guess as to why you can see the shadow, and Rick can't. I believe it's because you're gifted."

That made me pause, but not for long. "We need to find him," I looked at Talon, steel in my eyes. "I'm worried for my family."

Nodding, Talon leaned over to kiss me on my forehead. "I will protect you and yours with my last breath."

The next morning, I set to work making eggs, toast and a large pot of coffee. I had a feeling Rick would need it.

He ambled down the stairs looking embarrassed. Talon had spent most of the night out looking for Frances, but I knew he'd return soon.

Pouring a steaming mug, I slid it over to Rick, who smiled appreciatively. He sat comfortably on a stool at the island, and I gave him a few minutes before speaking.

"How are you feeling? Want some aspirin?"

"No," he answered. "I'll be fine. This helps," he gestured with his coffee. "Last night… that's not like me."

I waved a hand, dismissing his concerns. "It's okay to let loose once in a while."

"The truth is," he began, but Talon entered the kitchen and Rick immediately cut off.

"Good morning," he greeted Rick before kissing me on the cheek. Handing him a mug of coffee, I scooped eggs onto plates and passed them around.

"What were you saying?" I asked Rick.

He looked embarrassed again. "The truth is, I have feelings for… someone. I've had some trouble recently reeling them in."

With a knowing look at Talon, I nodded sagely and encouraged Rick to go on.

Before he could begin again, however, my phone rang.

Speak of the devil…

144

"Hello?"

"Jade! I… I didn't know who else to call."

"Emma? What is it?" I glanced at Talon, who could hear the same panic in her voice that I could. Rick visibly paled.

"It's Gerry," she cried. "He's… he's gone insane."

"We're on our way. Is he there?"

"No," Emma managed. "Suzy and Mikey are upstairs. Mikey's sleeping, and I have Suzy watching TV.

We were in the car in an instant, Rick on our tail, all signs of a hangover forgotten. I spared him a glance as we took off, but didn't argue.

"Stay on the phone with me, Emma. We'll be there in just a few minutes. Everything will be okay." I kept up a steady stream of encouragement, not sure if what I was saying was even made sense. Talon stepped on the gas, and I'm sure he was frustrated by the limitations of the car.

When we pulled up in front of Emma's house, Talon pointed towards the door. "Go inside. I will check around the house to make sure it is all clear."

I nodded, dragging Rick with me. More than likely Talon would shift to employ all his senses, and Rick couldn't be around for that.

It didn't take much encouragement, as I knew it wouldn't. We were inside in an instant, and I turned the bolts on the door to be safe.

Rick went straight to Emma, embracing her in a hug. Feeling slightly uncomfortable, I mumbled something about checking on the kids and ran up the stairs. Suzy was sitting happily in her room, the small television showing cartoons.

"Auntie Jade!" She squealed, running and jumping into my arms.

Taking a deep breath, I used my best calm voice to speak to her. "Hi, Suzy! How would you like to visit Auntie Pearl?"

"Yay!" She exclaimed, wriggling out of my arms, immediately collecting toys to bring with her.

"Pick out three toys," I told her. "While I get Mikey."

Leaving her to her decisions, I found Mikey sleeping in his crib, his face blissfully serene. His portable carrier was in the room, so I grabbed that and carefully transferred him into it, wrapping him up with a blanket. Snatching the diaper bag, I called to Suzy and headed down the stairs. Emma and Rick were seated on the couch, Rick holding Emma's hands in his.

Suzy ran to her mom, giving her a hug. "We're going to Auntie Pearls!"

Emma looked at me, her tear streaked face uncomprehending. "Just until we figure this out," I told her quietly.

Emma nodded, squeezing Suzy tight. "Be a good girl." Standing, she came over to kiss Mikey on the forehead.

Just then, there was a light knock on the door, and I checked to make sure it was Talon before opening.

"I will drive you and the kids to Pearl's," he began. "Rick, will you wait here with Emma?"

"Of course," Rick responded immediately.

"We will return shortly," Talon assured them.

Talon scooped up Suzy and held the door open for me. "Secure the deadbolt," he reminded Rick before shutting the door.

We settled the kids in the car; I'd grabbed Emma's keys so we wouldn't have to worry about car seats. On the way, I called Pearl, to warn her we were on our way. I hung up before she could ask too many questions and looked over at Talon.

"How are we going to explain this? To my family? The police?"

Talon gripped the steering wheel hard. "I was not planning on involving police."

Reaching over, I placed a soothing hand on his arm. "He's still their father," I reminded him.

He sighed, looking in the rearview mirror. With one sharp nod, he replied, "We will think of something."

The rest of the trip we remained quiet, not wanting to alert Suzy to anything more wrong.

Pearl met us at the door, worry in her eyes. She took Mikey's carrier from me and sent Suzy to find the girls in the living room.

"What is it? What's going on?" She asked, as soon as it was clear.

"As you know, Gerry has had some problems with alcohol. He had too much today and became a problem," Talon explained. "He did not hurt anyone, and Emma was quick enough to send the children upstairs so they did not see their father that way."

Pearl's free hand went to her throat. "Poor Emma. He needs help."

"He does," Talon answered again. "I will personally make sure of it."

Something in his hardened gaze had Pearl nodding in agreement. "Thank you, Talon. Where is Emma now?"

"At home. Rick is with her," I told her. "We'll let you know what's going on as soon as we can," I promised as we turned to leave.

Once we were back in the car, I asked, "So what is your plan?"

"Frances must be controlling him," Talon answered. "That makes him extremely dangerous."

He looked at me from the corner of his eye before continuing.

"The police will not be strong enough to hold him."

I shook my head adamantly. "We can't hurt him."

Talon sighed. "I have a way of holding him until we deal with Frances. Once Frances is taken care of, the hold on Gerry will disintegrate. At that point, we can make sure Gerry gets the help he needs."

146

"Rehab," I muttered. "He would need that whether Frances got a hold of him or not."

Giving my hand a squeeze, Talon waited until I met his eyes. "Is this acceptable to you?"

Weighing my options, I realized there wasn't much different we could do.

With a deep breath, I answered, "Yes."

"I will need you to stay with Emma and Rick while I find Gerry."

"Alone?" I squeaked out before I could stop myself.

"I assure you, I can handle Gerry."

It didn't sit well with me, but I trusted in Talon's abilities.

Arriving back at Emma's, I knocked and waited for one of them to answer the door. "It's me," I called out to help.

The locks twisted, and Talon and I entered the living room. Talon went straight to Emma, kneeling before her.

"Emma," he said quietly. "Gerry needs help, and I am going to help him. Do you trust me to do that?"

She nodded, watching him carefully.

"Jade has convinced me not to turn him over to the police. With your permission, I will keep an eye on him until he sobers up, then we can admit him to rehab together."

Emma's eyes closed, a single tear streaked down her cheek. Steeling herself, she nodded again.

"I'm coming with you," Rick spoke for the first time.

Both Talon and I stared at him.

"Rick, I don't think..." he held up a hand, effectively cutting me off.

"I'm coming," he reiterated, keeping his gaze steady on Talon.

Talon studied him for a few moments, and I held my breath. "Fine," he finally gave in.

Turning to me, he placed his hands on my upper arms and a kiss on my forehead. "Be safe," he whispered, just to me.

"You too," I whispered back, my hands clutching at his sides.

Talon turned to Rick with a sharp nod.

"Let us get this done."

After watching them leave, I turned to Emma. "Everything will be all right."

She nodded, not quite looking convinced. "I just don't understand. Gerry wasn't like this when we met. There were little things, after we got married and we had Suzy, but Mikey seemed to anchor him. The way he's been acting the last few weeks..."

I put an arm around her, trying to soothe. Leading her to the couch, I guided her into the seat before switching my hold to her hand. "It was nothing you did. He's sick, Emma, and now we're going to make sure he gets help."

It was difficult lying to my sister, and I felt horrible for doing so. The alternative, though, was not feasible.

You see, Emma, there's these shadow creatures that are trying to find me because I have supernatural powers. They took control of Gerry because he already had the root of evil in him.

Right. Looney bin, here I come.

Instead, we planted the idea that Gerry was mentally disturbed, which was mostly true. Not all his actions could be explained away by shadow creatures.

I got up to make tea, busying myself in the kitchen.

When the kettle whistled, and I scooped it off the counter to pour into the waiting mugs. As I began to walk carefully into the living room, there was a knock on the door.

Emma stood, a slight frown on her face. "I wonder who that could be," she said.

There was a bad feeling in the pit of my stomach as I realized what was happening. Before I could call out not to, Emma cracked the door open and gasped as it was shoved open. Gerry charged in, his eyes glazed and angry, his every step lurching.

Jumping back, I reached immediately for my phone.

"I don't think so," he growled. Producing a gun from his belt, Gerry waved it between the two of us. "Give me your phones."

Hesitantly I reached toward the table, where the phone sat, and threw the phone on the carpet near Gerry's feet. I wasn't going any closer to him if I could help it.

Emma followed suit. She attempted to speak to him.

"Gerry, what's wrong with you?"

"Shut up," he growled again and gestured towards the couch with the gun. "Sit."

Emma and I sat, squeezing each other's hand for support. Gerry perched himself by the window, immediately closing the blinds.

My heart was racing but I forced my brain to think. Talon and Rick would be back soon. I had to believe that. Until then, we had to stall.

Emma and I sat together, hands clasped. I knew my heart was racing; she had to be just as terrified.

He peeked out through the blinds, clearly on edge. The gun was held loosely by his side, the trigger finger flexing spastically. My eyes cut to the side, focusing on the landline Emma still had. It was our only chance to reach Talon, or Rick.

Catching Emma's eye, I looked to the phone and back until I knew she understood. Gerry was still staring out of the window, muttering to himself. Releasing Emma's hand, I slid carefully over on the couch, closer to the portable phone.

One more slide put me next to the table the phone sat on. Emma rose, moving the opposite direction.

"Gerry," she said softly. He spun around, the gun pointed in her general direction. I froze, ready to leap and tackle if need be.

Emma paused, taking a deep breath before continuing. "Gerry, talk to me. Maybe I can help."

Slowly, not wanting to direct any attention to myself, my hand slid over the side of the couch until it came in contact with the phone. Continuing to watch the exchange, I pressed the speaker into the couch to muffle any noise the buttons would make and began to dial.

Emma kept up her dialogue, hoping, as I was, to distract Gerry enough that he wouldn't see or hear my actions. My fingers felt along the buttons, pressing each lightly. When they were all in, I repositioned the phone so the speaker could pick up the conversation.

"Gerry, please, put down the gun," Emma pleaded. "Let's talk about this, what's going on with you. Let me help."

"You can't help me," Gerry's voice was without inflection. It worried me even more. This was not a man in control of his own actions.

"I still want to try," Emma pressed on. "You're my husband. The father of our children. I want to help you. Just put down the gun."

The arm with the gun swung up, pointing directly at Emma's heart. For the first time since he'd burst in, his hand was steady.

"Sit. Down." He bit out each word in the same dead voice.

Emma glanced at me and I nodded. She returned to the couch, grabbing my hand again. Hers was shaking.

Squeezing gently, I tried to convey without words that we would get through this. I was in amazement that Emma had been able to face a gun head on and manage to keep her wits about her.

Gerry began mumbling to himself, pressing his hands against his head as if he was in pain. Then he would glare at us before starting all over again.

Praying harder than I'd ever prayed that Talon would appear, I realized he wouldn't be able to use his incredible speed with Rick beside him. Somehow, I knew he'd find a way.

Finally, after what felt like an eternity but I'm sure was only a few minutes, I saw a shadow in the hallway that led towards the bedrooms. Talon looked cautiously into the room, gauging the situation.

Taking my cue, I began to speak. "Gerry, please tell us what's wrong."

Swinging towards me again, Gerry growled at me. "I thought I told you to shut up!"

Emma caught sight of Talon and joined in. "Please, Gerry, we only want to help you."

Talon crept closer, just a few steps away now. My heart was in my throat.

"What do you want?" I asked. "You can't keep us locked up in here forever."

He glared at me for a beat before turning to Emma. "Where are my kids?"

Emma seemed to stutter. "They're with Pearl today."

149

"You're lying!" Gerry burst out. "You're hiding them from me! I'm their father! I have a right to see them!"

Talon was just a step away now, and began reaching for Gerry just as Gerry turned. They went down in an ungainly heap, and both Emma and I launched to our feet. Emma screamed, and somehow, Gerry was able to swing his gun arm out of the tangle of limbs, aiming it directly at Emma. Part of my mind pondered that, realizing he must have some kind of other-worldly strength to even be able to put up a fight with Talon.

The rest of my mind registered that the gun pointed unerringly at Emma's chest, and Gerry's finger squeezed the trigger as if in slow motion. A shot rang out, an explosion of gun powder throwing forth a tiny metal object that could wreak such havoc.

There was no more thinking. Pushing Emma out of the way, half a breath later an immeasurable pain blossomed, radiating out from my stomach. Both hands clutched the spot as my breath released in a final huff and I collapsed to the ground.

The last things I registered where my name on Emma's lips, Rick appearing to restrain Gerry, and Talon's face filled with stark fear.

There was darkness surrounding me, yet I forced my eyes open one last time. There was something important, something I had to see...

"Talon," I breathed. "You came."

"Of course, love. I will always come for you." His voice was strained as I felt his strong arms wrap securely around me. "I am taking you away from here."

As his arms began to lift me from the floor, a groan of pain was released from my lips. Immediately he paused, assessing my condition.

A weak hand lifted to his face, to touch perhaps for the last time. "It's too late," I croaked, my throat clogged by blood. I coughed, my insides feeling on fire. "Just hold me," I mouthed, unsure if he was able to hear.

"No," he growled, the sound torn from his very soul. "I have waited too long for you. You will stay with me. Do you hear me, Jade? You will stay with me."

And just like that, the decision Talon had been so avidly against suddenly became his salvation. It was a purely selfish decision, but he was beyond rationality.

First, he bent his head to my neck, his lips sending sparks across my skin. Then, there was a prick of pain, and I began floating along it. My eyes slid open again, as he focused on the tip of his finger, watching his nail grow to a point. Quickly he slashed a line across his chest, pressing my mouth to it. "Feed, love, feed to live. Feed for me."

His soft voice was seduction itself, winding its way through my mind, my body. Everything inside me wanted to respond, comply to that beautiful voice.

150

Physically, I wasn't able to. I was too far gone. It was there in my mind, the need, the will to live. *I choose life. I choose Talon.* But my body betrayed me. The darkness crept over me until, finally, I succumbed, my mind screaming for life.

I was floating on a sea of pain. There were hazy images shooting past my peripherals, but it took too much effort to focus on any one. Everything hurt. I had succumbed to the darkness, and yet it wouldn't let me go. Wouldn't release me from the pain of life.

A small voice argued from somewhere in the darkness. *No. You want to live.*

That's right. I chose life. I chose...

But the thought was gone again.

Without warning the pain increased, as if every limb was on fire, the flames rushing to my core.

It lasted for an eternity. Or perhaps a few moments. It didn't seem to matter in this darkness. My past, my present, my future was darkness and pain. No other memories sustained me, no other thoughts interceded.

Yet...

I had something to live for. *Yes,* the voice inside me whispered like a cool breeze along my burning flesh. *Life. You chose life. You chose...*

"Jade," a voice fought through the layers of dark, of pain. "Jade..." but it was gone again.

Remember, the voice inside me chanted. *Fight,* it encouraged.

.

CHAPTER 19

My body was on fire, and I drifted in and out of awareness of this fact. Was this the change, then? Or had the bullet done its work too quickly?

It was impossible to grasp and hold onto any one thought. There was a reason I was fighting. There were people in my life, but I couldn't recall one of their names, their faces. This pain became everything to me. Nothing before, nothing else since. My future only consisted of this darkness and agony.

Minutes, hours, days, I couldn't be sure how long I struggled against this ever-present pain. There came a point that I truly believed this was how my eternity would be- never changing. Then, something changed.

It became worse.

Searing fire spread through my limbs, rushing towards my center. I could actually feel my organs reshaping, my heart near exploding to keep up with the demand of new blood. If I could scream, my voice would be hoarse with use.

Think, I encouraged my brain. Imagine yourself rolling around in the first snowfall of winter. Taking a dip in the cool lake during spring. Being showered with ice cubes. Anything to cool the fire that licked along my skin.

Using all the concentration I possessed, I kept the images coming. The reshaping was almost complete. I could feel it slowing, slowing, until, finally, it stopped.

There was silence. Silence, I realized, which included my heart. I really was dead, then. All that fighting, for what? Talon. His face was so easy to pull up now. My sisters, parents, grandparents, cousins… I flipped through each face, feeling the love for them and wishing, praying for more time.

Thud. One sticky, thick, struggling beat. *Thud*. Another, easier, and another. It was different than my heartbeat used to be. *I* was different.

"Jade," the velvet voice that I would walk through fire for. I moaned slightly, wanting to crawl inside its warmth. A hand squeezed mine, cool to the touch.

Brow furrowed, I forced my eyes open for the first time since I'd been shot. Talon's face was there, real this time. I could see each perfect pore, the crease of worry, the shadow of sleeplessness. One hand rose to wipe away the evidence of my ordeal, and as our skin touched I realized his seemed cool compared to mine. Made sense, since I'd felt like I'd been on fire for days.

My hand was perfectly smooth, and pale, not the crisp red I'd been imagining. I gazed into his eyes again, eyes that I'd be perfectly happy staring into for the rest of time.

"I love you," I told him, barely above a whisper. My voice was hoarse, and I wondered briefly if I had been screaming as much aloud as in my mind.

Tears brimmed in his eyes, and I felt my heart reach out to him, wanting to sooth.

"As I love you," he responded. His lips met mine, soft, but I could feel all the emotion there.

When he pulled away, he reached for something out of sight of me. It was a glass of water. He held it to my lips and I gulped it down greedily.

When I laid back again, I realized I was in our bed. I'd missed a lot.

"How long?" I asked, knowing he'd understand.

He gulped. "Five days."

I shot up, and immediately felt dizzy. "Five days!"

His hands restrained me. "Jade," he admonished. "You are still very weak. You need to rest."

Taking a breath, I worked on calming but remained sitting up. "I've been laying here for five days?"

"Yes," he nodded, watching me carefully.

"What have I missed? Is Gerry in rehab? How's Emma?"

"Before I begin, are you still thirsty? Hungry?"

"Talon," I warned.

"It's a long story, my love. I just want to make sure you're comfortable, and then I will tell you everything."

Hesitating, I looked away, one hand feeling my throat. "I'm... thirsty."

"But not for water," Talon said knowingly.

I didn't know how to respond. Instead of speaking again, however, Talon pulled off his shirt. My body reacted in two very distinct ways.

Stretching out beside me, Talon explained calmly, "You will feed from me, for now, until you have your full strength."

As he focused on a fingertip, extending it out to a point, I was hit with a memory that had gotten lost somewhere in the fire.

This wouldn't be the first time I drank his blood.

He guided my head towards him, towards the dripping red liquid. It should have repulsed me. Made me squeamish.

My lips made contact, and I took a pull like I would through a straw. With a groan, I pulled away.

"It's okay, Jade, you don't have to do this right now."

"No," I answered him quietly. "That's not it. It tastes... *good*."

He grinned, and I became momentarily distracted by the way it transformed his face. "That's good. Remember, you are not merely human anymore."

Rolling my eyes, I lowered my head, licking up a trail of blood that had escaped before pressing my lips against him again. This time, it was Talon that groaned.

Encouraged, I drank my fill, and was amazed at the way my body felt when I was done. Not only did I feel stronger, but it was an intensely erotic action, and I was feeling very much alive with my man laying shirtless beside me.

"Does it... does it always feel this way?" I asked breathlessly.

"No," he answered immediately. "At least, not for me. Never before."

154

"It's a mate thing?" I asked with a grin of my own, sliding a finger suggestively down his abs.

"It would appear so," he replied, catching my hand and bringing it to his mouth. "Jade," he began, then had to take a deep breath. "We cannot, not so soon after your transformation."

I pouted, but knew it would get me nowhere. Though I felt 100 times stronger infused with his blood, I also knew I had a long way to go.

"How about a shower?" He asked to distract me.

"That sounds lovely."

Talon rose first, helping me out of bed. Standing on my feet, I felt weak but managed to stay upright. Glancing down, I noticed for the first time I was wearing a long shirt of Talon's, and nothing else.

Raising a brow, he shrugged, unrepentant. "You needed to be comfortable."

He helped me to the bathroom, and into the shower. I still felt weak, and took this opportunity to coerce Talon.

"You might as well join me," I told him. "I'm not sure I'll be able to stand on my own."

With a narrowed gaze, he gave in, eyeing my cheesy grin as he stripped us both of our clothes.

"No funny business," he admonished.

"Me?" I asked, all innocence.

Talon began helping me wash my hair, keeping his assistance very clinical. To distract myself, I began asking questions.

"How long does it normally take someone to... change?"

"I don't really know what is normal. It took me six days. Since you were already weak from blood loss, I believe perhaps, for you, it took hold quicker."

I pondered that for a minute before asking my next question. "How long did it take for you to have... abilities?"

He thought about that before answering. "Again, it was different for me. Since my mother was fully Elemental when I was born, I was half and half." He smiled a crooked smile. "I already had control over the elements, to a small extent, before I was changed. I believe that you could begin experimenting now, though I would prefer to wait until you're stronger."

Thinking about that, I gazed at the spray of water washing over us. "What if I try something small?"

He narrowed his eyes at me. "What did you have in mind?"

"Water is an element," I stated.

Talon seemed at war with himself. "All right," he finally succumbed to my puppy dog eyes. "But if I say stop, you will do so immediately."

"Yes, sir," I saluted.

155

He rolled his eyes at me, then stood behind me, wrapping his arms around my waist. I was momentarily distracted.

"Focus," he murmured into my hair. "Imagine in your mind what you want the water to do. Will it to happen."

Closing my eyes just briefly to concentrate, I popped them open and stared at the droplets. My hands moved in a circular motion, and to my amazement, half the water spouting out followed suit.

"Whoa!" I spun around, wrapping my arms around Talon's neck. "I did it!"

"That you did," he grinned. "You're a natural."

Doing a little happy dance, I turned again.

"Jade," his velvet voice was a warning.

Sighing, I flicked my hand with a smirk and watched as a chunk of water hit Talon squarely in the cheek.

"You will pay for that," Talon growled. He wrapped his arms around me again, turning the tap to cold while I squealed.

"I surrender!" I gasped.

With a smirk of his own, Talon shut off the water. "We will practice with each element, as you feel stronger. I am also curious to see how your gift will expand," Talon said, wrapping me in a large, fluffy towel. "Let's have some breakfast, and I'll catch you up."

Nodding, suddenly serious again, I dressed quickly in comfortable pajamas and followed Talon downstairs. He got busy making tea, toast and eggs. Suddenly ravenous, I wolfed down the food and asked for seconds. Talon eyed me, clearly nervous about feeding me too much, too fast.

"Give it 20 minutes," he bargained. "I just want to make sure you're processing everything."

I agreed, though my stomach rumbled. It was like I hadn't eaten in a week.

"Start talking," I finally prodded him, sitting back and sipping my tea.

He folded his hands on the table and began recounting to me the last five days.

"When you were... shot..." This was difficult for Talon to talk about, and I could see the tension in his body. "You were my priority. Once we exchanged blood, I knew I would not be able to leave your side. I tossed my phone to Rick, who had restrained Gerry but was still struggling with him, and asked him to call Lani.

Forgive me, but I used slight hypnosis on your sister. She was hysterical, and was attempting to call 9-1-1. For obvious reasons, I could not let that happen. Once she calmed down, I explained to her that I would be taking you home, where my private doctor would care for you."

I raised a brow at this, but let him continue.

"Lani arrived within minutes, and I quickly explained to her what needed to be done with Gerry. I have some property that has been sitting empty, so she took him there and set up a perimeter."

"That's what you explained to me before, basically detoxing Frances out of his system?"

"That's right," Talon answered. "Lani made sure Gerry was comfortable and fed during those first 24 hours. I brought you home, where you began your transformation. Your family wanted to see you, of course, but luckily because of my help, Emma downplayed the situation."

"My poor parents, they must be frantic," I suddenly felt entirely guilty for not wanting to contact them as soon as I woke up. Talon seemed to read my mind.

"I allowed them to visit after three days. It reassured them to see you on the mend, and I explained that you were heavily sedated to help with healing."

"So," I began, not wanting to ask this, "I wasn't... screaming?"

Immediately I regretted asking as Talon's eyes tightened, his entire face transforming into rage. Knowing it wasn't directed at me, I held up my hands, "It's okay, honey. I'm okay. I wanted this, remember?"

He took several deep breaths before answering. "No. You were perfectly still, perfectly silent for all five days. If it weren't for your steady heartbeat, I may have gone crazy."

Huh. I'd have to examine that later.

"I only left your side once," he continued with the story. "Lani came and stayed with you. There was no way I was leaving you alone. After the 24 hours were up, I brought Emma and Gerry to a rehabilitation center in Bryantsville. It is an excellent facility, and far enough away that Gerry should be able to heal fully."

He hesitated, and I cocked my head to the side wondering why. "Before leaving him, I placed a protective layer of magic around Gerry," Talon finally explained. He watched my reaction carefully. "It is not something I would normally do, but I was concerned Frances would try again."

Processing that, I nodded. "I understand."

Talon relaxed, then continued. "He's doing well so far. I've been getting daily checkups. I know you must be anxious to speak with your family."

I nodded, glancing at the clock. It was early evening; my parents should be home. "Will they be able to come visit?"

"Yes," Talon answered. "But you will have to be a good girl, pretending to still be in recovery."

He slid me a phone, and I dialed my parents' house. After two rings, my mom picked up.

"Hey, Mom," I dropped my voice, hoping it sounded sick but on the mend. The scream protruding from the opposite end of the phone had me pulling it away from my ear.

"Jade! Oh, honey, it's so good to hear your voice. Are you okay? We're coming over right now. When did you wake up?"

157

She kept talking, so I finally interrupted her mid-question. "I'm much better, Mom, I promise. The doctor said it was okay for you to come visit for a little while. I'd love to see you."

"We're on our way. Isaac! Get your shoes, we're going to visit Jade!"

She yelled out at my dad, and I winced. "Mom," I tried to grab her attention again. "Just you and dad for tonight, okay? Maybe tomorrow Amber, Emma and Pearl can come over."

"Of course, honey, I'm sure the doctor doesn't want you overwhelmed. We'll be right there."

Hanging up, I raised my brows at Talon. "Looks like we're about to have company."

We made our way back upstairs, and I noticed for the first time the collection of flowers on the bedside table. My family was so sweet.

I snuggled into bed, propped up by a few fluffy pillows, and practiced looking tired. Talon laughed at me.

"I'm still hungry, you know," I complained to him.

"As soon as your parents leave, I will make you more food."

Faintly, the sound of tires on gravel could be heard. "They're here," I announced.

Talon paused, raising a brow. "You can hear that?"

I shrugged. "Tires on gravel is a pretty distinct sound."

"Jade," Talon explained patiently, "they only just turned off the main road. The beginning of my driveway is a half mile away."

At this I started, trying to comprehend what that meant. Talon merely grinned.

"You are healing quickly. I expected nothing less. Not to worry, love," he bent forward to kiss me on the forehead. "I will help you learn to control it. Imagine a volume control, like on a radio. Turn the volume down to appear normal, and up to eavesdrop."

This made me laugh. "I'll work on it."

He disappeared down the stairs while I continued to marvel at my acute hearing. If I concentrated, I could hear each footstep as he went down the stairs, where before I could never even hear him when we were in the same room. The car made its way up the drive, two doors slammed, my mom's excited talk and my dad's more subdued answers.

Though I wanted nothing more than to experiment more with my newfound skill, I snapped myself to attention. It wouldn't do well to be listening to chipmunks a mile away while my parents were here. Using Talon's advice, I imagined in old fashioned dial, and concentrated on lowering the sound I could hear.

Amazingly, it worked. I could no longer hear my parents.

They entered the room, and my mom ran directly to me, wrapping her arms carefully around me.

"Oh, honey, I'm so happy you're awake," she was still babbling like she had been on the phone. "We've been so worried, and didn't really know what was going on and then you were unconscious when we saw you and..."

My dad patted her gently on the back, and it quieted her small rant. "You're looking 100 times better," my dad said, leaning over to give me a gentle squeeze.

"I'm feeling pretty good," I told them. "But I know I'm not ready to do cartwheels or anything."

"The doctor has recommended a few more days of bedrest," Talon added. "We'll take it from there."

My mom shook her head sadly. "I just can't believe Gerry. How could he have brought a gun into the house, with those precious babies in there?"

"He's getting the help he needs," I murmured to comfort my mom. "He's sick."

She nodded, still looking troubled. "Emma's been staying with us, just for a little while. I can't imagine how she feels being in that house alone."

My dad agreed. "We've actually been looking for a new place for them," he confided. "They need a place to start fresh, with new memories."

"That's a great idea," I squeezed their hands with a small smile. "I love you guys."

My mom hugged me again. "Oh, honey, we love you, too."

"Jade needs her rest now. Tomorrow you will visit again, with her sisters?"

"Yes, of course," my mom gushed. "Rest well, honey."

"Let us know if you need anything," my dad added before guiding my mom out of the room.

Talon walked them out, and I rose to find some durable clothing. Though I was unconscious for most of it, I'd been inside far too long.

When Talon returned with a sandwich, I was pulling a sweatshirt on over my t-shirt and jeans. He raised a brow at me. "Where do you think you're going?"

"You're taking me out," I told him, sitting to pull on socks.

"You think so," he commented, watching me.

"Yes. I know I'm not strong enough to shift yet, but I was hoping you would." I took the sandwich from him and took a big bite.

His interest was piqued. "Jade, you need your rest," he began, but I cut him off.

"I've rested for five days, Talon." Standing, I wrapped my arms around his waist. "I just feel like I need the open air."

A piece of memory flitted through my mind, and I suddenly made a connection.

"You're claustrophobic, aren't you?" I asked him.

He seemed taken aback. "I suppose you could say that. It's more that I lived for so long in the open, I have trouble indoors."

The night at Pearl's finally made sense. When I'd gone into her basement and was overcome with anxiety, I was already having dreams about Talon. Connecting with his memories.

"Hm," was my response. "Apparently, so do I, so I know you understand. I'm not asking to do anything crazy myself."

He gave in to my hopeful smile. "What did you have in mind?"

CHAPTER 20

We stood outside, behind his workshop where the woods began, looking out towards the direction of Black Bear Lake. I had a nervous energy that had me bouncing from one foot to another.

Talon eyed me, an amused look on his face. Finally, taking a deep breath, his form shimmered before disappearing completely. I held my breath as a large shape took his place. The dark horse was majestic, and huge, at least seven hands. He shook his black mane and blinked an eye at me before lowering enough for me to comfortably get on his back. As I adjusted, I realized his clothes remained intact on the ground. That moment of nothingness between Talon's transformation now made sense. He must become the air before changing forms, so as not to rip out of his clothes. Smart.

He whinnied, which I took to mean hold tight, and started off at a light gallop. It was mind boggling that I was riding through the woods on the back of a horse, who was also my boyfriend.

Boyfriend. What an odd word to associate with Talon. Mate? Ugh, there was that word again. Soulmate? I suppose that would work.

We whipped through the trees at an easy pace. I knew Talon was holding back, but as long as I felt the wind on my face and could breathe in the fresh air, I was fine with that. Thoughts of my transformation were finally starting to hit me. Rubbing a hand along his sleek body, the realization that soon, I would be able to do this, hit me hard. We would have a lot of decisions to make about our life together.

It would be years before my family began to notice my lack of aging. I still had my house in Miami, and of course we promised to accompany Lani to help her find her family. The most pressing concern, however, was finding Frances.

He messed with my family. He would be sorry for that.

For the moment, though, I was content to ride, a carefree laugh floating on the wind. Talon and I would figure out the rest, together.

We reached a small field near the lake when Talon stopped, his head whipping back and forth. He whinnied again, lowering himself, and I immediately jumped off, also on full alert. He immediately transformed into his wolf, and that's all I needed to know- we were under attack.

My eyes searched the trees around us, looking for some sign of an intruder. Talon stiffened beside me, and I turned to where his eyes were focused.

Frances.

All the hackles rose along Talon's back when soft laughter reached us. Two more figures appeared, more large cats, much like the first time I'd been attacked.

Sucking in a breath, I tried to calm my fear and assess the situation. We were not only outnumbered, but I knew Talon would do everything to protect me, which left him more vulnerable.

My fault, a small voice nudged at me, but I pushed it away. I could deal with blame later. Right now, we had to win.

Frances began murmuring to himself, and I used my newfound talent to turn up the volume. It sounded like some kind of spell. I had to distract him.

"Frances!" I bellowed out, knowing he could hear me but wanting more than his attention. "It's me you want. Tell me why."

His head came up, focusing unerringly on me.

"Why, my dear, to save my soul, of course."

A growl emanated from deep in Talon's throat, but I ignored him.

"I can't save your soul," I told him. "I'm not your mate."

"No matter," he waved his hand as inconsequential. "You will be."

Those three words sent chills down my spine.

A figure ran in from the direction of town, skidding to a stop on my other side from Talon.

Lani. Talon must have called to her. Though I'd never thought to ask, I imagined he could speak to her telepathically while in his animal form.

It helped our odds, but we were still outnumbered. Frances sent me a dark smile. "Even better. I'll have two of you."

A snarl ripped out of Lani. I didn't need to hear her voice to understand her sentiment.

At some unknown to me signal, Lani and Talon launched their attack. As they clashed with the shifters in the middle, a scream wrenched from my throat.

They were circling again, and it was tearing me apart. I couldn't simply sit and watch Talon and Lani get ripped apart.

Closing my eyes to center myself, I focused all my energy on Frances. Imagining his essence as glowing threads, I latched onto one and began to pull. The instant I knew it began to work, his attention suddenly snapped back to me.

With a hiss, he began stalking across the wooded enclosure, and through our new connection I could feel the ripple of a shift running through his body. Wanting to keep his attention on me, I began sorting through the threads, searching, searching… and found his memories.

Abruptly he stopped, shock crossing his face as I watched visions flash across my mind's eye. The rest of the world had fallen away, existing in a blur of color, shapes no longer sharp on my peripheral. I shuffled through the memories, a seemingly happy childhood, his parents attentive and loving. Then, the memories had a dark quality to them, as if I were looking through a screen door.

I heard a gasp, realizing Frances had stopped several feet from me, wrapped up in his own memories right along with me. The death of his parents, the ensuing darkness that overcame his every thought. My heart was breaking right along with the little boys, and I struggled to stay conscious through the wave of emotion. My hands clutched at my chest, but I remained upright, focusing. In the darkness, I found that little boy, huddled in a corner. Taking his hand, I led him into the light, shielding him from the horrors of the world.

Releasing his hand, he walked through the open doorway, but I was now sucked into the room, darkness threatening to swallow me and nowhere to exit. No windows, no doors, only darkness.

I could no longer see Frances in the clearing before me. I was completely, utterly alone.

Jade.

The voice was faint, but I grasped it tightly.

Jade. Come back to me.

I reached out, tentatively, afraid of sucking my savior into this world of darkness with me.

Jade. Give yourself to me. Trust me.

Talon. My eyes closed, and I wrapped myself up in the safety of his voice. *I trust you.*

Instead of the dark room, I imagined Talon's arms, wrapping around me. His scent, campfires and evergreens. His eyes, sinking down into the warm chocolate of his soul. The tiny light inside me, so lost in Frances' memories, found its safe haven inside Talon's mind. Curled up there, I allowed him to carry me out.

"Jade?"

I felt the warm ground beneath me, a cool breeze ruffling my hair. Carefully I slid my eyes open, not missing the moment of Deja-vu. Talon's arms were around me, and I'd fainted. Again.

"Talon," I breathed his name, my solace in the storm.

Looking around, I realized the two attackers were gone, but Frances remained. He sat on the ground, his head in his hands, while Lani stood guard.

Sitting carefully, I allowed Talon to help me stand up.

"What did you do to him?" Talon asked calmly, belying the angry fear I knew was rolling beneath the surface.

"I..." I paused. "I think I healed him."

Talon gazed down at me, amazement prevalent in his expression. "You went into his mind. Do you have any idea how dangerous that is?"

"I've got a pretty good idea now," I told him. Then I flashed him a disarming grin. "You rescued me."

163

He let out an aggravated breath. "Barely. I'm not even sure what happened."

"You spoke to me," my brows creased, trying to recall everything we'd just been through. "In my mind. Telepathically. Your spirit found mine, and I..."

"You climbed into my mind to get out of his." Talon's mouth twisted into a smirk.

Does this mean? I pushed the thought out of my mind and into his.

Yes, I believe it does.

I was caught so off guard by his response that I nearly fell over again. My cheesy grin was back. "That is so cool!"

"What is?" Lani called out, clearly annoyed by being left out of the conversation.

"We can talk," I gestured between Talon and I. "In our *minds.*"

"Of course you can," Lani commented offhand. "You're a mated pair."

Talon and I stared at her, completely taken aback. Her expression mirrored ours.

"How did I know that?" She asked, seeming to point the question at no one in particular.

"What is with you people?" Frances muttered from the ground.

Talon and I approached slowly, ignoring him for the moment. "Are memories coming back?" I asked Lani.

"I'm not sure," she hedged. "That came out of nowhere."

I was having a thought, but didn't want to say it out loud quite yet.

No.

Startled, I glanced up at Talon. *Can you read my mind now, too?*

No, I just know how you think. It's too dangerous.

Ignoring Talon now, I looked down at Frances.

What happened to the other cats? I asked Talon.

They fled as soon as Frances collapsed. He was controlling them.

He didn't look so dangerous now, huddled on the ground. I felt an odd connection to him, which I'm sure was fallout from being in someone else's mind and memories. Chewing my lip, I gazed at him thoughtfully. When his eyes met mine, we judged each other for a long time.

Talon squeezed my hand, but didn't speak, in my mind or otherwise. This was my choice, and it made my heart swell that he would leave this to me to decide.

"You've done bad things," I said aloud. He hung his head. I glanced once at Talon, and then over at Lani. As if reading my mind, Lani raised her brows at me with a look that said she thought I was nuts.

"I believe you can do better," I told Frances softly. His head came up again, hope shining from his eyes. "You choose the life you want. You can choose darkness again, but believe me, we will take you down. You can choose light. You can find a happy life. You can find your mate. I truly believe she's out there, Frances."

Crouching down before him, I continued, "She's out there, and she deserves a good man. You can be a good man. So, you will stay here for the time being, and we're going to keep an eye on you. You will get a job which benefits other people."

"I will take your blood," Talon added. "To be able to track you."

Watching Frances carefully, I realized I wasn't looking at the man right now, but the small boy I'd led out of the dark room. All of his confidence was gone, and I wondered how long it would be before he came to terms with his childhood.

"Do you agree to these terms?" I asked him gently.

He nodded. "Yes."

Standing, I gestured for Talon to do his part. Frances extended his wrist, which Talon gripped with both hands before piercing his skin. He took just enough, I supposed, for tracking purposes, before straightening again.

"I will take him from here," Lani spoke up. "Jade should go home and rest."

"Thank you," Talon said to her before turning to me. I realized for the first time that he was wearing pants, and Lani was wearing a sundress.

Where did you get the clothes?

This is my land. I have caches of supplies scattered about.

Wonders never ceased.

Talon still didn't agree with me trying this, but I had this gift for a reason and I was going to use it. I had done nothing but rest for several days, and I was ready to do something.

"This will get... personal," I explained to Lani. "We will be connected in a way that I can't quite explain. I will have access to your memories, your thoughts, your feelings, and I believe you'll have access to mine. I just want to be sure you agree to that."

Though she looked nervous, Lani nodded her head decisively. "I need to know. Let's do this."

Glancing at Talon, he also nodded, though I could see his trepidation there.

"Talon and I are going to connect first, but he is only there as my anchor. He wasn't able to see Frances' memories before, so I don't believe he'll be able to see yours. Our main goal is to unlock your early memories."

We both took a deep breath, and I closed my eyes to concentrate. I built the image of Lani in my mind, how I saw her, and imagined her essence in threads of colors. They were earthy colors, dark reds, browns and green. I reached out lightly pulling on one, and I felt myself being sucked in. From somewhere in the distance I heard her gasp, and I knew she could feel it too.

Talon?

I'm here.

Opening my eyes, I focused on Lani. She was now glowing, the same colors I'd been picturing in my mind swirling around her being, and it was easy to find the thread I wanted. We delved into her memories together. I flipped backwards through time, catching glimpses here and there of a very lonely life, until I came across a block shrouded in black.

I kept searching, looking carefully now, for any thread, the slightest spark of color. Time fell away while I searched, trying not to let my annoyance at finding nothing show through. There had to be something, there just had to.

Finally, a small spark of white stood out starkly against the black, and I paused, watching it cautiously. The last thing I wanted to do was approach too quickly, scaring it away. Imagining a small spark of my own, I gently nudged it out, putting all the warmth and promise I could muster into it. For a long beat of time, they hung there, two matchsticks in a cave beating back the darkness surrounding them.

Then, like two magnets, the sparks slammed together and lit up the entire space in a bright, white light. It was so glaring after the darkness that my eyes closed reflectively. Once I managed to open them a slit, I looked around in amazement.

We were standing in a thick wood, very different from the woods of Wisconsin. Here, the trees were more tropical, and there was a dry heat. Standing along the edge of a river, I looked up and realized we were at the base of a beautiful waterfall. Laughter tinkled through the trees, and I glanced over to see a small, dark haired girl running, and not because she was being chased, but for the sheer joy of it. Following behind her was a similar dark haired boy, a carefree smile on his face.

Brother.

Unsure if the thought came from Lani or the memory, I watched as the two splashed into the water. The boy paused, concentrating, and a dragon made of water sprang up, circling Lani once before crashing back to earth.

His casual use of power at such a young age shocked me. Young Lani put her hands on her hips with a pout.

"Why can't I do that?"

"You will, one day," the boy responded.

"I'm still faster than you," Lani taunted, taking off at a sprint back into the woods.

Snapping back to real time, I blinked slowly, bringing the world back into focus. Talon's arms were around my waist, grounding me, while Lani sat before me in the same position we'd started. She was blinking fast too, and I saw tears in her large eyes.

I'm here, love.

Wrapping myself in Talon's voice, I was able to shake off the hazy dream world of memories.

"I have a brother," Lani breathed.

"You seemed very close in age," I commented. "Do you think you're twins?"

166

Talon spoke, "It is very possible. My mother told me it is very common for Elementals to be born as twins."

Lani let out a breath. "I have no idea, but it did seem as if we were the same age. He was so powerful," she looked at me wide-eyed. "We must have been only 6 or 7, don't you think?"

Nodding, I looked up at Talon. "Are you telling me we'll have *twins*?"

He grinned before looking at Lani. "Would you mind telling me about the memory?"

Lani explained it best she could, and when she talked about the water dragon Talon seemed as surprised as we had been.

"My mother told me it takes longer for Elemental children to mature, usually not until their mid-twenties." Talon explained. "For your brother to be showing such power at so young an age," he shook his head. "I can only imagine how powerful he is now."

"Any idea where that waterfall is?" I asked. "Those trees were not like any I've come across."

Lani shook her head. "No, but it gives me something to research."

"Hang on," I told her, and stood for the first time. I was a little wobbly on my feet, and I suddenly realized how hungry I was, like I hadn't eaten for hours. Looking at Talon, I asked, "How long have we been sitting here?"

He raised his brows at me. "Almost four hours," he answered.

Exchanging a surprised look with Lani, I asked her, "How long did that feel like to you?"

"I thought perhaps half an hour, tops."

"Good to know," I murmured. Turning again, I went off to find my sketch pad and some colored pencils. I didn't draw much, but I had some talent for it. Sitting back down, I did my best to sketch out what I remembered of the scene, from the style of tree to the river and waterfall. Lani added in her own perspective, and when I was done, all three of us stared at it.

"What now?" I asked. "Do we just google *tree* and see what matches?"

"Or waterfall," Lani suggested. "I have lots of time."

With a wry smile, I slid the sketch over to her. "That you do."

"I was thinking," Talon said, "that perhaps we could begin our search in the southwest. I would like to wait until Jade is completely healed, but then we go."

"Why the southwest?" I asked. Pointing at the sketch, I added, "That is definitely not the desert."

"No," Talon smiled. "But, I know there must be others there, and since those living on the reservation are technically my extended relatives, we have a better chance of finding out information. Plus, I would love to show you where I was raised."

"That's a good idea," I said, looking at Lani. "What do you think?"

She nodded. "I'm going to do some research while you are healing, and see if I can narrow down where this might be. If I can, then I might make a trip on my own, just until you're ready to join me."

"All right," I agreed. She stood, getting ready to leave, so I got up and gave her a hard hug. "You're family now," I whispered. "So, anything you need, you just have to ask."

Lani nodded, thanked us both and left.

Turning back to Talon, I sat myself on his lap, wrapping my arms around his neck. "Thank you," I told him.

"For what?"

"Helping me delve into Lani's memories. I know you didn't want me to."

"Your health and safety will always come first, Jade. But, I understand your need to help others, and you've been given this gift for a reason. I would never stand in the way of you fulfilling your destiny."

Not knowing how to respond, I kissed him. Just as I was going to badger him more about his protective streak, and how he didn't need to have one when it came to our physical relationship, my stomach growled.

"You're hungry," Talon said, using the excuse to break the kiss.

I pouted, but couldn't argue with food.

Talon brought me into the kitchen, and I propped myself on the counter, my favored position to watch him cook for me.

"I'm not sure I can handle pretending to be sick much longer," I confided in Talon, looking down at the ground. He immediately approached me, cupping my face. Gripping his hand, I stared into his eyes, trying to convey my deepest feelings through them. "Isn't there something we could do?"

He brushed his free hand gently along my cheek. "I don't feel comfortable moving you until you are at full strength," he told me quietly, though I could feel his strain at not being able to give me what I wanted.

A brilliant idea hit. "Miami," I said excitedly. "My house. I need to go and prepare it for sale, anyway. Why don't we go spend a few months down there? We can be alone," I rubbed my hand up his arm lightly, suggestively. "And my family will believe we're off at some special clinic to help my healing."

"I am still concerned over you traveling so soon," Talon began to accept my idea, with reservations.

"We'll charter a private jet. You can fly it, if you don't trust a pilot. I know you know how," a small smile lifted one corner of my mouth.

"This is truly what you want?" Talon asked, brushing back a strand of hair from my forehead.

"Yes," I told him quickly. "Absolutely."

"I will see to the details. Eat, and then rest, while I do."

I nodded. "Of course. Actually, I may as well start the phone calls. Let my family know we'll be out of town for a while."

"And then rest," Talon pressed. I rolled my eyes, but nodded. He bent his mouth to mine, meaning, I'm sure, to kiss my lips lightly. My body immediately reacted and it deepened into almost a frenzy. I clung to him, trying to press my body to his even after he pulled away.

"Soon, my love," he whispered. It satisfied me that he was as affected by me as I was by him.

However, he had more control than I did. I understood Talon worried about me, but I also knew that in a very short time I'd cease to care. My body craved his.

With one more lingering look, Talon left the room in his silent way. I lifted my phone from the counter, took a bite of pasta and started with my parents, letting them know I would be recuperating at a private facility in Miami, while also preparing the house for sale. My mom was thrilled with my decision to make my move home permanent, though I could hear the stress in her voice at the thought of my needing special care. I kept my voice upbeat and the conversation short, hoping to alleviate her fears.

I called Emma last, knowing she would be the most difficult one to explain this to. She took all the blame for the incident on her shoulders, and no amount of reassuring could convince her otherwise.

"Are you okay?" Emma asked immediately, her voice trembling. "It's worse than you've been letting on, isn't it? Oh, Jade, let me come with you, help out..."

"Emma, I'm fine, I promise," I cut her off. "Really. You know how protective Talon is of me, he just wants the best therapists he can find. Unfortunately, they just aren't available here. I was planning a trip down to sell the house anyway, and this just gives me a good excuse."

"You promise it's not worse than you're letting on?"

"I swear. Probably I'll just be hanging out on the beach, soaking up the sun before I come back here for winter. Please don't worry, okay?"

She took a deep breath. "Okay."

"Are you doing okay?" I asked her, hearing the underlying stress that went beyond her worry for me.

She hesitated, then answered. "I filed for divorce today. Even though I know it was the right thing to do, obviously I'd never trust Gerry again, but it was still difficult."

"Oh, Emma, I'm so sorry. Of course, it's difficult for you. I understand."

Talon and I made sure that Gerry would recuperate in rehab, and I convinced my family, with Talon's help, not to involve the police. I didn't feel it was right to blame him for Frances' actions. If Frances deserved a second chance, so did Gerry.

"I'm just a phone call away," I reminded her.

"I know, thank you. I love you, Jade."

"Love you too, Ems. I'll see you as soon as I get back and I'll keep in touch on my progress."

"Okay," Emma agreed. "Safe travels."

Talon glided back into the room as I hung up. He grinned mischievously at me. "So, I am overly protective, am I?"

"Yes," I answered him. "But I was just trying to alleviate Emma's guilt."

I took a deep breath, inhaling the warm, sticky air. Talon's arm was wrapped securely around my waist, alert to the people surrounding us. We made our way from the tarmac to a waiting car, complete with driver. Raising a brow at Talon, I allowed him to lift me into the back seat. Moving quickly around to the other side, Talon nodded to the driver before sliding me under his protective shoulder once again.

"This is unnecessary," I said, but there was no censure in my voice. He was amused by my obvious uncomfortableness being chauffeured.

"Your safety will always be necessary and a priority." He breathed the response against my neck, sending chills waving out through my body.

I knew he was aware of how my body reacted to him, yet I found it difficult to be embarrassed. There was too much need, both for myself and for him.

When the car pulled up in front of my condo, I was surprised to find I didn't feel a sense of relief, as I should when I arrive at home. Obediently I waited for Talon to come around, assisting me out of the car. When his arms were once again wrapped around me, I realized I had found home. It wasn't a place, a house, it was this man. Talon.

He looked down, meeting my gaze. I knew my heart was in my eyes and I watched his own soften as that registered.

The chauffeur followed us inside with the luggage we'd brought. I didn't need much, as the clothes I'd originally brought with me to Wisconsin were for cooler weather. My summer clothes were still in my closets and drawers.

I'd had someone come in once a week to make sure things stayed clean and no issues arose. The scent of fresh flowers met us as we entered, a welcoming sight.

Talon slipped the chauffeur a tip before turning his attention fully to me. "You have a beautiful home here," he commented.

"Thank you," I smiled at him.

He approached me slowly and in a lightning move whipped me into his arms, cradled like a child. I laughed, feeling carefree. Talon fastened his mouth to mine, moving through the halls so fluidly I hadn't realized we'd moved until I was pressed into my soft bed.

His hands were running along my body, memorizing each curve along the way. I moaned, pressing myself closer to him, my hands burning their own trail. The fire was all consuming, my blood boiling in my veins.

Too soon he released me, lifting his head to gaze down at me. Our heavy breath mixed together, and I was angry at the distance between us.

He pressed a shaky hand to my cheek. "We cannot," his voice came out husky with need. It encouraged me.

"We can," I argued. "I want to."

"I cannot risk your health. I will not."

"I feel fine, Talon. I swear to you." I brought his lips back to mine. "Please," I whispered against them.

He continued to fight his own urges. I felt the difference the moment he succumbed.

Though Talon was just as consumed as I was, he was infinitely gentle, tender in his movements. Quickly our clothes were gone, allowing me to feel his body against mine as I craved.

His hands, his mouth were everywhere, raising my already terrible need to a fevered pitch. I was begging him, both aloud and in my mind, to unite us as one.

When we joined, my body shuddered and rippled, savoring the release I had long been seeking. Talon moved then, slow and gentle even while the firestorm demanded more.

It built again within me, or it never stopped, small spirals constantly rocking my frame until finally we both exploded, falling together in pleasure.

Talon's head came to rest below my chin, though he was still careful not to crush me with his weight. I wanted the closeness, was never bothered by his weight against me.

Lightly I trailed my fingers across his back, feeling completely at peace in the moment.

I spent most of my days on the beach, soaking up as much sun as possible in the short time we remained. A few hours a day, when the sun was at its highest point was when I felt most lethargic. Talon and I spent that time inside, wrapped in each other's arms. I found the night to be beautiful, walking hand in hand with Talon. He'd never spent much time in Miami, and I showed him all of my favorite spots.

As the sun set a week after we'd arrived, I snapped a picture of myself, the sea at my back, and sent it to my family. Knowing they were still worried for me, I wanted to alleviate as much of it as I could.

Each new day I felt stronger than the last, and I practiced with the elements until I felt comfortable calling upon my power. Eventually I would use blood bags, as Talon did, but for now I continued feeding off him, and the same feelings I experienced the first time I'd fed from him were still prevalent. Talon told me I would need it more often when I used magic, but regular food would also sustain me.

A few days before we were set to go home, we walked along the beach, hands clasped, as the sun set over the deep blue water. My condo was packed and sold, and I felt completely at peace, happy. Talon had done that.

He paused suddenly, spinning me to stand in front of him. "I love you, Jade Callaghan."

My answering smile lit my face. "I love you, Talon Wolfchild."

His hand cupped my cheek, a move that always made me feel cherished. "I have waited for you for a very long time. Now that I have you, I will never let you go. You are my heart, my soul."

He knelt, and my heart leaped into my throat. In a smooth move, he pulled a small velvet box from his pocket and had it flipped open, the ring glinting blindingly in the sun. "Will you do me the great honor of being my wife?"

I flung myself at him, wrapping my arms around his neck, my mouth finding his. He pulled away, laughing. "Is that a yes?"

"Of course," I laughed with him. "Yes. It would be my honor to spend my life with you."

Grasping my left hand, he slid the ring on the third finger. It was gorgeous, a large piece of turquoise surrounded by diamonds. The band was white gold. With sudden insight, I dragged my eyes from the ring to look at his beloved face.

"You found this stone, didn't you?"

"Yes," Talon answered. "I found it for you. It is unique, as are you."

"I absolutely love it," I told him, my lips meeting his once again. We fell back onto the sand, and I prayed Talon had stopped us somewhere secluded, because I was past noticing if we had an audience.

EPILOGUE

"Hey, Rick," I said into the phone.

"Long time no hear," he replied genially.

"I know, I know. I'm going to make up for it. How about dinner and drinks?" He hesitated. "Where?"

"Why not The Spade? Pearl said she would take Cassie for the night, something about wanting to practice."

He laughed, but was quick to recover. "No, I couldn't do that to her. She's seven months pregnant, for goodness sakes. She could go into labor."

"Unlikely. Besides, Micah's there, and Aspen would love to have another girl on her side."

"All right. You got me. What time?"

"Meet me in an hour?" I suggested.

"Sure. See you then."

Hanging up, I glanced over at Talon. With a wicked grin, I lifted the phone again. Talon lifted a brow at me, but I ignored his unspoken question. When the voice came on the other end, I composed myself and spoke.

"Hey, Emma. What are you up to tonight?"

She sounded surprised. "Nothing, really. Pearl actually took the kids for the night, something about wanting to practice."

I laughed, pretending to be hearing this for the first time. "Well, with twins on the way, it sounds like a good idea. Why don't you come with me to The Spade? You deserve a night out."

"Oh, well, I..."

"Great, I'll pick you up in half an hour," I told her, not giving her a chance to argue.

"Okay, I guess I can do that."

"Perfect. See you then."

Hanging up, I let out an ecstatic laugh. Talon's arms wrapped around my waist, nuzzling his face into my neck.

"What, exactly, are you up to?"

"Oh," I said nonchalantly, "Just a little revenge."

Twenty minutes later, I pulled into Emma's drive and strode into her new house. She was at the computer, dressed in jeans and a baggy, flannel shirt. There were still several boxes stacked in the living room, evidence of the recent move.

"Hey, Jade," she said, glancing at her watch. "Oh, you're early. I guess I'm ready to go."

"Oh, no," I told her, shaking my head. Before I left, I'd made sure to dress for my part in a slinky black skirt with a matching black, sleeveless vest that showed off just a bit of my stomach. To offset the black, I wore fire engine red heels that I was having some trouble walking in. My hair hung, as usual, straight down my back. "Come with me," I told her, and grabbed her hand before she could react.

Dragging her into her room, I scrounged through her closet and finally found a form hugging dress shoved into the back.

"What are you doing?" Emma asked from behind me.

"We're going out," I told her. "And I'm getting you ready for it."

"Really, Jade, that's not necessary," she began, but I cut her off.

"Emma, this is the first time I've been out in months. Are you really going to ruin that for me?"

She hunched her shoulders. "I guess not."

I felt a little bad about throwing that on her, but it was the fastest way to compliance, and time was short. "Go put this on," I told her, rifling through her underwear drawer. Finding black lace, I threw that at her as well. "With these."

She walked, bewildered, into the bathroom while I picked out jewelry. When she was dressed, I walked in and handed it to her.

"Now," I said. "Time for make-up."

Twenty minutes after I walked in, I walked back out with Emma on my heels. I was proud of my prodigy, and couldn't wait to show her off.

Pulling into the busy parking lot, I led Emma into the front door. I spotted Rick immediately and waved, then turned and shoved Emma in front of me. To my satisfaction, I watched Rick's jaw drop and eyes bug out just slightly. Emma stood frozen until I nudged her along. Their eyes stayed locked until we reached the table, and Rick managed to stumble out of his chair to hold out hers.

"Thanks," Emma said softly, sitting.

"Hi." Rick replied.

Stifling a giggle, I held the back of my hand to my mouth in feigned surprise.

"Oh, no!" I said dramatically. Both pairs of eyes landed on me. "I forgot, I was supposed to help Mom with something! You two don't mind having dinner without me, do you?"

Both fumbled for words but I beat them to it. "Great," I said again. "Rick, could you do me a favor and drive Emma home? Thanks a bunch." I kissed Emma on the cheek and sent Rick a wink before sauntering off.

The rest, they would have to figure out on their own. I was going home, to Talon.